'I NEED TO KNO
WHO ESPECIALL
AND SUPPORT O
TONIGHT – SOMEONE WHO FEELS IN A BAD
PLACE, OR IS FACING ANYTHING
DIFFICULT . . .'

Stella waited for someone to speak. How easy to be loving, she thought, when you are in love.

Shall I say something, thought Sandra? Because I am facing something difficult – half-term with my parents. But no, she thought. She didn't wish to dominate the group, and felt certain that someone was sure to have a worse difficulty than hers. The temptation, however, to pass everything, her whole dilemma, over to the group, to rid herself of the responsibility, was so overwhelming. Perhaps if no one else spoke, for someone had to start the ball rolling; otherwise what was the point of having a meeting at all?

SHERRY ASHWORTH

PERSONAL GROWTH

A SIGNET BOOK

SIGNET

Published by the Penguin Group
Penguin Books Ltd, 27 Wrights Lane, London w8 5tz, England
Penguin Books USA Inc., 375 Hudson Street, New York, New York 10014, USA
Penguin Books Australia Ltd, Ringwood, Victoria, Australia
Penguin Books Canada Ltd, 10 Alcorn Avenue, Toronto, Ontario, Canada m4v 3b2
Penguin Books (NZ) Ltd, 182–190 Wairau Road, Auckland 10, New Zealand

Penguin Books Ltd, Registered Offices: Harmondsworth, Middlesex, England

First published in Signet 1993
1 3 5 7 9 10 8 6 4 2

Copyright © Sherry Ashworth, 1993
All rights reserved

The moral right of the author has been asserted

Typeset by Datix International Limited, Bungay, Suffolk
Set in 10/13 pt Monophoto Plantin Light
Printed in England by Clays Ltd, St Ives plc

Except in the United States of America, this book is sold subject
to the condition that it shall not, by way of trade or otherwise, be lent,
re-sold, hired out, or otherwise circulated without the publisher's
prior consent in any form of binding or cover other than that in
which it is published and without a similar condition including this
condition being imposed on the subsequent purchaser

Thank you to all my friends;
friends are, after all, the best therapists!

This novel is for Molly and Jack.

'With all its shams, drudgery and broken dreams,
it is still a beautiful world. Be cheerful.'

Desiderata

CHAPTER ONE

The morning began badly. Stella forgot to thank the refrigerator. So she paused, her fingers hooked around the handle, and thought, consciously, thank you, refrigerator, for looking after my food for me during the night. With renewed confidence she opened the door and reached for the milk.

Only coffee this morning. Not – heaven forbid! – that she was on any form of diet. All that was over with years ago, when she left her job as group leader of the Slim-Plicity slimming club. Coffee only this morning, because she really was too excited to have anything else. Just for a moment she missed Richard, as she wanted to share her anticipation.

But no, it was better like this, she admitted to herself, with a delicious spurt of guilt. Better alone. For Richard, her husband, was now living – only for six months – in Los Angeles, at the request of his company. She glanced up at the pinboard to look at the postcard he had sent her, and then looked at the slip of paper next to it with the address: 8 Lincoln Grove. A new beginning.

Now, stirring her coffee, she found she could actually be grateful for all that had happened to her. It was as if everything had gone round in one big circle. Four years ago she had left Slim-Plicity, forcibly disillusioned with the dieting game, and had met Gill Goldstein. Gill was her therapist. While her friends Liz and

Emma had taught her that the slimming business exploited women, Gill had shown her that Stella's own desire to slim stemmed from unresolved conflicts within herself. And with Gill Stella had embarked upon a voyage of discovery. She had relived her childhood, shedding oceans of tears en route, given vent to her anger, got in touch with her feelings, and almost forgiven her parents. She hardly missed Slim-Plicity because Gill had encouraged her to attend workshops and courses, and it was in this way Stella had gained her qualifications. And so much more. She breathed deeply, picked up her coffee mug and drank.

She lifted her eyes to the pinboard. There were her little messages to herself. 'You are a star, with the ability to accomplish your purpose in the universe.' 'Self-acceptance is the beginning of change.' 'There are always beginnings – and there is always now.' How lovely, now, not to have to wonder what Richard was thinking about all this.

It was true that, at first, when she had started in therapy with Gill, he had been supportive; at least, he had not complained about the cost, realizing, as she did, that a good therapist would naturally be expensive. He was happy, too, when Stella took courses in counselling, Transactional Analysis, Gestalt, stress management, assertiveness training, dealing with anger; he wondered slightly about the Swedish massage, but thought the circle dancing was innocent enough; balked slightly at 'A Learning Experience with Crystals'. Gradually, she knew, she was leaving him behind. Gill had suggested that one solution to this might be that Richard should go into therapy too. And Stella had agreed; how could she possibly manage to maintain her new-found serenity with Richard sighing behind his newspaper as she practised her calming breaths; how could she grow when her attempts to forgive him were met with 'I should think so!'?

But he had gone – at least for six months. And so – she experienced a sinking feeling – had Gill. Gill had returned to California to fulfil her life's ambition – the setting up of her TransFormation Foundation. And here am I, thought Stella, beginning my new career too. Stella Martin, Group Therapist. If 8 Lincoln Grove is suitable, I can begin as soon as next week.

If? Stella flicked the elastic band she was wearing round her wrist, giving herself a short sharp sting. Tut, tut! No negative thinking, please! And certainly not today. Stella could feel that she needed time for her affirmations and creative visualization and, as she placed her empty mug in the dishwasher, began to say to herself, 'I, Stella Martin, love and approve of my-self ... You, Stella Martin, love and approve of yourself ... She, Stella Martin, loves and approves of herself . . .'

Stella knew that if she was in a good space she would have no trouble with the journey to Lincoln Grove. So sitting in the driver's seat she took the added precaution of sending her love to her car and, it seemed to her, the engine purred responsively as she turned the key in the ignition. She moved off in the direction of Chisholme.

Stella couldn't find the bell. Right in the centre of the door was a large red knob, and that was it. No visible

3

means of announcing her entry, so she rapped with her knuckles against the wooden door. Silence. Had she got the right day? Yes. Was this 8 Lincoln Grove? Yes: a figure 8 was painted on the gate post. Nobody's in, thought Stella. She took off her gloves, and rapped this time with bare knuckles, stepping back after doing so. She stepped forward to listen for footsteps. Nothing. Checking that the street was empty, she pushed open the metal flap of the letterbox and looked inside. She could see a long corridor, and to the left a flight of stairs without a carpet. Stella felt certain that the house was empty.

A bad beginning. No! No, it wasn't. There wasn't such a thing as a bad beginning. There wasn't such a thing as a mistake. There are only learning experiences, she thought to herself, in a quasi-American accent. Only learning experiences. I am learning now to cope with disappointment. I mustn't feel foolish, she berated herself. She sensed the presence of someone behind her and turned to find a woman of about her own age, in a long black coat, and multicoloured scarf.

'Are you Stella Martin?' she asked.

'Yes.'

'Oh, I'm late! I'm so sorry. I'm so disorganized.'

Negative self-fulfilling prophecies, thought Stella.

'I do apologize. There was a rush of customers at the shop and I couldn't get away sooner. I hope you've not been waiting long.'

'It's all right. I've only just arrived this minute.'

The woman felt in her pocket for a key and, as she inserted it in the lock, she continued to talk to Stella.

'I'm Carol Thorpe. Did Eric explain to you? I live

on the first floor, and I'm a sort of – well, not a caretaker exactly, but I keep the other rooms clean and have the keys – in exchange for a reduction in the rent. So I said I would show you round. I work part-time at Illuminations too. It's a bit stiff. Aah!' The lock gave and with a push on the doorknob, the door finally opened.

The corridor was bare, and the wallpaper gave way to patches of bare plaster. It wouldn't take long, thought Stella, to strip the walls and paint them over in a light peach or grey, something soothing. Then a few posters saying something inspirational. To her right was a door standing slightly ajar, and this Carol pushed open, saying, 'Here it is.'

Stella entered. The room was quite empty. Its carpet was speckled green and black and the walls were painted in a garish green. Stella mentally painted them over again in a soft pastel. Like the prow of a ship, the bow window expanded on to the street, filling the room with winter sunlight. Studio cushions and bean bags, thought Stella. I'll get plenty of those and scatter them around. I'll need a small table for the box of tissues and some literature, and lamps – yes, and a few spotlights – and I can burn some incense too.

'There's a small kitchen behind,' added Carol. 'You can make coffee and there's a fridge for milk. No cooker, I'm afraid. Do you like it?'

Stella nodded slowly. She could see it all now. She would sit in the middle – no – just below the bow window, against a bean bag, and her group would be around her; she would exude love and serenity, and there, in that room, her clients would –

'Would you like a coffee now? I've decaffeinated, or a herbal tea?'

'Thank you,' she said. 'Coffee – no milk or sugar.'

Carol's living room looked out over a square of back gardens with rotting sheds and tangled trees. Stella sat by the window, a mug of black Nescafé in front of her on the table, too bitter to drink. Carol stood by a dresser, extracting the last few drops from a mixed fruit teabag. The aroma was rich and pungent.

'Will you be taking the room?' Carol inquired.

'Yes,' said Stella, delighted at her own certainty. 'I think I can make it just as I like it. I don't have a room in my own house large enough for a group.'

'Is this your first group?'

'Yes. My first therapy group.' Stella underlined the word 'therapy' as she spoke it. 'But of course I have led other groups.' She wished to impress, and hoped that Carol would not inquire further.

'What other groups?'

'Well, not exactly personal growth,' Stella said, carefully. Carol gave her an encouraging smile. Stella filled with that now familiar, irrepressible desire to confess, to tell all. And why not? One look around Carol's room, her shelf full of books on healing, her *Trees for Life* calendar, her poster explaining the Bach Flower remedies – all this revealed a kindred spirit. Why not?

'The group I led – it was a slimming group.' Carol's eyes widened. Stella thought quickly. 'You see, I have an eating disorder – had an eating disorder.' (An eating disorder was much more respectable.) 'And before I went into therapy myself – a long time ago – I was addicted to slimming. So much so I ran a group. It did very well. But I realized – I was made to realize – that commercial slimming clubs exploited women like me.' Now Carol nodded vehemently. This was better. 'So I joined a group that campaigned against fattism – they've disbanded now, and I went into therapy with Gill Goldstein.'

'Gill! Oh, I know her. You lucky thing! Everyone says she's super. I would have gone to her myself but I couldn't really afford it. I bet she helped you.'

'Oh yes.' Stella felt herself warming to Carol. 'She's an excellent therapist. I – I think of her more as a friend now, except that she's gone back to the States, you know.'

'Has she? Why?'

'She's got the money together to start up her own Foundation. She's calling it the TransFormation Foundation for Inner Peace and Self-Awareness. She's running it as a therapy centre where all kinds of healing can take place. In Los Angeles.'

'So you don't see her any more. Do you miss her?'

Stella felt the customary pang. How dare Gill leave her! TransFormation was all very well but – She tweaked her elastic band so that it inflicted another sharp sting. No Negative Thinking!

'No, not really. She's put me in touch with a friend of hers, who I'll probably continue with: Roland Temple.'

'Oh, Roland Temple. I know a couple of people with him. He's very, very good. But how do you feel about seeing a man?'

'That doesn't bother me. I mean, a number of my clients are men. It isn't a problem for me.'

7

Carol nodded, taking it in. 'And you, yourself. What sort of therapies do you use?'

'A mixture. I'm qualified in counselling, in Transactional Analysis and Gestalt. And some techniques from hypnotherapy. And self-esteem of course. And I teach meditation. And I like Louise Hay, that sort of thing. But really for each client I try an individual approach. Personal growth is an individual matter.'

Carol nodded again. 'Do you have room in your new group?' she asked. 'I'm sort of interested. I'm between therapists at the moment, and I'd love to make a new beginning. I think I feel quite an affinity with you, Stella.'

'Oh, please. Yes, of course there's room. What – what exactly is your problem? That is, why do you want to join?'

'Personal growth.' Now it was Stella's turn to nod. 'I feel stuck. Blocked. I've made nothing of my life. I look after this place, work part-time in Illuminations. I've hardly any money, no meaningful relationship – but it's not that. I *know*, just *know* that I could achieve so much – I mean, I know I have it in me – but something, something is stopping me stepping out. And I'm still not sure what it is. There's something – some impediment.' Carol shook her head. Her eyes filled with tears. Stella reached out and took her hand. She felt wonderful. For not only had she found a room, but a group member too.

You see, it works! she said in her imagination to Richard. It works, despite all your scoffing. You must think positively – thoughts create your future. Look at me. I

spent months, visualizing this. Remember that morning, when you came in, and you told me I'd spent long
enough in bed, and I said I was working, visualizing
what was to be? Those meditations have created this
here and now. It works!

Stella filled with righteous anger as she drove home.
Yes, she was right to be angry with her husband. He
had turned down every opportunity, flatly refusing to
take any sort of course in self-awareness. He wouldn't
even read *Feel the Fear and Do It Anyway*. She had
spent hours and hours with Gill, shouting at the cushion that was meant to be Richard, 'I resent you. I
resent your attitude.' She began to long for the times
he went on his business trips, imagined what it would
be like alone. Thoughts create reality. Richard was
asked to work for six months on the audit in California.
And he had gone three weeks ago. And she didn't miss
him, except to say, I told you so! It works! I'm going
to have my own therapy group.

As she approached the city centre, she thought for a
moment. She had two choices. She could either go
home for lunch and come back to town for her meeting
with Roland Temple, or stay in the centre and perhaps
do some shopping. Shopping was still a word that
electrified Stella, and Richard had not left her short of
money. Yes, she would look round the shops, perhaps
get a sandwich, and then go on to Roland. It was so
easy to make decisions these days.

Never, thought Stella, have I felt so happy as I do
right now. Her car took its place in the queue of traffic
along Deansgate. Everything is perfect. I have space.
She thought of her house, all of it, for the moment,

9

hers. The car behind her hooted to encourage her to move on. I have my lovely house. I love you, house, she thought. Houses need love too. And a new career, and I shall be so successful. I shall write too, articles for magazines, she thought. She moved ahead, into the box junction. And perhaps a book one day. Cars moved round Stella as her Renault sat in the junction. She checked herself in the mirror. I'm glowing, she thought. Recently Stella had visited a colour analyst. She was Spring. She had subsequently had her style analysed too, and for the third stage the analyst had accompanied her to the shops, and selected the clothes that would be most suitable. I look good, thought Stella, and best of all, I'm normal about food. I'm cured. She turned right towards Piccadilly.

In fact, not for the first time that day, she wondered about Roland Temple. Did she really need another therapist? She had posed that question to Gill, and Gill had refused to be drawn. Perhaps, she had said, if Stella arranged to meet him, she could judge whether they had a rapport. Roland had been in therapy with Gill a number of years ago, and Gill thought very highly of him. Stella had felt a pang of jealousy. *She* was Gill's favourite client, surely? She did not want to meet this Roland. And yet, life without a therapist . . . No one to support you . . . No one to pat you on the back . . . No one to listen. She supposed there would be no harm in simply seeing this man. A father-figure might make a nice change.

Stella stood by the sandwiches in Marks & Spencer. She picked up the packet labelled 'reduced calorie', just to see exactly how reduced it was – not that this would affect her decision. She would have precisely what she wanted. The coronation chicken looked nice. She read the calorie value and put it down. If only there was something in between. What would Gill have said? Stella picked up a salmon sandwich, put it down. It contained mayonnaise. Ought she to confront the mayonnaise? Would choosing a calorie-counted sandwich – which would keep her slim - kick her into dieting obsessively again? It was all so hard. I need a therapist, she thought. The woman beside her picked up the plain chicken salad, and so did Stella, and she made her way to the check-out.

What impressed Stella was that Roland had a secretary, who sat outside the suite of rooms behind a small desk, and was actually typing. The clatter of keys made it all seem so impersonal. The secretary smiled widely, got up from her chair, and took Stella along the corridor, knocked at a door, announced her, and Stella went in.

Roland Temple rose to meet her. He was tall – over six feet – and Stella noticed immediately that he was very thin. This was accentuated by his clothes – black trousers, a black shirt open at the neck – but he was so thin. Stella had never seen such narrow hips. Had he dieted? she wondered. Do men diet obsessively? Or did he just have a high metabolic rate? He peered down at her through small round gold-rimmed glasses, and smiled nervously. Stella immediately felt as if she wanted to put him at his ease.

'Shall I sit down?'

'Yes, yes. Do. Good.'

Stella sat, perching on the edge of an easy chair, and Roland settled into his director's chair, crossing his legs. He picked up a clipboard, glanced at the notes on it, and put it down. He looked at her again and grinned.

He's my age, thought Stella. Or possibly even younger, or perhaps it's just his hair. Roland Temple's hair was cropped; in one ear he wore a small earring. She wondered what Richard would have to say about that.

'Good,' he said. 'Do you want to tell me a bit about yourself?'

Stella smiled and gave a small laugh. 'Where shall I start?'

'Wherever you feel is right.'

'Right.'

There was a silence. Then Stella was distracted by the faint sound of a lavatory flushing. She stole another glance at Roland, who was looking at her. He really was thin. She wondered what his waist measurement could possibly be. Then she breathed deeply to centre herself.

'Good!' he said.

She continued to breathe deeply, filling her lungs with air, panting slightly as she let out her breath.

'I don't know where to begin.'

'That's OK.'

'I'm Stella Martin. You know that.' She laughed. 'I was in therapy with Gill Goldstein. You know that too, of course. When I first saw her – about four years ago – I had an eating disorder.' She glanced at his hips. 'You see, I used to run a slimming club. I was addicted to dieting, and I was obsessed with food and weight. I needed to break all that. So Gill took me back through my childhood . . .'

Roland propped his chin on his long tapering fingers, his hands pressed together as if in prayer.

'. . . in fact, I could see that I didn't have a childhood – that is, I was an only child, and my mother wanted me to be her adult companion. And she wanted more than that; she needed to know exactly what I was doing so she could make it all her own. You see, she wasn't – isn't – happily married. My father is a weak man, avoids issues. I can see now I was a victim of emotional incest. But it was my mother who wooed me with food. And so you see, I resisted her control with dieting. And – oh! – I feel guilty!'

'Good, good. Stay with it. Stay with the guilt. What do you feel guilty about?'

'Telling you about my mother. I'm disloyal. She'd be outraged. And hurt. And I can't bear to hurt her. I feel responsible for her. Gill said I learned to care for my mother, as my father was inadequate, and . . .'

Roland pushed his glasses back on to the bridge of his nose.

'. . . some equilibrium, but still when I see her, I feel my stomach knotting, a resistance – here,' Stella said, placing her hands on her midriff. 'My inner child is bruised, you see. I remember an occasion, when I was four . . .'

Roland clasped his hands; unclasped them; clasped them.

'. . . so my growth has been a process of grief for my lost childhood, expressing and dealing with the anger and resentment, and developing an assertive way of handling life, becoming an adult. And right now I'm in a good place –'

'Good.'

'– for the first time, I'm able to be on my own. I accept Richard's absence; I can see the positive side of solitude, which represents real progress for me. But perhaps I –'

'Go on . . . Go on.'

Stella lowered her eyes. 'Perhaps I should miss him. Perhaps my marriage isn't . . .'

'Say what you want,' he said.

'Do I have a problem? I'm married, but I'm happy he's gone. It's . . . it's good not to have to retrieve socks from under the bed, not to have to put up with the American football, not to have to –' Stella stopped. For here was something she could not possibly talk to this man about. Yet. And up to this moment she had not really thought about his sex. To Gill she could have said, and indeed, had said in the past, that she didn't want Richard in *that* way any more. She was glad he'd gone. But what would Roland think? 'Not to have to . . . listen to his conversations about money. And now when I'm focussing on my new therapy group – I'm starting a group, you know –'

Roland looked up and smiled.

'. . . premises in Chisholme owned by Eric Hunter. Several of the clients I'm working with now have expressed an interest, and a woman I met today will almost certainly join. I was in Gill's group for a time and . . .'

Roland sneezed.

'Bless you! Do you have a cold?'

'No, sorry, carry on.'

'Yes . . . Do you realize it's nearly three o'clock?' she said, feeling obliged to take care of him.

Just then a buzzer sounded from beside Roland's chair. 'Aah!' he said.

'That's my time up, I suppose,' said Stella. 'Look, thank you. It's cleared my mind, talking like this. I've really appreciated the way you've let me clarify my situation. I value your support. I can see now that perhaps I need to do some work around my relationships. I will . . . I will see you again – if that's all right.'

'I'd like that,' Roland said, and blushed.

He blushed, thought Stella. How sweet. I like him, she thought, as she wrote out her cheque for £25. He's not at all like Gill, of course. Gill was the mother I needed, Stella diagnosed. Now I must move on. This is the right time for a man, she told herself as she swung her scarf around her neck and hurried along the road. The yin and the yang, she thought. And he's not threatening. A New Man. She saw his hips again in her mind's eye.

Two new friends in one day. Stella slid her ticket into the pay machine in the car-park foyer. She tried not to breathe in the fumes of disinfectant. Her ticket came back stamped. Thank you. Thank you, machine, for returning my ticket. Be grateful, Gill had always said. Thank you, Gill, for arranging my meeting with Roland. Thank you, universe, she said. I, Stella Martin, love and approve of myself . . .

CHAPTER TWO

Let's face it, thought Sandra, it can't be a sinus headache because my nose isn't running, and it can't be a
tension headache because it's only 8.15 in the morning,
so it must be a hangover. Again. Well, perhaps it was
half a tension headache and half a hangover. Tuesday
morning simply wasn't a respectable time to have a
hangover. And besides, she had had only two glasses
of wine. Two large glasses of wine. Sandra reviewed
quickly what she had to do that morning. Third years
– they could read silently; then a free; and then junior
drama. Damn. That would be noisy. She pulled into
the school car-park and looked for a space. As usual
everyone had avoided the area next to the Head's car,
so Sandra pulled in there. As she locked the front
door, it began to drizzle.

Two paracetamol, thought Sandra, with my coffee.
Or Nurofen, if anyone's got some. The door of the
boot lifted as she unlocked it, and it brushed lightly
against her cream pullover, smearing it with damp
grime. Oh no, she said. Sandra brushed the mark rapidly with her hands, only succeeding in working the
stain further into the material. She gritted her teeth
and swore repeatedly. The lights! The side lights were
still on and she got back inside the car to switch them
off. I'll be all right, she thought, with a large mug of
coffee and two paracetamol.

Dawn was only just breaking over the distant factory

roofs, and girls scurried in, hooded and bowed against the sharp wind, which brought the light rain directly into Sandra's face. Oh God, she thought, I'm miserable. And my head hurts. Perhaps it's flu, she thought with rising spirits, and pushed the bar to gain entrance to the school building. The cleaners sat smoking in their cubby-hole, resting from their puzzle magazines. Sandra smiled at them. It hurt. She made her way to the staff room.

There, at the entrance to the sitting and kitchen area, Sandra's way was barred by a group of women, reading the morning's notices. Once again, Sandra was convinced something important had happened. Some scandal – please! But no. Simply room changes; some second years out at an exhibition; girls had been seen wearing non-regulation T-shirts under their school blouses, so do be extra vigilant; and Tracey Jarrold's cat was run over last night, so please could staff be understanding . . . and the sitting list. Sandra noticed her only free had gone again. All the more reason to get the paracetamol now. She rubbed her brow.

'Morning!' said the Head of History, full of enthusiasm. She had only been at the school one term.

Sandra moved among the women ranged at the notice-board. 'Excuse me . . . excuse me.' She edged her way between bodies which did not acknowledge her presence. On the way to the kitchen she was stopped by her own head of department.

'Ah, Sandra! You had *Of Mice and Men* last, didn't you? I gave the set out to my group yesterday afternoon, and I was six copies short. I can't set any reading until I've got the full set, and I wondered if you could find out what happened to the other –'

'Sorry! Have you finished? I thought . . . oh, good,' Anne Palmer, the Deputy Head, interrupted. 'Sandra. I was in your form room yesterday, and I was a little alarmed at the state of the blackboard. I think someone has been throwing food at it. There were stains, you see, down one side, and I said in the staff meeting at the beginning of term, we really do have to impress upon the girls – because all the boards were replaced at the beginning of the school year – I do know you can't be there all the time – I'm not *blaming* you – but I do think if you had a few words . . .'

'Yes, yes of course. I'm sorry.'

'Don't be sorry. I know it's not your fault. I'm not telling you this because I hold you responsible in any way at all. I know how we can't be in several places at once, and the fourth years this year are difficult . . . How do you find Sally Mercer?'

Sandra tensed. I want my coffee, she thought. Shut up, you old windbag.

'She's fine for me.'

'Yes. She would be . . . for you. Has she been handing in her work on time?'

'Yes. Yes.'

'Good. Do you know, last week . . .'

Forget the coffee. But I must have the paracetamol, Sandra told herself, as she escaped from the Deputy Head and made her way to the cloakroom. She took off her coat and looked at herself in the full-length mirror. She saw a shapeless mass. Her dark green skirt was long, too long. It hung unevenly around the middle of her calves. Her baggy sweater, which she had worn intending to cover everything, simply made her look extra bulky instead. She folded it over in the centre to hide the stain. She turned and examined her profile. A series of random lumps. But I won't diet, she thought. I can't diet. Life's too hard.

And she remembered Slim-Plicity. Once she had belonged to that slimming club, when she was a student. A crazy thing to do. But she had made some good friends. Helen. And Emma, who told her what a good teacher she would make. Sandra permitted herself a rueful smile. She had to admit, the teaching wasn't bad. It was just school. Her smile cheered her up, and she looked in the mirror, mussed her hair, pulled in her stomach, and went back to get herself some water. And the bell rang. I'll do without the paracetamol, Sandra thought. I take too many anyway.

As she took her register from the rack, Zoë came up beside her.

'Hi, Sandra. Are you all right?'

Sandra smiled, her first real smile of the morning, for Zoë was her friend. When Zoë said, are you all right?, she meant it. If you wanted to, you could say no.

'Surviving,' Sandra said.

'Shall we go out for a drink at lunchtime?'

'Not more alcohol. But we'll go anyway.'

Anne Palmer, full of concern, advanced upon them. 'Ah, you've arrived, Zoë. Bad traffic, was it? Are you on your way to registration?'

'Yes – but it's all right. The girls know to start taking the register if I'm a bit delayed.'

Sandra braced herself.

'Ah, but Zoë, you do know that technically speaking,

and I think it might even be a DES regulation, that the form mistress must be there in person to take the register. I'm a little alarmed to think –'

Sandra thought, should I defend her? Doesn't Anne realize that she has to take her daughter to school before she gets here and there's no one to help? And was there any point in defending her? For there was no getting away from it, Zoë should be on time, should be there to take her register. And Anne would make absolutely sure she realized that.

'– I'm sure you'll make a greater effort to get here now you realize that, Zoë. Now I shan't delay you further. Remember there's a brief staff meeting at break, and that all the money for the photographs has to be in by tomorrow – quite a lot of yours is missing.'

Zoë Swann took off her coat as the Deputy Head was talking, apologizing, nodding and reassuring her. She opened her briefcase to get her diary and mark book, and caught her breath, as she saw that Laura's sandwiches were there. Not again. She thought quickly. Was it possible to pop out of school later on and get them to her? Out of the question. She had only one free today, and that was after lunch. Laura would never eat a school dinner. Think, Zoë, think!

The bell rang that signalled the end of registration. Zoë flew along the corridor with her diary, mark book and sandwiches and met her form as they were leaving the form room.

'It's all right, Mrs Swann. We've taken the register and Kelly's taken the money to the office. You don't have to worry.'

'You're a treasure, Kate.' Zoë thought, I have the

lower sixth next for a double, and if I set them an unseen I could nip over to Millbank View, pop Laura's sandwiches into the school office, be back before the end of the lesson and run through their translation with them. The classics room lay at the other side of the main school building and Zoë broke into a run, ignoring the discomfort in her bladder that suggested the advisability of a visit to the toilet. Her three A Level students were sitting, slumped at the back of the classroom. They smiled as they saw her.

'Would you like to try an unseen this morning? By yourselves?'

They groaned.

'All right. Look. Why don't you work on it together – um – borrow my dictionary – it's good practice – I don't mind if you make a mess of it. I – I think you'll be all right if I leave you to it. I need to take my daughter's lunch over to her school as I put it in my bag rather than hers, so – I'll be back before the end.'

And she slipped out of school by the side entrance, furtively, like a criminal. Guilty. Of forgetting Laura's lunch; of not teaching her A Level girls – and they were the only three girls in the school prepared to take Latin A Level; guilty of not taking her own register. Well, she thought, checking her rear mirror, at least I don't have the time to feel sorry for myself. And she probed the wound inflicted by Mike's departure and found it numb today. Thank God for that.

Zoë Swann was forty. Old to have a six-year-old daughter, but then she had only married Mike seven years ago. He had left her three years ago – and this was the part that was strange – for an older woman.

They had gone to Spain, but Zoë had accepted that because she was a little surprised that a man as glamorous as Mike had wanted her in the first place. Now it was difficult to meet men, especially in a girls' grammar school, and besides, there was Laura, her teaching, and the cat. My life, she thought. All that promise – she remembered her own Latin teacher telling her she would go far, achieve things – and now this. A single parent, teaching a subject nobody wanted to study, with retirement the only thing to look forward to.

I must be expecting a period, she thought. Not like me to be so maudlin. She shook her head to dispel her thoughts and turned up the heating in the car, as she had forgotten to return to the staff room for her coat. I'm getting older, she thought, there's no doubt about that. She had gone for a facial the other day. It was Sandra's idea. Sandra had said that she ought to do something for herself, and a facial was just the thing. So Zoë had laid herself down on the beautician's table, ready to be made to feel good. Oh dear, said the beautician, you've got broken veins, look. You'll need a corrective concealing cream for that. If I were you, I'd get a better moisturizer – it's probably worth it for you to get something expensive. Have you thought about colouring your hair, she had said. She sympathized with the cheese mouldering slowly at the back of her fridge; she too had passed her sell-by date.

Which was not surprising, really, for she never had time to rest; her life seemed to her to be a constant cycle of activity. Never stopping – Laura and marking, and cooking and cleaning, and feeding the cat and taking him to the vet, and paying the bills, and remembering to renew the library books and Laura's eye clinic appointment. She felt like a character in a 1920s silent movie, moving at a preternaturally high speed, never quite catching up with herself, unable in fact to sit down at the end of the day as the habit of rest had been lost.

Because, she thought, I'm so disorganized. If I'd remembered the sandwiches, I wouldn't be missing this lesson. If I'd remembered my coat, I wouldn't be sitting here freezing. I forget things. If I could train myself to remember things, if I made lists and stuck to them, I know I could manage. And people would respect me. Zoë raised her head slightly, being that other woman. All my marking would be up to date. Zoë, the Head would say, the Latin results have been so excellent this year that I am going to develop a policy of actively encouraging our best girls to take it. And Laura would stop fighting at bedtime. That long letter from Mike would arrive, full of regret and recrimination. But it would be too late, because that subtly attractive highly intelligent rich single man who had never fully committed himself to any other woman yet would be chasing her. Sometimes bouquets would arrive in the school office, addressed to her, from him. And Zoë pulled up in front of her front door.

No. That's wrong. I had to go to Millbank View. I've been driving automatically and I've come home. And she threw her head in her hands.

Sandra looked around the saloon bar with frank appreciation. Her eyes took in the rotund publican with his shirt unbuttoned at the top, the quiz machine; she glimpsed the snooker table in the adjoining room, and her eyes rested on the gloriously ordinary people at the small tables. Such a refreshing change, she thought, from the intense middle-class aspirations of Millers' Company Grammar School for Girls. She breathed in the stale cigarette fumes and inhaled deeply. If only she hadn't given up smoking. She waited her turn at the bar. Zoë was in the Ladies; she didn't have time to go before they left school. Sandra had deliberately not looked at the dinner supervision lists, having a suspicion that Zoë might just be on today. She ordered a cider for Zoë, and hesitated when it came to herself. Certainly something non-alcoholic after last night, but not a diet drink as she was certainly not dieting. But then half a bitter was not many more calories than a coke. She ordered the bitter.

The Sun did a good cheese and onion pie. That was partly why Sandra liked to go there; partly it was the name of the pub. 'I'm going to the Sun' sounded particularly corrupt, conjuring up Page Three girls and scurrilous stories; moreover, when it was a department lunch, most members of staff went instead to the Prince William, which was much more salubrious. Hence Sandra and Zoë felt safe here.

'I need this,' said Sandra, as her pie arrived.

Numbed by the warm stupor of eating, she did not want to talk, and besides, she had a guilty suspicion that she had come out this lunchtime to pour out her troubles to Zoë, and had paid little attention to her friend's problems. Whatever her motives, she offered Zoë the opportunity to speak. 'How are things with you? OK?'

'Just about. I've had a chaotic morning.' And she recounted her earlier adventures to Sandra. 'I thought it was all over. Then at break Debra Wentworth saw me.'

Sandra pricked up her ears. Debra was always bad news. Sandra would have preferred almost to be her acknowledged enemy, but instead the three of them shared this pretence that they were all friends, all professional. Debra Wentworth was Head of General Studies, Head of Careers, in charge of Industrial Liaison and Economic Awareness, and was planning to get Information Technology across the curriculum too. Sandra wasn't sure whether the Head liked her, or was terrified of her. For Sandra, even the mention of Debra's name was enough to knot her stomach and prevent her full enjoyment of the pie.

Zoë continued. 'She wants me to take on more General Studies next year. Greek and Roman Culture, she said, and European Awareness.' She smiled apologetically at Sandra.

'European Awareness?'

'She said that with my background it would be easy to construct a course. But Sandra, I know nothing about Europe – I wouldn't know where to start – and God knows where I'll find the time to get the material together.'

'Is the other course all right? The classical one?'

Zoë frowned. 'That's easy to teach but none of the girls are interested. It's the last choice the girls make, and the ones I get never participate, and I spend half my time finding out where they were when they should have been at my lesson.'

'Have you told the Head?'

'Not yet. The problem is, since they've taken Junior Latin off the timetable, they don't know what to do with me. Hence these general courses.'

'The bastards!' Sandra speared a chip ferociously. 'Don't they understand the value of Latin? And a grammar school too!'

Zoë smiled, cheered by Sandra's loyalty. 'I'm sure they do really, but it's the National Curriculum. I think there simply isn't time for it. I'm afraid I'm not very fashionable any more.' She thought of her broken veins and drying skin. 'Extinct,' she said. 'There are times when I feel like a dinosaur.'

Sandra glanced down at herself. 'I feel like a mammoth.'

Zoë looked at her quizzically.

'My figure, I mean. I shouldn't have really had this pie, but I did. And what's worse, the beer. It hasn't done my hangover any good at all. I don't know why I do it!' Sandra answered her own question. 'It's just that some days are so exquisitely awful I feel that I need little bits of pleasure, like something nice to eat, and then when I get home, after the marking and everything, a drink is so tempting. I keep meaning to get hold of myself, but I don't.'

'It's hard,' Zoë spoke gently.

'I'm so miserable.'

'Why don't you try for another job? You're an English teacher, you'd find it easy.'

'Yes, but I don't want to teach in a school without a sixth form. Millers' is the only 11–18 round here. Full-time English jobs rarely come up in sixth-form colleges, and if I don't have a full salary, I can't be independent of my parents. Besides, I like the girls at Millers', and the lessons. It's just –' Sandra shrugged. Zoë remained silent.

Sandra continued: 'I don't know how to put this. I like teaching but I hate school. It's funny – when I was at school myself, taking A Levels, I felt like that – liking learning, but deliberately taking days off school. But I can't decide why I feel like this. Is it because everyone in our school is so middle class and traditional, because it's a fee-paying grammar school? Or is it because since education's been made a political football you've got to be bang up to date if you want to be taken seriously, and know what SATs and cohorts and appraisal and everything are?'

Zoë laughed.

'Sometimes I blame the school and the way people nag you and are so petty, and careerists like Debra keep sticking knives in your back and the way people stop whispering when you go into the staff room. But then I think, is it just me who feels like this? Is it my fault? Am I expecting too much? I just get so confused. I became a teacher because I *like* kids, and you know the way they talk in the staff room – Jane Bloggs is so *arrogant*, and, you've got Mary Smith in your group, poor you! – as if the worst thing in the world is to be in contact with these kids. And then I think, who am I? How come I know better than anyone else how to behave? I wonder if it's me who's arrogant, and I wonder if I'm jealous of Debra because we've both been in the school the same time and she's got on so much further than me. But then, would I want to be Head of General Studies? And I don't know!

'I don't know anything! And this is the worst thing. My father rang last night. He said he'd had a discussion with my mother and that they'd agreed that if I wanted to give up teaching they would support me if I was to take my CPE, which will convert my English degree to law, which is what he's always wanted. For a moment I was tempted. He said I didn't have to decide right away; the offer was open. Which is the last thing I need, because now I really can't decide what to do at all.'

Sandra ran her hands through her hair. She waited for some calming words from her friend. Subconsciously Sandra had always selected friends who were older than her, friends who beat a path through the jungle for her. Sandra was twenty-four to Zoë's forty.

Zoë spoke. 'It's a good offer. But I'd hate you to leave.'

'Why? All I ever do is talk at you and go on about my problems, and – Zoë, I'm sorry - I forget about you. I'm so selfish. I never let you get a word in edgeways, and I know you've got it so much worse than me with having to look after Laura by yourself and no one at school giving a damn about that and not being able to teach proper Latin any more. Look, you talk now.'

There was a silence. 'I'm all right,' Zoë said.

'No you're not,' Sandra said.

'We both seem pretty fed up.'

'Yes, but you've got reason to be. No, I didn't mean that! I meant that my problems are my fault.'

'I feel like that too.'

The two women were silent again. Sandra considered

that talking about your problems was supposed to make you feel better, but here she was, feeling decidedly worse. Something had to be done. But what? She thought aloud. 'Zoë, I knew a woman once – Emma – who had a weight problem like mine. She went into therapy with a woman therapist. She said it was wonderful and that she was different afterwards, you know, more able to handle her own life . . . and make decisions . . .'

'And become more organized?'

'Yes. She ended up living with this lovely man. I met him once. A mini-cab driver.'

'Really?' Zoë's interest was apparent.

'Does it appeal to you, being psychoanalysed? I've often wondered what it would be like and what you would find out.'

'Can it really – help you get organized, and turn your life around?'

'Oh yes,' said Sandra, conscious at one level that she was making this up as she went along, but then two halves of bitter often had that effect. 'I've read articles about therapy. You discover what it is that makes you tick. You see what's been stopping you getting the things you want – like a new job or a relationship or self-respect or something. Yeah.'

'Really?' Sandra couldn't decide whether Zoë was incredulous or impressed, but she was certainly paying attention.

'You know, it might be fun to try. Finding out about ourselves. I don't see we'd have anything to lose. Maybe if I could find out why I have this problem with food and booze I could solve it. They might show me how to make decisions. And Zoë, wouldn't you like to be more assertive?' Sandra checked her watch and saw that time was running out. 'You know what I could do, I could ring Emma – I have her number somewhere. She lives in Hebden Bridge. Find out who she saw, just make some inquiries. Shall I?'

'Would it be expensive?'

'I'll find out. I can't see that it would be,' said Sandra, willing it not to be. 'Fancy being "in therapy" with someone. It sounds like "in love" or something. And I don't see what's wrong with it,' she said, addressing an imaginary adversary, 'some people go to the doctor when they feel depressed and others to the priest. We'll go to a therapist!'

'Here we are!' said Sandra. 'Tea for you and coffee for me and now I'm going to tell you what happened last night!'

Zoë was conscious of some not unpleasant anticipation. All morning Sandra had promised her some interesting news and she had guessed that it might have something to do with this new idea of Sandra's of seeing a therapist. At first, Zoë admitted to herself, she had been reluctant. Imagine having to tell a stranger all about yourself! It all seemed a little too American, but if it really did do what Sandra had claimed . . . Therapy, she knew, came from the Greek word, to heal. An ancient art. That made it more acceptable. And really, life couldn't get any worse. She sipped at her tea.

'Right! I'll start at the beginning. I rang Emma last night and it was lovely hearing her again. She has a little girl now. And she gave me the name of her old therapist, who is called Gill Goldstein, an American.'

'Oh,' said Zoë.

'No, listen. So I rang this Gill, and the woman who answered the phone said she'd gone back to the States, and that she only did massage. But Gill had left the names of two therapists who she could personally recommend if anyone rang for help. So she gave me two names. One was a man called Roland Temple, but I didn't fancy that because I think we'd need a woman, don't you?'

'Why? I think a man –'

'So I decided to ring up the woman, whose name was Stella Martin, which sounded sort of familiar to me, but I couldn't think why. Oh, Zoë, she was so nice! She sounded pleased to speak to me, asked me why I was interested in therapy. I told her that I wanted to cure myself of my indecisiveness and my overeating. She said that was her speciality. Imagine! Then I told her about you – that I had a friend who was also interested. I didn't tell her *all* about you. Now this is the interesting thing. She's about to start a group. A therapy group. For people who are interested in personal growth. And because it's a group, it's cheaper.'

'How much is it?' Zoë asked nervously.

'Oh, you decide how much it's going to be by attunement.'

'What?'

'Apparently Stella and you instinctively agree how much you can afford.'

'But what if she thinks I can afford more than I can?'

'It's not more than ten pounds a session anyway, even if you're rich. That's once a week. Individual therapy is more, and Stella recommends that to start with, but she said that the group is starting very soon, so if we wanted we could join that from the beginning. What do you say?'

'Join a therapy group?'

'Mmm. A change from this place. And we might meet some people.' Zoë hesitated, and Sandra added, 'Some men.'

'Men – in a therapy group! They'd have something wrong with them!'

'Zoë! *We*'re thinking of going and we're perfectly normal. Apart from my eating,' Sandra added as an afterthought.

'When does this start, this group?' Zoë asked, maintaining a studiously neutral tone.

'Next Thursday. I've got the address, 8 Lincoln Grove, in Chisholme, just south of the university. I know it well. I had a friend who lived round there. I'll take you. Please, Zoë. Just try it once and if it's awful or silly or something we'll leave it.'

'What about Laura?'

'Go on. Get a babysitter – the sixth form are always looking for employment. It starts at seven-thirty and goes on for two hours.' Sandra paused. 'I told Stella Martin that we'd both be there.'

Zoë laughed.

'Great! I'll pick you up and take you there. I'm so excited. It's like an adventure, isn't it? An adventure inside yourself.' The bell rang, announcing the end of break. 'And here's a funny thing. I remembered later on why her name sounded familiar. I'm sure the leader of the slimming group I went to once, was called something like Stella Martin. Huh! It can't possibly be her!'

CHAPTER THREE

'But it's somebody's house!' cried Zoë.

Sandra's car had pulled up in front of 8 Lincoln Grove, a large semi-detached house, half hidden by an overgrown hedge. In the bow window, which protruded into the front garden, the curtains were drawn, although a thin line of light between them indicated that someone was in. The house sagged comfortably next to its neighbour, substantial, elderly, brick-built. But Zoë was right. It did look like somebody's house. Sandra too was expecting – well, it was hard to say what she was expecting, something official perhaps, a clinic, or a suite of offices.

Silly, really. She knew Chisholme well. It was composed mainly of large Victorian houses either divided into student lodgings, or sold whole to university and polytechnic lecturers. It had no centre as such, just occasional rows of shops, with mostly take-away restaurants, and Sandra had sampled not a few of them. Chisholme library had been re-named the Chisholme Cultural Centre by the Labour council. The Women's Group and Black Writers' Group flourished. As did alternative therapies.

Zoë leant over to check her lipstick in the driver's mirror.

'Come on, Zoë. I don't think we're *too* early.' Sandra opened the car door with her characteristic nervous impatience. The two women made their way to the front door in darkness, for the street light opposite was not working. There was no bell, and Sandra rapped loudly on the wooden door. Zoë stood a few paces behind, her hands in her deep pockets.

The door was opened by a young woman with long fair hair and a fringe that almost fell into her eyes. Her face, Sandra thought, looked older than her hairstyle, and she wondered if this could be Stella Martin.

But the woman spoke and put her mind at rest. 'Hello! I'm Carol. Are you for Stella's group?'

'Stella Martin?'

'Yes.'

'Yes.'

Sandra swelled with awkwardness. Always when she was unsure of herself she felt ungainly, clumsy, and liable to do something obviously wrong, but she made her way inside, to stand in the hall, painted, she noticed, in a pale grey. The smell of fresh paint competed with the thread of incense in the air. Unusual, she thought.

'Stella said to come inside and make yourselves comfortable. She won't be very long. I'm Carol, as I said before, Carol Thorpe. I'm also starting in the group tonight –' she ushered Zoë and Sandra into a room leading off the corridor '– and this is Angela, who's also new, like you.'

In the room Sandra saw a beautiful woman. She sat near the wall facing her, resting against a black velvet studio cushion. Her hair was raven-black too, and was swept to one side. Her face was completely heart-shaped; her eyes, large and expressive. Worst of all was her figure. Her jeans revealed a completely flat stomach, a tiny waist, and a perfectly formed bust. No woman should look like that, thought Sandra, it's ideologically unsound. Besides, with a figure like that, what sort of problem could she have? She glanced at Zoë, who had moved over to a small table by one wall, where some leaflets were displayed.

'Stella says please help yourself. All the local therapists carry each other's literature.'

Sandra guessed that Carol must be some friend or assistant of Stella's, as she seemed to know exactly what was going on. She persuaded them to part with their coats, which they left over the back of an upright chair in one corner of the room, and she brought them to sit along the wall near the woman called Angela. Sandra noticed that they were all expected to sit on the floor; there was an assortment of bean bags and cushions; beneath the bow window was a small canvas contraption that looked quite unsittable-on. Sandra wondered what that was for. She would have loved to look around her, and read the poster on the wall with a photograph of the earth from space, but she realized it was necessary to make conversation with these other women. But what does one say? Why are you here? What if they say something like, I'm suicidal; or, I'm a rape victim; or worse still, it's none of your business? What *do* you say to people in a therapy group? There was a silence.

Carol spoke first, looking down. 'I live upstairs – that is, I rent a room. The house belongs to Eric Hunter. Do you know him?'

'No,' Sandra said.

'How did you get to hear of Stella?'

And Sandra launched into a long explanation, to which Carol nodded sagely. Then she continued.

'Angela's a friend of Eric's,' she giggled. 'A sort of friend. But really she's more my friend. We've known each other since we were at school.'

Angela said yes, with an enigmatic smile. I wonder what's wrong with her, thought Sandra. There was another rap on the door and Carol sprang up. Sandra could not think of a single thing to say; she swallowed hard.

A man entered, in a red check lumberjack jacket. His hair was pale ginger, and he looked chilled to the bone. He smiled quickly at the seated women, and moved over to a radiator. He was followed quickly by a woman in her late forties, a large flowered scarf draped over her coat. Sandra immediately noticed her nose; it was Roman – no, it was more than Roman, it formed a large regular triangle. Splendidly ugly, Sandra thought. She noticed Carol leave the room and run upstairs. Perhaps the therapist would be on her way.

This is silly, thought Sandra. I wish we'd never come.

'Are you all right?' asked Zoë.

'Yes,' Sandra whispered.

The door opened to reveal Stella.

It *is* her, Sandra thought.

Stella moved among them, in a long black pullover and purple leggings – no shoes. Sandra and Zoë rose.

'Tell me who you are!' she beamed at them.

'Zoë Swann.'

'And I'm Sandra Coverdale. It was me who rang you. Look, I think I know you from somewhere.'

'A course, perhaps.' Stella frowned in thought. 'Was it the reflexology workshop? Or was it "Script and Aspiration"?'

'No, no.' Sandra lowered her voice. 'Didn't you use to lead a slimming group? Slim-Plicity? In Heyside, about three or four years ago?' Did Stella blush?

'Yes. Oh, yes. Just for a short time. Wasn't it you who spoke of having an eating disorder?' Stella said loudly.

'Well, not exactly an eating disorder. A sort of problem with food.' And a thought struck Sandra: if Stella was the leader here, would she be expected to diet? For that was one thing she was simply not prepared to do. What if therapy was a euphemism for dieting? She had to ask.

'Is this . . . is this a dieting group?'

'Not in the food sense! But don't be surprised if I ask you to go on a thinking diet – a diet of positive thoughts. It's the only way. I've given up counting calories, Sandra. It doesn't work. But I'm so glad you've come here. I think you're in the right place.'

And Sandra felt her excitement rise. Perhaps all this was more than a coincidence – perhaps it was meant. Look at Stella. She was thin and said she didn't diet. A thinking diet. Interesting! Whatever did she mean? Do you think about low-calorie food, and not eat it? She felt envious as Stella moved to speak to the other group members, and Sandra squatted down on the floor next to Zoë.

'She's much younger than me,' Zoë said.

'But I think she'll be good,' said Sandra.

And then suddenly it seemed as if they were going to start. Another man had arrived, had divested himself of a jacket, and was speaking to Carol. His hair was curiously old-fashioned; it fell in a quiff over his forehead. He was just a little shorter than Carol, but stocky, with a pigeon-chest. His fawn jumper seemed slightly small, as if it was not his, but borrowed. He's odd, thought Sandra. Stella had moved over to the bow window, and sat on the low canvas stool, her legs tucked under it, her back erect. She was taking deep breaths. She looks lovely, thought Sandra. So serene and self-assured. I think I'm going to enjoy myself.

Sandra's eyes travelled around the assembled group. They were seated in a circle. Sandra found herself longing to know why everyone was here. Stella looked around her group too. She saw them ill at ease, waiting for something, waiting for her: an exquisite moment, poised on the brink of creation.

'Before I talk to you properly, I want you to take a few moments to centre yourselves,' Stella said. 'I want you to realize where you are and who you are. Take a few deep breaths, forcing the breath down into your abdomen. Like this!' Stella exaggerated her breathing; Sandra watched, entranced.

'Breathe in through your nose, and out through your mouth. It doesn't matter if you make a noise.'

Sandra tried to do it, and felt, odd making a little exasperated sound at the end of each breath. She glanced sideways at Zoë, who whispered, 'Just like ante-natal classes!' It was easy to breathe properly,

Sandra thought, but not so easy to centre yourself. She liked the phrase, centre yourself. Perhaps it was hard to do because she didn't know what it meant.

'Good. Now I hope you feel you're really here. The most important thing tonight, I think, is to get to know each other, and get to trust each other. Of course, I operate a confidentiality rule; we never repeat what we hear here. On the day you come to group, you are not to have any alcohol or other mind-altering substances. And –' Stella paused '– there are not to be any sexual relationships between group members.'

Sandra immediately felt constricted, and then reminded herself that she could always have a drink *after* meetings, and that might be a very good idea. Besides, there were only two men in the group and both looked considerably older than her.

'Now, as you can see, there are seven of you here tonight. In fact there is an eighth member – Kevin – but at the moment he's not quite ready for meetings.' Sandra was fascinated. 'He's an agoraphobic. But I'm hoping he'll join us in the not-too-distant future. As far as the rest of you are concerned, I want to leave it to you to get to know each other, and that's what we'll be focussing on tonight. Names first. This is how I want you to do it. We'll go round in a circle, and as you say your name, think of a word that rhymes, or that begins with the same letter, that sums up how you feel right now. It'll help us remember you.' The group shifted around uncomfortably. 'Look. I'm Stella, so tonight I'm –' Stella paused, her hands prayer-like under her chin, in a gesture unconsciously reminiscent of Roland Temple '– I'm starry-eyed Stella!'

Sandra thought rapidly. What could she say? It had better be good. She was an English teacher. Nothing rhymed with Sandra. Then, sad Sandra? No, she felt quite happy. Studious Sandra? Sounded boastful. Sweaty Sandra, more like.

The dark-haired woman, to Stella's left, spoke first. 'Amorous Angela.' Carol giggled.

Sandra immediately felt competitive. Sexy Sandra, Randy Sandy . . .

'My turn, is it?' questioned Carol. She looked down and thought; there was a moment of suspense. 'Care-worn Carol.'

Serious Sandra, severe Sandra, spoilt Sandra, stupid Sandra . . . Sandra felt the eyes of the group on her. She looked at Stella for help.

'How do you feel right now?' she said.

And the answer came: 'Screwed-up Sandra!'

'Silent Zoë,' said Zoë, stretching a point.

The man who came in with a check jacket announced himself as drowsy David. The man in a fawn jumper next to him ran his fingers through his quiff, smiled lopsidedly, and said, 'Jilted Jim.' Finally, the elegant woman with the remarkable nose proffered, nervous Norah.

Norah, thought Sandra. She could have said nosy Norah. She reprimanded herself.

'That's lovely,' said Stella. 'Now there's something else I'd like you all to do. When you feel ready, I want you to tell the group either why you're here or, if that is too difficult for you right now, just explain how you feel at this moment. Just to give you all the experience of communicating with the others. OK?'

41

Sandra had to fight an impulse to leap in. In discussions when she was a student, or even in staff meetings, she always made the first contribution, then normally regretted having spoken. But tonight, feeling her way cautiously for once, she waited, to see who would speak first. Stella smiled benignly at her group. The silence held them all suspended. Sandra curled with embarrassment, but Stella did not seem to mind.

'I've come for two reasons really,' began Sandra, falteringly. 'One is to help me stop overeating, and the other is so I can decide what to do about my job – whether to leave it or not. You see, I'm a teacher, and although I like it – teaching, I mean – I find being in a school difficult – you know, the teachers, the other teachers, and –' Sandra trailed away, hot and cursing herself, exposed and defenceless.

'That's wonderful, Sandra!' breathed Stella. 'You were so honest!'

Sandra felt mollified. Then Carol spoke.

'Hi, everyone. I'm Carol. Right now I feel – scared, I guess, and hopeful too. I hope that something will grow from this group tonight for me and for all of us. Thank you, Stella, for being here. Yes, I feel scared of you all. Scared of what you will think of me. I feel inadequate too. I felt inadequate when you said you were a teacher, Sandra. Part of my problem is my lack of achievements. You see, I feel a failure. I have a dead-end job, no relationship, no house of my own – I feel surrounded by negativity, as if someone is saying to me, Carol, you're worthless, you don't have a right to exist. And I' – her voice quavered – 'and I'm powerless to defend myself, to rewrite the script – and now I

42

feel sad, very sad –' She sobbed. 'Oh God!'

Stella left her seat and came and put her arm round her. Angela too moved over, and Sandra watched as Carol rocked and sobbed, rocked and sobbed. She heard Stella murmur, 'Good, good. Let it out.' What do we do now? she wondered. And she looked at the carpet, with its speckled green and black pile; just in front of her was an old cigarette burn. Should I have cried? she thought. Then Stella moved back, and the circle resumed.

Drowsy David spoke next. 'Why am I here? I'm quite interested in this sort of thing, read a few books. I suppose I just want to know what makes me tick.' He yawned. 'Sorry. Just what makes me tick. Sort of –'

'Personal growth?' suggested Stella.

'Yeah, yeah. You could call it that, personal growth.'

'That's lovely,' Stella said.

'I'm Angela,' said Angela. 'I joined the group because of my entanglements with men, unsuitable men. It's beginning to cause me problems. Carol suggested it; she says that I'm probably a Woman Who Loves Too Much.' Carol, red-eyed, nodded.

Sandra looked at her with interest. She had read an article in a magazine once, about a book called *Women Who Love Too Much*. It was apparently about women who were fatally attracted to the wrong sort of men. At the time she had thought, aren't we all, but now, faced with the real thing, she suspended her judgement and resolved to read the book.

'I suppose I should speak after that,' said Jim. Jilted

43

Jim. 'I've come here because I need to put my life in some sort of order.' He spoke easily, sure of the attention of the group. 'My mother has acute senile dementia and needs constant supervision. Some time ago I managed to get her put in a private home, but it was expensive, and I couldn't keep up the payments on my mortgage. It was around that time I first started on the horses, thinking that maybe a big win would help me pay my way and support my mother, and I began to see Patricia – the nurse who looks after my mother – on a serious basis. The building society repossessed my house and I moved in with Patricia's brother, who is a clairvoyant. It was he who warned Pat to avoid me. She broke it off. I was furious, I got drunk one night, and picked a fight with him. I broke his jaw. Then two weeks later she got engaged – to my bookmaker. That cured me of my betting. I've got a good mate who's lent me some money to tide me over, but he's having to take time off work as his health's not been good. I feel I need to start over: I need a good job, and I need my self-respect. I need a woman too. That's why I'm here.'

This is like listening to a short story on the radio, Sandra thought. This is fun. And immediately she felt guilty.

Norah looked straight ahead, and spoke each word with pain. 'My problem is quite simple. My GP has advised against plastic surgery, and has told me I shall have to learn to live with it.' Sandra knew what she was talking about. 'He suggested some form of therapy.'

'I'm sure he knows best,' said Stella.

Knows, thought Sandra. Nose. She glanced at Norah.

And Zoë still hadn't spoken. Feeling the group's expectation, she shifted uneasily. She couldn't tell these strangers how she felt, or worse still, why she was here, why she had come to a therapy group. She couldn't even think why she *had* come to this therapy group. She sensed Stella's eyes upon her, knew she had to find something to say, and echoed the words she had heard earlier, 'Personal growth.'

'What is personal growth?' Zoë asked Sandra later in the car as they drove beside a row of high-rise flats, windows lit at irregular intervals.

'Well, it's not growing in the physical sense, obviously,' replied Sandra, with authority. 'I suppose it's shorthand for getting to know yourself better and . . . developing. Developing your good points. I liked your painting, Zoë. You're actually quite good at art, aren't you? You've got a good eye for colour. What was it Stella said about your painting?'

'That the purple in the background reflected my suppressed spirituality, and the lack of red showed I had a problem with unexpressed anger, and that it was interesting how each colour mingled with the next, and that I might fail to keep certain parts of my life separate from each other.'

'I think that's true.'

'How could she tell all that from a painting? Honestly, Sandra, I felt as if I was back at infant school. All those little pots of paint and brushes.'

'Yes, but it was fun. Stella said she was trying to liberate the child in us, anyway. We feel with our inner child, she said. And I liked that stuff about

45

having to acknowledge our inner child before we are ready to move on. I'm looking forward to my individual therapy session with her. It's on Monday. She said she had a book for me to read, too. About emotional eating. And I'm to keep a diary, you know, of how I feel when I eat. What emotions I experience. Shall we stop for a pizza or something before I take you home? You rarely get a chance to go out to eat without Laura.'

'Perhaps my inner child would prefer a box of Smarties and a knickerbocker glory,' Zoë remarked.

'Don't be silly, Zoë. Don't make fun. I think it was all very interesting and I feel really encouraged. Don't you?'

This was a dangerous question. For Sandra knew that if Zoë demurred, expressed dissent, dismissed it, she too would suddenly feel cynical, contemptuous. She held her breath.

'It was interesting, Sandra, but I feel I made a mess of it. I couldn't think of anything worthwhile to say· I felt so humdrum and ordinary compared to everyone else.'

'But you're not.'

Zoë laughed. 'Yes I am.'

'You will come next week, won't you?' Sandra slowed the car down as they approached the roundabout.

'I'm committed to it now, aren't I? Don't look so upset, Sandra. In my own way I enjoyed it, if only to listen to all the other people. Did you see how Angela was making up to Jim?'

'Oh, did you think so too? But why? He was so

peculiar-looking – like he stepped out of the sixties. That quiff! And Angela – she's amazing.'

'Amorous Angela!' Zoë guffawed.

'No, stop it, Zoë. You know what Stella said. We're a support group. We've all got to give each other unconditional positive regard. We could have a bottle of wine with that pizza.'

Pastissimo beckoned enticingly, and really, Zoë thought, this was better than staying in with a set of GCSE papers, and a child who woke to complain she had had a nightmare about a big friendly giant except he wasn't friendly and please could she sleep in mummy's bed. Inner child, thought Zoë. Wait till you've got a real one.

Waiting for Sandra who had gone to the Ladies, she berated herself for her scepticism. You're cold, she said. A crusty old classicist. Show some enthusiasm for something, for Sandra's sake. And she had to admit that although the Anglo-American jargon irritated her and the emotion embarrassed her, there was something compelling about the readiness of that group of people to speak about themselves. She would love to be able to do that. Perhaps that was her problem. She needed to open up. When Sandra returned, she smiled brightly. She would give this therapy a try.

CHAPTER FOUR

Boots' in Chisholme had recently been refurbished, and stood now, clinical and pristine, along the High Street. Even the cosmetics counter at the front of the shop spoke of cleanliness and purity rather than beauty. Soft grey cases of eye shadows and face powders, soft grey lipsticks, grey eye pencils were displayed with a meticulous regularity. Lines of bottles with pastel-coloured liquids, pinks, pale blues were ranged along the rear shelves. Gentle promises of perfection.

The counter formed an oblong, with the Nº 7 cosmetics at the front of the store. At one corner was a large pillar of mirror, four sides of clear bright mirror, trapping the unwary shopper into confronting all her physical imperfections. One side of the mirror faced the assistants behind the counter, and by it were make-up brushes, a box of tissues for blotting lipstick and a stocklist. Angela regarded herself. Her hair was tied back into a high pony-tail, and two wicked tendrils of hair escaped to frame her face. Her complexion was perfect; her eye make-up, perfect; her lips, delicious. Her blouse was crisp and white; her badge read *Miss A. Leach, Nº 7 Consultant*. Her skirt was navy and fitted tightly across her hips. Angela enjoyed looking at herself.

Fortunately the store was not very full. The chill mist had thickened and deterred many of the Chisholme customers. Only the pharmacy seemed to be busy. Michelle, the Almay consultant, had taken an early lunch, and Angela was left on her own; today she did not mind. She looked briefly at herself again, and smiled prettily. It was very important to look nice, she told herself. This was why her job meant so much to her. Carol was sweet, but untidy, and worked in an ordinary shop, if you could call Illuminations ordinary. And fortunately the other women in the group last night were nothing special. Someone really ought to advise that Zoë about basic skin care; at her age a woman has to be careful. Sandra, she had noticed, was overweight. She doubted whether a therapy group could solve that, and she smoothed her skirt over her stomach, and observed her trim waistline. Stella was pretty, she conceded, but then she could not imagine herself being helped by anyone who was not.

Not that she needed help. It was Carol's idea. It had come out of that awful night when she'd discovered that Eric was seeing Linda again. Linda was Eric's wife. She had understood that their separation was final, and that he only saw her briefly when he visited his daughters. Eric had told her that he had never loved his wife as he had loved her. Quite. But he had spent a weekend with Linda. It was unforgivable. No man of hers would dare . . .! She lifted her chin as she looked in the mirror. He had actually told her that for the sake of the girls he thought he might give his marriage a second chance. As if seeing the girls once a fortnight wasn't enough. She had been betrayed, and she knew it. What she could not understand was how she could let it occur. Nothing like this had ever happened to her before. Men chased Angela Leach, men lusted after her. She selected, de-selected. With Eric, something had gone fearfully wrong. She was scared.

That was when Carol had asked her in for a herbal tea and told her that she was a Woman Who Loved Too Much. Angela liked the label. Carol had suggested she join the group, said Stella could identify the roots of her behaviour and help her to combat it. Two things had then occurred to Angela: perhaps she could find out why she had made such a mistake with Eric, and secondly, she had established that there might be men in the group. She had to admit, she liked alternative men. She had found Eric's Buddhism attractive, but it goes to show you can't trust a Buddhist. And Spencer was a poet. Spencer was a friend of Carol's too. He was unemployed, wore very thick glasses and had an unusual accent because he came from south London. He belonged to a writers' group in Chisholme and once he had had a poem published in the group's anthology. He had written a poem to her. It was her first poem, and she knew it off by heart:

> An angel
> Who illuminates my dreary life
> not a wife.
> No wings.
> But my heart sings
> As she brings
> Things
> Which delight my soul.
> You've stole
> my peace of mind
> Angela

I can't unwind
Angela
Be kind
Signed
Spencer.

   She liked the last bit especially and thought it very
clever. Fancy being able to rhyme so well. Spencer
was her reserve, but first there was Jim. 'I work in
Boots',' she had said, 'on the make-up counter. It's
not very busy on a weekday.' That should be bait
enough. That he should visit her once was all she
wanted: it was nice to have confirmation of her
attractiveness.
   Two middle-aged women approached the counter
and Angela spoke to them: 'Can I help you?' They
declined her assistance, but stood by the lipsticks, talking quietly to each other. Angela watched them test
several on the backs of their hands. Once more they
stood indecisively and she approached again. 'Have
you looked at our range with added moisturizer?
They're particularly good for harsh weather.' She
selected a tester. 'Now this shade has pink undertones;
or this,' selecting another, 'if you prefer red.' She knew
that the more attention she paid the women, the more
likely the chances of a sale. 'This shade – Sunset Bou-
levard – I wear myself.' That usually clinched it. One
look at Angela, and the customer reached for her purse.
Angela took the five-pound note over to the grey IBM
till at the back of the counter.
   On returning to the ladies, and handing them their
purchase and their change, she became aware of

another presence, a man. It was Eric. What on earth could he want to speak to her about? She felt her whole body tighten with anger. And then, from the corner of her eye, she saw another male figure push the glass door and enter the shop. It was Jim.

'Eric,' she said, 'I'm busy. Go away.'

Jim came up to the counter, smiling to himself, and fingered the cosmetic brushes with curiosity. Angela moved over to him. 'I'll be with you in a moment. I have an awkward customer.' She returned to Eric. 'It's over. Now go.'

'Carol told me that you've started Stella's therapy group. It's not because of me, is it? You know I still care about you.'

'You don't care enough, Eric. Now go. I suggest a blusher to go with the foundation, sir. Your wife will be delighted.'

'Stella will help you. I believe she's good. Roland Temple knows her, apparently. You know Roland Temple, the one who –'

Through clenched teeth she said, 'Eric, go away. I don't want to talk to you. That's seven pound sixty.'

'I'm sorry, Angie.'

'Don't call me that. Go! I can't stand the sight of you.' She moved sharply over to Jim.

'He's decided against a purchase,' she said brightly. 'These older men, so indecisive. Can I help you?'

'Maybe,' Jim said, enigmatically. He smiled his lopsided smile. 'I like you with your hair up. Come out for lunch.'

'When Michelle gets back.'

She noticed Eric standing a little way off, looking at

her. This will do him good, she thought. Fancy suggesting that I thought I needed help. I'm the only sane one in that blasted therapy group. I know what I want. She glanced at Jim and noticed his expensive leather jacket. Today he had groomed his hair with Brylcreem, and wore a white polo-neck top. He fingered the bristles of a blusher brush.

'I've had some good news,' he said. 'A windfall. Four years ago an uncle of mine died. Owned a shoe factory down in Leicester. He left me a bequest, but the will was contested. My sister's always been pathologically jealous of me — she can't help it. Plus which he kept all the money in an offshore account. Takes that bit longer. Got a cheque this morning, didn't I? Twenty thousand pounds. Where can I take you for lunch?'

Eric pulled up outside Illuminations, as he had run out of bread. So Angela was angry with him, which was better than indifferent. He had to admit, he still wanted her. He did not see why he could not have some sort of open marriage with Linda, some kind of alternative set-up, which would free her too. For when you think about it, what is the individual? Nothing. We all need the freedom to transcend our limitations. Linda nearly understood that. Carol might know if Angie would understand that too — how desirable the impersonal was.

Chimes tinkled softly as Eric pushed open the door. Illuminations was not properly his shop; he had indeed lent the co-operative a sizeable sum to start the venture and it had been a shrewd investment. Illuminations

53

was the mecca for all environmentally-aware, veget-arian, New Ageist Chisholmeians. Even now the shop was fairly busy. In front of him was a long-haired man, wearing a T-shirt inscribed 'Jesus had long hair', who browsed along the row of pulses and lentils, all sealed in biodegradable Cellophane. To his right Sebas-tian stood behind the counter that dispensed herbs and spices from rows of large bottles. He served a woman in a fisherman's smock. Carol, at the bread counter to his left, was busy too. At the back of the shop a few steps led to a quieter area, where there was: a rail of multicoloured clothes and scarves; ethnic jewellery; shelves of books - vegetarian recipes, homeopathy, New Age philosophy; rows of tapes *Increase Your Self-Esteem*, meditation music: 'Enfold yourself in this haunting cocoon of sound and experience a transcend-ental serenity'; Bach Flower remedies in little dark bottles, homeopathic remedies, essential oils; incense, candles, crystals; and a notice-board where leaflets and posters were pinned on top of earlier posters, making the whole unreadable. It was this Eric chose to peruse, though most of its contents were familiar to him. The Buddhist Meditation Centre advertised its courses, various practitioners offered shiatsu massage and craniosacral therapy, and Greenpeace encouraged him to fight the by-pass. There was Stella's group adver-tised too, and Roland's extra-mural class in Trans-actional Analysis. Eric loved the richness of it all, the colours of the clothes, aromas of the oils, the promise of lasting youth.

Carol came up to him and hugged him, and he hugged her back. Ever since Carol had been to

Findhorn she had greeted her friends this way, and Eric appreciated it.

'How are you?' she asked, and paused for a reply.

'Good today. I've been to see Angela. She seems angry with me. She won't admit that I've hurt her, and she doesn't seem to understand – as you do, Carol – that love is essentially an infinite thing. She and Linda aren't mutually exclusive.'

'You must give her time, Eric. I think it's OK for her to focus on her anger right now, to give it vent. I'm sure the therapy will bring her along. Then she must grieve for what she feels she has lost. Coming to terms with loss is important. Understanding herself will help her to understand you.' She took Eric's hand and held it, and looked at him, greying but distinguished, lines now around his eyes, but curiously attractive. 'Go home,' she said. 'Centre yourself. Relax.'

Eric smiled at her. Noticing a queue forming at the bread counter, Carol returned down the steps. She felt good. She knew she had a strength in counselling her friends. Eric was a dear friend, an ex-lover too, but now purely a friend. She too could not see why Angela could not share him with Linda. She did. But then, she thought, as she wrapped the organic wholemeal loaf, perhaps that was a mistake. She knew she undervalued herself. That was her problem. Stella had told her that, and so had her previous therapist. And her masseuse. Don't settle for so little, she had been told. You have the potential for change, someone else had said. You can change.

'Excuse me! You've given me the wrong change!'

Carol looked at the customer, her reverie broken.

'I gave you a ten-pound note and you've only given me change for five.'

Carol thought, and did not remember. The lady had certainly given her a note. But there were plenty of notes in the till. What, oh what, should she do? She felt her stomach knot, the muscles tighten at the back of her neck. 'Are you sure?' she asked.

'Yes. I had only this ten-pound note in my purse!'

The customer is always right. You have the right to exist. You have the right to say no without feeling guilty. You have the right to change. The right change. I can't change.

'I'm sorry,' said Carol. 'Let me think.'

What would Stella say? Accept and advance. What would her meditation teacher say? Be still. Carol breathed deeply. I accept that I am confused, she told herself. I accept that I am embarrassed. And I remember, once, when I was at school . . .

'I'm sorry,' she repeated, 'but I find this hard to cope with. Once, when I was at school, a teacher accused me of keeping part of the dinner money that I had to take to the office. I hadn't taken it. She hadn't counted it correctly. But I can access back to that humiliation, you know. It just overpowers me. I feel like that right now. I feel like I'm nine again. Thank you for letting me hang on to that.'

'Can I have the right change, please?'

'Her name was Miss Hawkins. It was just that she reinforced that feeling of worthlessness which I'd learnt at home. But you want your change. I can understand that. You must be experiencing pain too. That's OK. I'll get Sebastian to open the till. I need some space.'

Carol made her way into the back room, after alerting Sebastian, and took her coat. It was her lunch break, and she felt like going back to Lincoln Grove. She would write it down. This helped her focus on what was going on for her. She was pleased, for she would have something to say at the group next week. And it was only Friday. Miss Hawkins. She would need to work on that one. It would be nice to try a role-play in the group. Didn't Sandra say she was actually a teacher? And that middle-aged woman, her friend, Sue, or Zoë, or someone. Either could be Miss Hawkins. What was it she had read once? Thanks from a student to a teacher: 'To the person who destroyed all of my dreams.'

CHAPTER FIVE

'No,' said Sandra, 'I don't think Ted Hughes is exactly sorry for the pig. He's just saying how absolutely lifeless it is.'

'But Miss Coverdale, it's awful, that dead pig. And it says, look, "The gash in its throat was shocking" and in our group we think Ted Hughes is a vegetarian.'

'No. I don't know but I don't think so. The poem's not about that, anyway. It's just a description of a dead pig.'

'Miss Coverdale!' Philippa swung back on her chair. 'But how do you *know* that's what he meant? Why are you right and not us? You said poetry was sometimes a matter of opinion!'

'No, a matter of taste. But this is just a poem about a dead pig.'

I hate Ted Hughes, thought Sandra. I hate him for writing about dead pigs, I hate him on behalf of Sylvia Plath, and I hate him for appearing in every bloody poetry anthology in the English stockroom. When I get out of here I'm going straight to the tuck shop for a Mars bar. She stopped in her tracks. Ah! Emotional eating. Stella was right. Fascinating. But I'll still have that Mars bar, she thought.

'Miss Coverdale. Stacey says that if we put our pork rinds in the food-only bucket in the canteen, then it goes to the pigs and that's like cannibalism.'

Sandra shuddered at the thought, and looked forward to her Mars bar. 'OK girls, let's get back to work. Find me the two verses in the poem that are intended to contrast with the rest of it . . .'

Sandra saw Zoë as she left the classroom and came up to her, her eyes shining. It was impossible not to tell Zoë how she was feeling. Together they wove around lines of girls in navy skirts and white blouses, and Zoë listened as Sandra spoke.

'Now I'm becoming aware of it, I can see how much I think about food and booze. Just now, right, when I was teaching the third years, I was fixating on this Mars bar. And then before, with half of my mind I'm leading a discussion on Mr Rochester, and with the other half, I'm thinking, I shall stop at the garage on the way home, fill up with petrol, and get some things – I mean, food. And if I finish my marking I can open that bottle of Liebfraumilch my mother left. Stella is right, you know. I'm not properly hungry, but I think about food to get me through the lesson. You know, Zoë, I read somewhere that men think about sex every four minutes. Well, I'm like that with food! This is going to work, I know it. If I can discover *why* I do this, I'm almost there. I'm looking forward to my session with Stella tonight. Oh, are you in Room 4?'

Zoë waited at the door. Her Latin GCSE set – all five of them – sat along the radiator. She smiled wearily at her friend, glad for her.

'Have you booked your session with Stella?' Sandra asked.

'No, not yet.'

'You should. I've got to go now – I'm invigilating.'

As Sandra made her way to the hall, she pushed to one side a sense of unease. She'd done it again – bombarded Zoë with her own selfish concerns. And Zoë, being so long-suffering, had withstood it all. I must make it up to her, thought Sandra. She remembered, with even more guilt, that it was this morning that Zoë was scheduled to have her appraisal interview with the Head. Zoë was dreading it. And she had not even said to her, good luck. She knew that Zoë found the Head difficult.

She pushed open the door to the hall slowly and quietly, and the teacher that she was relieving picked up her marking and prepared to leave. Sandra liked examination duty. It sent her into a trance. She watched the fifth years bowed over their desks, their pens chasing across the paper. The large clock on the wall ticked audibly. All was quiet. I wonder what would happen, she thought, if I were suddenly to shout, very, very loudly? Then she had to make an effort to stop herself doing that. She watched individual girls working, felt her mind wander, her eyes grow heavy. Could I, she thought, just close them for a moment? It would be so wonderful. She looked across the hall to see who was on duty with her. Debra Wentworth. Sandra shook her head to dispel the sleepiness. She knew that if she shut her eyes for a moment, Debra would notice, and would mention it in the staff room, or worse, put up an anonymous notice on the bulletin board, saying something like, 'All teachers on examination duty should ensure that their attention never strays', and Sandra would know it was meant for her. Debra caught her eye and smiled.

Sandra watched the girls. Twenty minutes until the end of the exam, and break, and the Mars bar. There I go again, she said to herself. Debra stood up, to survey the girls. Sandra looked at her. That's power dressing, she thought. Debra wore a black suit with a waist-length jacket. Her blouse was powder blue, and her shoes matched exactly. Her hair, in a short bob, was immaculate. What was more, she knew she looked good, and Sandra could almost imagine that she stood there in front of the girls to make them aware of that fact. She wondered if the girls liked her, if they saw through her hypocrisy. Sandra reached into the pocket of her cardigan and found, as she expected, half a packet of extra strong mints, and slyly inserted one into her mouth.

One by one the girls put down their pens. Sandra stood too, and picked up the instructions for ending the exam from her desk. She read them through. It was simple enough; there were three biology sets, and each set was to be collected in separately. One minute to go. She watched the clock so as to call out 'Stop writing' at precisely the correct time. Debra Wentworth joined her at the front of the hall. Debra looked up at the clock and, stepping in front of Sandra, said authoritatively, 'Girls! Stop writing now.' She took the instructions from Sandra. 'Right. Miss Coverdale will collect sets one and two, and I'll take in the third. May I remind you there is to be no talking until you leave the examination room.'

Bloody typical, thought Sandra, as she stomped around the hall, collecting papers in both arms. Give the orders, and let someone else do all the work. It wouldn't matter, she thought, if the Head saw through her. She wasn't popular in the staff room. But the Head loved her. She spent hours closeted up in his room, discussing new initiatives and policies. Although Sandra would have liked to think they were having an affair, she was certain that wasn't the case. Debra spoke frequently about her affection for her husband – 'Justin and I never argue'; 'We've decided not to have children because they would intrude'; 'When I came home there were a dozen red roses . . .' The Head liked her simply because she was such an expert flatterer.

It was unusual for an independent girls' grammar school to have a Headmaster. Two years ago, when the governors announced his appointment, there was an outcry. The girls won't talk to him openly, some feared. More work for us, said the deputies. Sandra was outraged too. There were few enough top jobs for women, and surely in an all-female institution there ought to be positive discrimination. But, Zoë had argued, the best person ought to get the job.

Ironic, really. It was Dr Young who had progressively cut the Latin courses. And poor old Zoë was there now, ensconced in his room, discussing her career. Millers' Grammar did not have a proper appraisal system – only state schools need have those. But the Head saw each member of staff once a year for a little talk. Sandra had not had hers yet, and was glad. Because really she needed to decide before then what she was going to do with her life. In her mind she tried saying to the Head, 'I've decided, Dr Young, to leave teaching. I'm taking up law.' He would be utterly taken aback. Delicious. Sandra ignored Debra and took the papers to the staff room.

★

Dr Young leant back in his reclining chair and smiled reassuringly at Zoë Swann. She looks like a drowned rat, he thought.

Let this be over as quickly as possible, thought Zoë. She sat, her legs tightly crossed, on the edge of her chair, and pulled at her fingers. She had nothing she wished to say to the Head. She despaired of ever being understood by him. She only wanted to be left alone. She correctly identified the nutty aroma in his study as fresh coffee, and focussed her attention on the photograph of his wife and three daughters on the desk. They oppressed her in some undefined way.

Dr Young picked up his gold biro from his desk set and tapped it three times on his desk. He inhaled slowly. 'And how have you been coping this year, Zoë?'

'All right.' What else could you say?

'Because, as you're no doubt aware, I see appraisal as essentially a two-way process. It's every bit as important for me to hear how you see yourself, and your role in the school, as it is for me to give you my opinion of your contribution to Millers'. In fact I like to base my opinion on what you have to say. I readily admit that, as a doctor of physics, I have little expertise in your – ah – field.'

Dr Young liked the sound of his own voice. For a scientist, she thought, that was impressive. But, as he never tired of informing the staff, he was a cultured scientist. He played the violin, painted still lifes and read biographies.

'What do you enjoy most about your job?'

Zoë thought about her lunches with Sandra and her

lessons with the second years who actually enjoyed singing *Rudolph the Red-Nosed Reindeer* in Latin, and the occasional enthusiastic sixth former.

'Teaching,' she said.

'Of course, of course. And what have you done to incorporate student-centred learning techniques into your classes?'

Zoë experienced a mild panic. 'I don't . . . I mean . . . with my subject, it's best if I explain it all first, and then give them exercises . . .'

'So you prefer a more traditional approach. I see. This is a real problem with the classics, isn't it? Not very open to change. And how are you managing to combine – ah – motherhood and full-time teaching? I'm sure you won't accuse me of being a male chauvinist pig,' he laughed a little, 'for asking that. I'm simply concerned about you.'

Zoë saw Laura tugging at her sleeve while she was marking, and asking for drinks, and watching unsuitable television programmes, while she was ironing and planning tomorrow's lessons simultaneously.

'It's fine,' she said.

'Good, good. But it can all get on top of you at times, I know. That's why I thought it might be better for you next year to do without a form. You do know that we value your scholarship, Zoë, but you would be the first to admit that administration isn't your strong point. That's why I thought I would ask you to take on lost property instead.'

Zoë's heart sunk. She smelt all the games socks and abandoned knickers. She saw piles of digital watches and rollerball pens.

'Good, good. I'm sure you'll also be glad to know that Debra Wentworth has offered to lead the sixth-form trip to Athens in the summer, as we both felt it might be difficult for you with your little one, Linda.'

'Laura.'

'Laura. Of course!'

Zoë wondered whether that hot, tight feeling in her chest was the beginning of tears. The one thing that she had been positively looking forward to was the trip to Athens. Her sister had offered to take Laura. And now it had been whipped away from her. Big girls don't cry, she told herself. Perhaps it's my inner child. She tried to catch the drift of the Head's remarks.

'. . . a very important part in the cultural life of the school. But whereas our parents can easily see the results of our drama, music and art departments, you do see that the classics is a rather moribund area. What we need to do is equip our girls for change.'

Change, thought Zoë. I need a change. I need to change.

'. . . so in my vision of the development of Millers', I see the classics as an option for the girl who – ah – likes that sort of thing, but I am hoping that you might begin to think of some new areas where you might make a contribution. Have you thought about learning Japanese? Or perhaps computing. Classicists are supposed to have fine minds. Ask Debra to let you have a play in the IT rooms. You haven't had any experience of computers, have you?'

Zoë shook her head. What was she going to do? She knew she had to say something. She couldn't let the Head railroad her like this. What would Sandra do?

Sandra would argue, she knew. Zoë cleared her throat. When she spoke, she noticed her voice seemed to be a thin, quavering echo from deep inside her.

'I think I would prefer to teach Latin.'

'And I'm sure there always will be some Latin for you to teach.'

'I'm not very happy about computers.'

'Change, my dear Zoë!'

The sharp ring of the Head's phone cut across their conversation. Dr Young picked up the receiver.

'Yes? Ah, yes, of course.' He put his hand over the receiver. 'It's the Chairman of Science 2001. I'd better speak to him. We'd almost finished, hadn't we? You can go now, Zoë. Ah, Mr Briggs. So glad to hear from you . . .'

Zoë left the Head's study quietly. She walked down the corridor towards the main entrance, and walked out through the double doors. The sharp winter air made her shiver. Out in the street she turned left and walked towards the canal. Hot tears stung her eyes. Why didn't she say anything? How could he do that to her? Why were all the things she had loved when she was at school – the teasing intricacies of Latin syntax, the elegance of Cicero's prose, Catullus's love poetry – thrown on to the educational scrap heap? She might as well give up now. Admit it, Zoë, you're finished. She came to the bank of the canal and stood there on the frozen mud. It felt hard and polished. The water was dark, sluggish. Going nowhere, used up.

I don't even have the courage to jump, she thought. And she thought of Laura and knew she was being very silly. She had to carry on. She had to go back to school and teach her GCSE set.

It wasn't fair. She allowed herself a spurt of anger. Other schools didn't value Latin as little as Millers'. Chris, her friend from university, was Head of a thriving classics department in Somerset. Zoë wondered, not for the first time, whether all of it might be her fault. And the conviction grew. She had said nothing effective to Dr Young; she had sat there and taken it all. And yet, the thought of fighting back . . .

She needed to change. To learn to be more assertive. She remembered the trip to Athens and again she felt a spasm of disappointment. What can I do? Who can help me? That was when she thought of Stella. Would she tell her what to do? For the first time since that Thursday evening when she sat on the floor at 8 Lincoln Grove, ashamed and writhing with embarrassment, she felt glad that she had the therapy group. She re-entered the school building, and noticed that it was still ten minutes off her next lesson. The telephone in the staff room was free. She had taken a note of Stella's number last week, and was glad she had done so, for now she was going to ring Stella, and arrange a private session as Sandra had done. It was the only way.

The telephone rang several times. Then, a click, a pause. Oh God, thought Zoë, it's one of those infernal machines. She wouldn't use the modern term, ansaphone, even in her own mind.

'Hello. This is Stella Martin. I'm not here right now, but my love is with you, strengthening you. Remember, this ansaphone is an extension of me. Don't be afraid of it. Tell it whatever you want. Leave your name and number and I will ring you as soon as I can. I love you.' And then the tone.

Zoë was about to replace the receiver, defeated. Just then Debra emerged from the sitting room and smiled at her.

'This is Zoë Swann. Please ring me at home as soon as possible. My number is 772 2737.'

CHAPTER SIX

Stella replaced the receiver and experienced a deep sense of satisfaction. She had even wondered whether Zoë Swann would come back to the next meeting; she had seemed so withdrawn, so defensive, yet she had rung to arrange a private appointment, had asked Stella to help her to change. That's my speciality, Stella had said. And she sent her love out to Zoë. Poor Zoë. Stella would make her better.

Not only that, but shortly Sandra would be arriving for her first appointment. Stella was still continuing to see clients individually at her own home, but had wondered, if her practice was to grow, whether she could use Lincoln Grove as her permanent base. Anything was possible, she knew. But this evening, Sandra was to come to her old consulting room, which was, in fact, a converted spare bedroom. It lay at the back of the house, overlooking Stella's garden. She had furnished it simply: two colourful easy chairs; an occasional table by each chair, each with a box of tissues; a small desk with her appointments diary under the window; and a number of plants. She kept the lighting low and burnt incense.

Stella used the room too for her own meditation. It was her safe room. And now she was here to write a letter to Gill. Stella's stationery was recycled, and printed with her name and address. The paper was a soothing shade of peach.

DEAR GILL

Thank you so much for your letter, which I received yesterday. Of course I am well but miss you so much. I am thrilled that the extension to the TransFormation premises has been started, but I'm sad to hear about your financial problems. But you told me, Gill, never to worry about money. Love leads to prosperity, remember? But if you do have difficulty raising a loan, why don't you contact Richard? He's in Los Angeles in the McWilliam–Mitchell headquarters.

My therapy group has eight members already, all of them special. I have one woman who has an eating disorder and feel –

Stella stopped writing. How did she feel about Sandra? She really did not remember her at all from the Slim-Plicity days. So many women had passed through her hands. And yet, it was embarrassing to think that she had known her in those days when she had been so misguided. It was necessary to impress Sandra. To prove how she had advanced. Naturally it would take Sandra some time to understand and accept a new way of thinking about food and weight. But Stella was perfect at it. Now she was able to eat precisely what she wanted and remain slim. (Of course, provided she kept to a few trivial rules: no sugar, no white flour, no eating between meals, no fried food.)

Yes, she had found freedom. She picked up her pen again.

I have one woman who has an eating disorder and feel delighted at being able to do for her what you have done for me. I took your advice, and contacted Roland Temple, and am seeing him once a week.

She put down her pen. How much to tell Gill? Was there anything to tell her? Although she was alone, Stella could feel herself blushing. At her last session with Roland, the subject of Richard had come up. Roland had asked her, how was she handling Richard's absence? She had said she was fine, that she preferred him away. And she knew that Roland must be thinking about the lack of sex, and Stella could not bring herself to mention it, but then realized not mentioning it was even worse than mentioning it, as Roland might think that she wasn't interested in sex at all! So she had said that her sexual relationship with Richard had deteriorated. Roland had said nothing. She had to carry on. She told him how she had invented excuses to avoid intimacy, that during sex she felt detached, disgusted even, but she was sure, she added quickly, that was because of problems with Richard, not problems with her own sexuality. Roland had simply nodded.

And she was scared. What if he thought she was frigid? I like men, she had said. He had blushed, which made Stella blush too. She had continued, Gill always said I possessed a tremendous capacity for passion. Roland said, she said that to me too.

So, thought Stella, two passionate people. And after that session, she had begun to daydream. What if? What if, after a session, he suggested she stay for a coffee, for a meal? What if they attended a workshop together, something like iridology, where they had to look into each other's eyes? When she visualized him, she could see him very clearly, his tiny hips, his black shirt, his cropped hair.

No, there was nothing to tell Gill.

I, Stella Martin, love and approve of myself. You, Stella Martin, love and approve of yourself. She, Stella Martin . . . sat at a corner table at the Cornerhouse and held Roland's hand tightly. You are beautiful, he said to her. Morally, spiritually and physically. Stella, we need each other. Our road to fulfilment must be together. The doorbell rang.

Stella ran downstairs. It can't be transference, she argued with herself. I've already been in therapy with Gill and I would have had my transference then. Anyway, she reasoned, I'm a therapist myself. And she opened the door to Sandra.

She's rich, thought Sandra, taking in the wide carpeted hallway, the large number of rooms, and the seductive atmosphere of affluence that permeated Stella's Greenfield home. Sandra wondered how she got rich. A good marriage? Wealthy beforehand? Does therapy make you rich? She did not have time to answer her own questions, as Stella ushered her upstairs and into a room at the rear of the house, smelling gently of musk. Sandra felt large and clumsy, awkward and ill at ease.

She sat on the edge of the armchair, and felt both as if she was at the doctor's and not at the doctor's. Stella was, she assumed, a figure of some sort of medical authority, able to tell Sandra, *this* is what is wrong with you, *this* is how to cure it. But Stella's look of loving concern offered something else too, a promise that whatever Sandra said would be taken very very seriously. That was nice.

Stella spoke softly, with a sort of hushed earnestness, 'In this session, Sandra, I want to begin to try to understand you and the areas of your life that cause you concern. I don't have any one method of proceeding. My basic analytical theory is informed by TA, although I use a Rogerian-influenced client-centred approach, with some Gestalt as appropriate.' That'll impress her, Stella thought. 'But all you have to do is talk to me about yourself, saying just whatever seems right to you. Think what you want to say most to me.'

What luxury!! A whole hour, in which to talk entirely about herself. This was worth paying £20 for. Sandra hardly knew where to start. What did she want to say most? She thought she had better start with her eating.

'From as early as I can remember, I've loved eating. I was fat when I was at school, and teased for it a bit, and that was why, when I was a teenager, I started dieting – you know, following the diets in magazines. But I could only stick to them for three or four days at a time – Monday I started, usually, and then by Thursday it was over, and I'd stuff myself at the weekend, you know' – no, I don't know, thought Stella – 'and I just began to hate myself. When I started at university I was still fat, and I had to do a lot of reading, and whenever I read, I ate. Sweets, or packets of biscuits, or bags of peanuts. And that's when I first met you – at Slim-Plicity – I thought I'd join a slimming group. But I joined the Fat Women's Support Group too, because I also thought that I shouldn't be ashamed of being fat.' Emma's group, thought Stella, surprised. Emma and Liz and Martha's group. 'But in the end things happened and I gave up both; and since then I've sometimes tried to curb my eating, and somctimes just not bothered; and not liking my job very much, I find I'm eating more and more, and my weight's going up and up; and the more I eat, the more miserable I get, and the more I eat. That's about it.'

Slim-Plicity, and the Fat Women's Support Group, thought Stella. She said – like Roland – 'Good!' She nodded. 'Now Sandra, I'm sure you realize, being a very intelligent woman' – I hate it when people say that, thought Sandra – 'that your overeating is a symptom of something that lies far deeper. I don't want to treat the symptom. I want to get to the roots of your dis-ease.' She pronounced the *s* softly. 'For your overeating comes from some wrong early decisions taken about yourself, and about food. My job as your therapist is to discover these early decisions, and then help you to make some new ones. Or to put it another way, we will see what emotions your overeating is suppressing, and then find other ways of dealing with these emotions. So now I need you to tell me about your earliest days. A person's character is virtually entirely formed by the age of six.'

Gosh, thought Sandra.

'So tell me your earliest memory – the first thing you are conscious of remembering.'

Sandra thought hard. Her first memory. Actually she often asked her second years this question when they read the opening chapters of *David Copperfield*. She herself had difficulty in remembering anything at all from her early years.

'My mind's a blank,' Sandra said.

'Aah!' murmured Stella. 'Perhaps there is something you are not yet ready to admit to yourself.'

Sandra considered that one. 'No, wait. Here's

something. My Aunty Lydia's wedding. When I was three. I don't recall the wedding, but my mother got me ready early – I wore a pale blue frilly dress with a real sticky-out petticoat – and I played in the garden as it was warm. I rode my tricycle round the garden path. When she called me in I had dirty marks all round the bottom of the dress. She was furious and called to my Dad, and they shouted, and I cried, and then they cuddled me.'

'Good!' said Stella. 'Now, have you a memory to do specifically with food?'

'Yes!' cried Sandra, enjoying herself. 'Banana-flavoured ice lollies that they sold at the corner shop by the entrance to the park. And those Blackjacks – two for a penny – they were liquorice chews – I suppose they'd be considered racist now – and there was a time when Mum invited round the Parents and Friends Committee and put out little bowls of peanuts and sweets, and I sat there listening to them talk and eating nuts very, very slowly, and thinking how happy I was.'

'Good, good.' said Stella. 'Now, do you remember a phrase or a saying that you associate with your mother?'

That was a hard one, Sandra thought. 'I suppose,' she said to Stella, slowly, 'the phrase, "be more careful". I was never very good at maths. I think I rushed at it rather, forgetting about remainders in sums and missing out bits. And Mum used to get very frustrated with me. So she got me to practise little problems at home – I must have been around eight – and she'd watch me work and she would say, "Be more careful."'

'OK,' said Stella, suddenly eager. 'I'm your mother. Think back to when you were eight. Be eight. You're doing a sum. Talk to me about it.'

This is fun, thought Sandra. Like drama. 'Right. Mum, I'm stuck.'

'Tell me the problem.'

'Five girls have three biscuits each. Eight are chocolate. How many plain biscuits are there? I don't know what to do.'

'How many biscuits have they got altogether?'

'Twenty-four?'

'No. Be more careful, Sandra. Be more careful.'

'I am being careful.'

Stella switched back suddenly. 'How do you feel, Sandra? What do you really want to say to your mother?'

'I *am* being careful!'

'Tell her again.'

'I *am* being *careful*!'

'Good, good. Now, really shout!'

'I AM BEING CAREFUL!'

And Sandra burst into tears. Stella sprang from her chair, and put an arm around her. Sandra felt very, very sorry for herself. Her mother had never understood. She did do the best she could. It was awful being a child again. She must have had a terrible childhood. And Stella, cool and fresh and smelling of a musky perfume, embraced hot, snivelling Sandra.

'I'm sorry,' Sandra mumbled.

'No!' said Stella, as she went back to her chair. 'You need to cry. You need to let it out. You're doing very well.' Sandra sniffed loudly. She felt shaky and strange.

'Tell me what you've found out, Stella.'

'I have some ideas,' she said, with a deliberate hesitation. 'Your mother seems to have made some impossible demands on you. Giving you messages such as "be perfect" and "try hard". And these made you feel overpoweringly inadequate. Perhaps food gave you the security and emotional well-being that you craved. Food became your safe house. I think you might be very angry with your mother. I think perhaps you need to off-load some of that anger. I think you have a problem with unexpressed anger.'

'Have I?'

'Your mother may not have met your needs. You may have felt she didn't give you the love you needed. So you went to food. For many women food equals love. Tell me, Sandra, do you love yourself?'

Sandra found this a very odd question. 'Not all the time,' she said.

'Do you love yourself when you overeat?'

'Certainly not.'

'Aah!' Stella looked at her watch. 'Our hour is nearly up, Sandra.'

'Oh!' said Sandra. 'I haven't given you my eating diary.' She fumbled in her sports bag and got out the red exercise book that she had been writing in all week. She offered it to Stella.

'I don't think I need that now.' Sandra felt cheated. 'I've already found out a lot about you. Can I give you some homework?'

Sandra nodded eagerly.

'Next time you overeat, I want you to say to yourself, "I, Sandra, love and approve of myself." Say it over and over again. Write it out. Put it on your bedroom mirror. Tell it to yourself over and over again. First, you see, you must accept yourself exactly as you are right now. You must love yourself exactly as you are right now. Practise it. If you want to pay by cheque I'd appreciate it if you'd write your cheque-card number on the back of the cheque.'

Sandra did. Bemused, exhausted, starting a headache, she allowed Stella to escort her downstairs, through the hallway and out into the tree-lined avenue. See you at the group meeting, she had said, as her farewell. She got into her car, and sat for a while at the steering wheel, thinking.

Thinking that for all these years she had been wrong. She thought she'd had a happy childhood. Affluent loving parents, who did everything to give her a good education. But no! She had had an *unhappy* childhood! Her parents had pushed her too hard. And her mother had given her an eating problem! Of course! Now it all fitted into place. Sandra ignored a slight feeling of betrayal. And I don't love myself, she thought. I suppose I don't. She thought, I, Sandra Coverdale, love and approve of myself. She felt silly. But she would get that book Stella had recommended. It was called *The Love Yourself Diet* by some American or other.

My head hurts, thought Sandra. It's all too much. And I'm hungry. I'll stop at the chippy on the way home. I, Sandra Coverdale, love and approve of myself.

I, Stella Martin, love and approve of myself. If Sandra belonged to both the Fat Women's Support Group *and* Slim-Plicity, Stella wondered, could she have been the one who told the Fat Women's Support Group about Slim-Plicity's celebration at the Carlton International? So, in fact, it was due to Sandra that Liz, Emma and Martha had been there when she had discovered the awful truth about Jo McKenzie? Did Sandra know? Stella felt most uncomfortable. She would prefer Sandra not to know about her humiliation, no matter how long ago it was or how far she had progressed since then. That was something she would have to address at their next meeting. For it was important, Stella felt, that Sandra should see her as perfect. How else could Sandra trust her and look up to her as she had looked up to Gill?

CHAPTER SEVEN

Sandra sniffed. She had forgotten to bring any tissues to the meeting, and Stella's box was empty. If she didn't sniff, she was sure her nose would run. She was acutely conscious of Norah. She sniffed again, more loudly.

'Is your friend coming this week?' Norah asked. In fact only the two of them had arrived as yet.

But Sandra was able to explain. 'Zoë's upstairs with Stella, having her individual session. She's coming straight to the meeting from that.' Sniff. Sandra watched Norah's nostrils dilate slightly. Dilate and flare like a horse.

'I find this painful, don't you?' enunciated Norah.

'Oh yes!' breathed Sandra, enthusiastically.

Some footsteps heralded the arrival of more of the group. Angela and Carol entered the room, Carol in a kaftan and Angela in either a very short black dress or a long jumper; Sandra wasn't sure which. But already she felt a warm intimacy with them, a funny sort of comradeship. The first time there was a knock on the outside door, it was so faint that Sandra thought she imagined it. The next time, she found the courage to inform the others that she thought she'd heard a knock. Carol got up to open the door.

The man who came in was unknown to them all. To Sandra he looked oddly out of place – greying sideburns, a drab brown suit and not much hair. He avoided eye contact.

He gave a slight cough before he spoke, with a rather effeminate lilt, 'Stella Martin?' Carol assured him she would be down soon. 'I'll wait,' he said, and stationed himself by the door.

Sandra wondered if this could be the agoraphobic. Quite an achievement for him to come all by himself. But then, Stella was obviously such a good therapist. Since her meeting three days ago so much had fallen into place. Sandra's eating was unexpressed anger, true, and a cry for love, *and* an act of rebellion against her mother's high standards *and* a feminist statement about not wanting to be seen as a sex object, probably. Sandra brooded; watched Jim arrive - tonight in a shell suit, his hair parted on one side - watched him go to sit by Angela; saw David settle by the wall, holding his head in his hands; waited for Zoë. The man waiting outside peered into the room, stared at Angela and looked at his watch. Sandra tried to think why it was that an agoraphobic should prefer to wait *outside* a room; perhaps he was claustrophobic too. She noticed he looked at her, and she did not appreciate the length of the look.

But then came Zoë, slightly breathless, dishevelled, excited. She whispered to Sandra, 'My parents wrote a script for me in which I was told not to react and not to exist. I've got to change the script, got to express my feelings. Be assertive. Rebel. I'll tell you more later.'

Stella stood at the doorway, speaking to the brown-suited gentleman. He brought a folded newspaper from his pocket and pointed to a section. Stella read it, nodded. He put his hand to her ear and whispered something. Stella shook her head vehemently. He

81

reached out and put his hand on her shoulder, at which point she slapped him round the face with a stinging blow.

'Get out!' she screamed. Stella was scarlet with emotion. Sandra scrambled up and ran to her. 'Oh God!' she said, and burst into tears.

'What happened?' Sandra demanded.

'He thought . . . he thought I was running a brothel!'

'What?'

'It was the ad. The ad I put in the *Chisholme Recorder*. The free newspaper. It said, "Relationship Problems. Sexual problems. I am a trained sympathetic therapist . . ." And he thought it meant . . . I feel so dirty!'

'It's not your fault, Stella!' said Sandra, outraged. The others had crowded around her. 'That's men for you. Desperately searching the small ads.'

Carol took Stella's hand. 'Let it go, Stella. Treat it as a learning experience. Sit down and let me run upstairs for my Bach Flower Rescue remedy.'

I'm overreacting, thought Stella. All my group saw me overreact. What shall I do? She thought of Roland, with gratitude. She would tell Roland. Tomorrow first thing. And she sipped at her Rescue remedy and concentrated hard on her affirmations. I, Stella Martin, am a fountain of love and serenity. You, Stella Martin, are a fountain of love and serenity . . .

'Tell the group, Zoë, what it is you told me,' Stella spoke encouragingly.

'All of it?'

'Just your decision.'

Zoë addressed the carpet. 'I've decided I want to fight back. I want to stop being trodden on by people and I – Stella said – I need to know how – how to –'

'Zoë wants you all to share with her your ideas on how she might become more assertive,' Stella explained. 'Use the group, Zoë. Listen to what they say and take whatever you find useful. Tell the group your affirmation, Zoë.'

Zoë told the carpet, 'I'm in control of my life.'

'Good. But do it as I showed you. "I, Zoë Swann . . ."'

'Oh. I, Zoë Swann, am in control of my life.'

'Again. Tell the group.'

She focussed on a spot near the ceiling. 'I, Zoë Swann, am in control of my life.'

'And state your feelings, Zoë. Experience your feelings. How do you feel?'

'Silly.'

'Good! Now, what can Zoë do to help her feel good about herself, and fight her negativity?'

Carol raised her hand and Stella nodded her permission.

'Do you meditate, Zoë? Try it. Try visualizing what it is you want to happen. Thoughts create results. You are what you think, you know. I've got some tapes, tapes of subliminal affirmations and creative visualizations. There are lots of courses too. Assertiveness courses. Or there's a psychodrama workshop next weekend.'

As Stella listened she jotted Carol's words down. She looked up and nodded at Angela, who smiled at Zoë.

'Have you thought of having a make over? A new look? I'd help you. I'm a cosmetic consultant.' Stella wrote that down too.

And Sandra felt uncomfortable. Because these women weren't Zoë's friends. She was. They had no right to tell her what to do. But Sandra wasn't going to be outdone. 'Take some action. Apply for a new job. Meet some new people. Or you could join something. Once you told me you'd quite like to do some work for the homeless.'

Stella stopped writing. 'Those are good ideas, Sandra. But we mustn't run before we can walk. First Zoë needs to learn about herself. Until you get yourself straight you can't be of much use to others. To take action too early is to risk failure.'

Sandra felt she had been reprimanded, and felt her colour rise. But Stella spoke again.

'This applies to you too, Sandra. It's pointless for you to take action over your food until you understand fully the reasons for your overeating.'

Sandra fell back in love with her. At least she didn't have to diet. Stella was wise. It doesn't do to rush at things.

It was 1.02 a.m. Sandra turned over in bed and her nightdress twisted around her like a sheath. She got out of bed and shook it free. It was impossible to sleep. Her mind was whirling. But she would not give in and make herself a cocoa; she had school in the morning and needed all the sleep she could get. She got back into bed and lay on her back, the back of her head resting on the palms of her hands, and thought.

Carol said that her shop – Illuminations – had *The Love Yourself Diet* in stock, and it would be a simple matter to drive down there and get it. What was it Shakespeare said? 'Thinking makes it so'? Yes! So it must be true. If you don't let one negative thought into your mind. I'll try it now. I will fall asleep. I, Sandra Coverdale, will fall asleep in a few moments. Zoë wants to learn about assertiveness and skin care! I don't want her to change. No, I do. I, Sandra Coverdale, will fall asleep. Fancy Jim being related to the housekeeper at Balmoral! How do you meditate? I'd like to try. What essay title can I give the lower sixth tomorrow? I've forgotten to do something. I, Sandra Coverdale, forgot to ring my mother. Because I don't want to. I love and approve of myself. I wish I was David. He never has any trouble sleeping. Is it a good idea for me to tell my mother what I've discovered? Fancy thinking we were a brothel! Funny, really. Stella didn't think so. Thinking makes it so. So it wasn't the agoraphobic. Stella said he might come next week. If you love yourself enough you don't have to eat.

It was no use. Sandra kicked off her duvet and made for the tiny kitchen. Cocoa, biscuits, and two paracetamol.

CHAPTER EIGHT

In fact Stella had regained her serenity. But she was glad, nevertheless, that she had arranged an emergency appointment with Roland. It was good of him to see her, as it was his morning off. He did not have use of the consulting room that he shared, so had agreed to see Stella at home, at the Quays. Stella appreciated that. She liked the Quays, too. It was modern, fashionable and fresh. She intended to dress with particular care that morning.

Her wardrobe was extensive. For Roland, nothing too businesslike; the real Stella was not tailored and severe, but feminine and flowing. She selected a soft grey angora sweater and her tight jeans. And she would miss breakfast. She felt much better before she started eating, as sometimes food had an unsettling effect. Sometimes it was better to avoid it altogether. As she completed applying her blusher, a dull thud at the door told her the post had arrived.

She looked through the letters. Most were circulars; Stella was on a number of mailing lists; all the local therapists mailed each other. Stella was aware that she had not been on a course for some time, and although she felt utterly confident in her empathetic skills and contemporary holistic approach, she thought it good practice to refresh herself. One letter in particular caught her interest. 'Modern Myth and Mickey Mouse', it was entitled. A weekend in Herefordshire. Expensive –

£250 for the weekend, tuition and accommodation inclusive – but Richard's allowance was generous. The theory was – she read quickly down the course description – that analytical identification with archetypes from myth and folklore was no longer applicable in the post-war generation; no one knew the classics any more, and what folk tales there were had been transformed by the film studios into something quite different. So for archetypal models it was necessary to study Disney films and children's television. Oedipus was dead; long live Mickey Mouse. Stella read with attention. This sounded good. She remembered seeing *Snow White* as a little girl and screaming at the Wicked Queen. Interesting. She took the leaflet and the booking form into the kitchen, leaving the other letters on the table, including the one with the Los Angeles postmark.

Roland had explained briefly how to find his house. He had suggested to Stella that she leave her car in the hotel car-park, and walk. This she was happy to do. It gave her time to arrange the final version of the incident last night correctly in her mind. A man had thought her group was a brothel; that she was the madam. It was that fact that distressed her. How could anyone – especially that revolting man – think she was available for general consumption? She was Stella Martin, who loved and approved of herself. She shuddered. Still, she was pleased to have a problem to share with Roland. She had been worried, it was true, that she didn't actually need a therapist, having so few problems now. Was there any real justification for seeing Roland? At least now he might be of some use to her.

Stella came to a small marina, the water inky black and hardly moving. There were no boats moored here. She looked beyond to the docks. All was still. But she knew very well that the point of living at the Quays was to have the address; the Quays was the place to live. Each house along the marina was three storeys, narrow, and built in a distinctive brick pattern. Only now, looking up at the first row of houses, and realizing that some were quite large, did it occur to her that Roland Temple might be married. He had said nothing about his marital status; why should he? Stella felt her stomach lurch. No, he simply didn't look like a married man. And here was the terrace that Roland had described. Salter's Wharf. Each property had a small front garden, just large enough for two chairs, and not at all private. Here, Number 4. Through the window Stella could see a large Wurlitzer jukebox, a black kitchen table and black chairs, and an abstract painting on the wall which looked something like a row of purple camels. As she approached the door, it opened, and there stood Roland. Her heart beat audibly.

She came in carefully so she did not brush against him. To do so would be just too forward. She removed her shawl, which he took and draped over a chair. There was no sign of any other woman; everything looked as if it belonged wholly to him. Their conversation was embarrassed, staccato. She thanked him for seeing her; and yes, she would like a coffee, but no milk and no sugar; and yes, she would prefer to move into another room as this was rather public; and yes, it was a lovely house, and how long had he lived here and did he like it? They moved into a small lounge with vertical blinds, which Roland closed. He then turned on a large lamp with a green shade that cast a glow over the room. Stella wondered where to sit. There was a two-seater settee – in black leather – and a director's chair under the window. She chose the settee, and watched Roland sit on the floor at the other side.

'I feel strange, sitting above you,' she said. Stella rose and sat on the floor too, opposite him. That was nice. Informal. She liked the gentle concern in his eyes. He looked at her with real interest, real attention, and smiled – an odd smile, as if he knew he shouldn't be smiling but he couldn't help himself. He leaned with one arm on the settee, his hand hanging free, his long pale fingers elegant. She noticed how clean his hands were, how his skin was soft and translucent. And he wore no rings.

'Last night you said something had happened that troubled you. Do you want to tell me about it?'

Stella nodded, but felt strangely reluctant to talk.

'OK. Just do what you want to do.'

Stella shook her head. She couldn't tell him after all, couldn't say that some man had thought she was . . . She felt Roland reach for her hand and he held it, across the settee. His hand felt cool, alien, a feminine hand.

'It was just that, some man, a stranger, came to my group. He'd misread the ad, thought I was . . . some kind of sex therapist.'

Roland nodded, full of concern.

'I mean, not exactly a sex therapist, but someone who called herself a sex therapist in order to . . . as a cover for . . . you know. It shocked me, I suppose. To be thought of in that way.'

'In what way?'

'That way!'

'Sexually?'

He had not let go her hand.

'I felt cheapened and dirty. To be thought of on that level!'

'Level?'

'Like a tart. Because . . .' Roland was silent. 'Because - oh, I see it now! It was unthinkable - when I was a child sex was unthinkable! My mother told me the facts of life and I didn't believe her - probably because she'd already conditioned me not to believe her - and there was never any contact - that sort of contact - between my father and her. She was fat even when she was younger. And when I did believe her - about sex - I couldn't think of her . . . and him. And I knew that when I got married I didn't want to . . . I would find a husband who didn't want . . . And I suppose I've succeeded. A husband six thousand miles away means I can be celibate.'

Roland removed his hand. Said nothing.

'But I don't want to be celibate!' Stella wailed. 'I believe in sexual fulfilment - with my adult self - although I can see now that my parental injunctions have suppressed that side of me. And that awful man put me in touch with my Shadow. With the whore in me. Who I don't want to know - yet. And I want to be slim, not to be sexually attractive - no, I want to be sexually attractive, as well as immaculate and pure . . .'

'Have you tried an affirmation?'

90

'What do you suggest?'

'Something about a right to sexual fulfilment.'

'I, Stella Martin, have a right to sexual fulfilment.'

Roland repeated after her, 'You, Stella Martin, have a right to sexual fulfilment.'

Stella looked at him. Behind his glasses – what was that she saw? – were those tears? She was transfixed. She said, 'I, Stella Martin, have a right to . . .' She took his hand.

'I'm sorry,' he said. They clasped hands. 'This is a difficult one for me.'

And Stella fell in love.

But you can't, a voice inside her told her. He's your therapist. If anything happens, you can't carry on seeing him. But if you stop seeing him – as a client – then nothing will ever happen. And she was curious, so curious, to know why he cried. Was it on her behalf? Or – please God! – was it *for* her? Did he want her? He's a tender man. A tender, vulnerable man. A tender, vulnerable, slim man. Dressed in black. With a jukebox and an abstract painting. But vulnerable. And she loved him because she was in control. He was so open, so pure.

She had with her a small fabric handbag, from which she extracted a tissue for him. She noticed in her bag the 'Modern Myth' leaflet.

'Have you seen this?' she asked. He had not, and read it attentively. 'I want to go,' she said with decision. 'Are you interested? Would you like a lift?'

'Yes,' he said. 'Yes, yes.' He looked at her and smiled. 'When you wish upon a star.'

*

He walked back to her car with her. He said he needed some fresh air. Then, he said, he had to go back and work. He was writing a book, he told Stella. (Imagine! He was writing a *book*!) It was about the place of ritual in male friendship bonds. He spoke a little about it as they made their way back to the car-park, past empty moorings and paved walkways and clumps of maisonettes. Words such as inadequate fathering and Robert Bly and rediscovery and the chains of rituals flew past her ears. She was only conscious of him. He was much taller than her. She had to look up to him. She would have loved to take his arm but knew that would be wrong, that would be a risk. They passed the cinema complex, silent and empty now, as it was mid-morning. Everything – the cinema, the Nautilus café-bar, the Croft Hotel, the office buildings – was just a backdrop for them both. She only knew the throbbing consciousness of him and her. They reached her car.

She put her key in the lock, and he grinned at her, almost, it seemed, against his better judgement. She wanted to embrace him, or rather, for him to embrace her, but he held out his hand. She took it and grasped it warmly, and they shook hands.

'I'll make an appointment for next week, then.'

'Good. Yes, do.'

'I shall look forward to that.'

'Good.'

'Bye, then.'

'Bye. Thank you for coming.'

She got into her car and drove off.

She leaned back against the seat as she drove, breathing shallowly, feeling slightly dizzy. She turned into the main road, but no, it was impossible to drive with due care and attention. She turned and parked a little further down the road, and walked. She needed to think. Beyond an empty office block stretched the canal, which Stella was surprised to find there. It was wide, and the waste ground on either side flat, littered with half-completed building projects. There was an air of hazy desolation. She stood and saw the city in the distance. With a tremendous effort she tried to recall his face. She knew it too well. She couldn't do it.

Roland was unlike any man she had ever been involved with before. When she was younger, living with her parents, she had gone out with a series of nice Jewish boys, more for the sake of telling the girls at school that she had a boyfriend. She had gone out for some time with the manager of a menswear shop in London's Oxford Street. Lawrence, that was. Her mother was keen on him. She finished with him shortly after her twentieth birthday, searching for something more. She met Richard about eighteen months later. The point about him was that he was not Jewish and her mother disapproved. So she really felt as if he was *hers*. When he was transferred to the north-west he proposed to her and she accepted gratefully. She loved having a home – a nice one at that – so far away from her mother.

But now – now that she had met Roland – she could begin to see that there were problems with her marriage. She had never wanted children, always putting it off to some later date, when she was slimmer, perhaps, or when she had passed her TA 101 exam. And

Richard was away so much. When he was at home, he never seemed to listen to her, not as Gill had listened, and then, there was his narrow-minded scepticism about her new way of life.

A voice – her mother's voice? – informed her that she was still married, children or no children. You have to work at a marriage. Marie had worked Stella's father to the bone. Now, now when she wasn't thinking of him, Roland's face came unbidden to her mind, and Stella's stomach contracted. That was one wonderful thing about being in love, your appetite went. Stella couldn't eat today if she tried. Roland Temple.

Were there any signs that he cared for her too? She thought hard. His smile, the way he held her hand, his tears, his ready agreement to go to 'Modern Myth and Mickey Mouse'. He loves me. 'Modern Myth and Mickey Mouse', his tears, the way he held her hand, his smile. All ambiguous. He loves me not. But his smile, the pressure of his hand, his tears – it all must mean something. Why else would she care so much? He would come and find her here, he could not concentrate on his writing, he would find her here, and take her in his arms. He would say her name tenderly . . .

She was filled with a delicious sense of sin, so familiar. She knew the feeling. How very odd! Sometimes, when she had lowered her customary restraints, and eaten something forbidden – like Belgian chocolates, or salmon *en croûte* – she would experience that melting, yielding, *wicked* sensation. But this was even better. And this didn't make her fat.

Roland, I love you. I, Stella Martin, am a fountain of love and serenity. You, Stella Martin, are a fountain of love . . . of love . . . Stella knew all about positive thinking. Your thoughts create reality. What you believe to be true, you create. You, Roland Temple, are a fountain of love . . . We, Stella and Roland, are fountains of love and, and – She turned, for there were footsteps behind her.

Despite his hair, now oiled and smoothed back into a short pony tail, she recognized him immediately.

'Jim!' she said, astonished. What was he doing here, on this waste ground by the canal on a Friday morning? He seemed surprised to see her too, but not particularly taken aback, apparently uninterested in what brought her there.

'Hello, Stella! It's all right here, quiet, if you like that sort of thing. They're doing a grand job of redeveloping it. I often used to take the dog for a walk round here, before they killed her. It was the debt-collecting agency. As a kind of threat. She took a third place in Cruft's one year, 1976. Having a break from your clients, then?'

'Oh, yes,' Stella said, having had time to collect her thoughts. 'My dentist has his practice round here. I've just had a check-up.'

'Is he good, your dentist?'

Stella smiled and nodded.

'My dentist used to treat Bob Geldof. When he was in London. Bob used to give him free copies of his records, but my dentist didn't go in for that sort of thing, more of a jazz fanatic. So he gave them to me. They were nicked, though, along with my boxing trophies. Well, I must be getting along. See you next week.'

Jim continued along the canal bank and crossed the main road, in the direction of the Nautilus café-bar, checking his watch as he did so. He rose on his toes as he walked, and quickened his pace as he mounted the mock gangway into the interior of the Nautilus. As yet the music was only at a moderate volume. Later it would be turned up fully, and conversation would prove impossible. Jim went through the bar and greeted his fellow waiters. He put on his mock sailor's jacket, which hid his pigeon-chest, and prepared for business.

'Why are you taking me to the Quays?' Carol asked. 'We could have had lunch in Beano's.'

Angela did not take her eyes off the road. 'It's my day off, I fancied a drink, and besides, it'll do you good to have a change of scene. It's smart in the Quays.' There was a pause. 'And Jim serves in the Nautilus. I thought we might pop in to see him.'

'I thought he wasn't working.'

'He is now. He was picked for this job from fifty-five applicants, he told me.' Angela paused before she entered the car-park to let the car which was leaving turn safely. Stella, not recognizing her, raised her hand in acknowledgement and drove off. Angela stepped out of her Mini, her hair in a chignon today. Carol followed her. Their footsteps crunched on the gravel as they made their way towards the Nautilus.

'Have you arranged to see him, Angela?'

'Not exactly.'

'Are you chasing him?'

'Chasing! Hardly. Just creating opportunities.'

'But you know what Stella said,' Carol warned. 'No sexual relationships within the group.'

'Oh, it's all very well for Stella, telling us to behave ourselves! I wonder what *she* gets up to in her spare time!'

'But Angela!' wailed Carol, pausing at the gangway entrance. 'You joined the group because you wanted to stop having problems with men!'

'Who's got problems?' Angela sucked in her cheeks, pouted slightly, and entered.

Carol, watching Angela sitting on a high bar-stool near the ship's wheel, was not jealous. She was not at all jealous. She watched Jim's attentiveness with detachment and pity. If Angela did not recognize that she had a problem, then her problem was even worse than it seemed. Carol knew that Angela was empowering men to create her happiness. This was like any other addiction. Angela was clearly incapable of coping with real life, and instead lived in a world of her own making, which consisted entirely of pursuing and collecting men, like trophies. Carol sensed the pathos in this. She was certain this behaviour concealed some deep inner sadness, something Angela could not admit to herself.

Of course, Carol had not always thought like that. When the two of them were at school, she did envy Angie a bit. She always got the attention when they went to parties, had a chain of boyfriends, and Carol listened to a succession of lurid confessions. But now that Angela was in her early thirties and still not married, and now that Carol had learnt so much about the mysteries of the personality, it was clear to her that it was Angela who was sick, and herself who was free of that particular illness. For Angela's pursuit of men, she knew, was an illness. A neurotic illness. It was much easier to put up with Angela's illness now she knew it was an illness. She could just pity her, and her victims like poor Eric. Poor heartbroken Eric. And poor Spencer whose last poem 'Love at first blight' was almost suicidal.

Carol felt glad that she had at least managed to get Angela prepared to accept some form of treatment for her illness. She watched Angela laugh and put her hand to her mouth. She watched Jim remove that carefully manicured hand and kiss her briefly. Carol shook her head. Although she knew she did not have a problem herself with Angie's behaviour she nevertheless felt an urge to return to safe ground, to get back to Illuminations. She did not really like it here. The music was loud and intrusive. People were eating meat – steak sandwiches – and she disapproved of these shallow business people who came here and ate dead animals for their lunch and never stopped to think about the damage they were doing to the environment with their petrol-guzzling cars. Carol wondered about leaving Angela there, but it was a long way back to Chisholme.

She didn't have enough money for the bus. But there was enough for a phone call, and Eric might be in. She could always ring Eric and ask him to pick her up. That would be a surprise for Angela.

'It's revenge, isn't it?' Eric said to Carol as they stood

outside Illuminations. 'She's seeing him because she wants to get back at me!'

'No.' Carol shook her head. 'It's her illness.' She hugged Eric, and thankfully opened the door of the shop. There was Sebastian weighing out the continental lentils. They pattered into the scales. How much nicer this was than the selfish materialistic world of the Quays and the Nautilus. Carol inhaled deeply the incense and spices. Who needed money and all the destruction it caused? Next week she would go to a day of lectures by Shantih Greenleafe who had come from America for a two-week visit to the north-west to spread her message of peace, ecology and personal fulfilment. She had been receiving messages from the spirits of nature that had shown her the way forward for the twenty-first century. She was known to be positively inspiring and the whole day of lectures was only forty pounds.

The chimes at the door tinkled, and Carol came out of her reverie. She smiled with pleasure. It was Sandra, Sandra from the therapy group. Both were pleased to see each other.

'Hello, Carol!' Sandra said. 'I hoped you'd be here. How are you?'

For Carol this was always a serious question. She thought hard.

'I'm feeling OK just now. I had a bad night,' she confessed.

'Why? Couldn't you sleep?'

'Oh no! That was the trouble. I slept too soundly. I couldn't do any dreamwork!'

'Dreamwork?'

99

'Mmm. I use my dreams as indicators of the present and guides for the future. It's not something Stella's awfully keen on, but it helps me. I think we have to listen very carefully to our subconscious and unconscious minds. Hear what they're telling us. What have you come in for, Sandra?'

Sandra found her attention drawn by the display cabinet of spinach bhajis, ricotta-cheese-stuffed pancakes, carob flapjacks, and date and banana cake. But no! That was precisely the point of her visit. She was here *not* to buy the food but to get her copy of *The Love Yourself Diet*. She told Carol the title of the book.

'Ah yes. Come here.' Sandra followed Carol to a free-standing display of books. Carol began to look along them. Sandra searched too. Here were books on vegetarianism, vegan cooking, and – horror! – slimming for vegetarians, meditation, crystal healing, *A Course in Miracles*, yoga and –

'Here it is!' Carol said brightly. She handed Sandra a thin paperback, its cover white, with a large red heart printed centrally, like a badly-designed valentine's card. *The Love Yourself Diet*. Sandra turned to the back. It was £8.95.

'That's a lot!' she said, impulsively.

'Ah!' said Carol. 'It's from the States. It's hard to get hold of over here. Only a few bookshops have it. But I've heard it's very good.'

Sandra opened her purse. She wondered why it was so costly to have an eating problem. While Carol got her change and wrapped the book, she looked around the shop. It made her feel nostalgic for her student days. Here were the Indian scarves and the candles and cheap food that were part of her life only four years ago. But now she was enmeshed in the world of work, respectable, a teacher who had to try to dress smartly and live conventionally. She suppressed a sigh. She knew she was being silly. People move on. She took the book with great anticipation. If this was to work, if through reading this book, talking to Stella, and positive, loving thinking, she was to overcome her weight problem, her life would be transformed. This was a historic moment. She received her change, just over a pound.

'How much are the ricotta-cheese pancakes?' Sandra asked.

Sandra made herself finish the set of second-year exercise books she had brought home with her. Then she turned off the main light in her room, put on the standard lamp, and sat in the armchair beneath it, curled up with her legs under her, and once again looked at the cover of *The Love Yourself Diet*. She wished the title didn't include the word 'diet'. It wasn't, she told herself, that she particularly wanted to become slim now. Just slimmer. Just less dependent on food as an emotional crutch. She had learnt from Stella that bad parenting had given her a food problem. Now she was going to learn what to do about it.

She flicked through the pages of the book. She was rather surprised. Much of it seemed empty. Or rather, there were spaces for the reader to write her own affirmations. 'My affirmations for Monday are ... my affirmations for Tuesday are ...' and so on. So you write your own book, Sandra thought, but berated herself for her scepticism; Stella had said this book worked.

Sandra had read a number of self-help books about weight; they all followed the same format, and this was no exception. First, a hagiography of the writer. Then, a preface. Then, a preface to the second edition. Then, a dedication. Then, the introduction. This is like the dance of the seven veils, thought Sandra, eager to find the promise enveloped in the book.

And here, on page forty-three, it was. Chapter One. Thoughts create reality. Negative thoughts create negative reality. Negative thoughts about food create obesity. So if you truly believe that the food you eat is not fattening, it is not fattening. If you believe your body is slim and beautiful, it will be slim and beautiful. Clap your hands if you believe in fairies, thought Sandra. This is ridiculous.

She read on. She had to re-programme her mind to respond positively to the food she ate. Which meant using affirmations. I, Sandra, can lose weight just by the power of my mind. I, Sandra, can eat chocolate and be slim. I, Sandra, deserve to be my ideal weight. She was to write out all her objections to these affirmations and then, when they were written, she was to burn them and scatter the ashes outside. She read on. She overate because she was afraid. She had inherited fear from the birth trauma. Until she dealt with that fear, she had a problem. She read of the woman who, while breathing deeply and healing herself, lost twenty-three pounds instantaneously. If you are frightened of a particular food, you must address it, talk to it, and tell it you are not afraid. This will disempower it. But above all, it is the power of your negative, hateful, destructive thoughts that creates blocked energy. And blocked energy means fat.

Sandra thought about this from a scientific point of view. She dimly remembered from physics at school something called potential energy. She'd never really understood that. But she could see now that if fat was composed of excess calories, then, in a way, it was potential energy, blocked energy, and that this could be released with the power of positive thinking. Thinking makes it so.

Sandra put the book down. She had read it all in just over half an hour. This book, thought Sandra, is the most ridiculous book I have ever read in the whole of my life. I shall try it, though, because it can't do me any harm, can it?

She imagined justifying herself to Zoë. Zoë, she said, somewhat sternly, one thing's for certain! If I don't try this, it won't work; if I do try it, it might. You get nowhere by being cynical. Everything, I, Sandra, consume, turns to health and beauty.

Including alcohol, she thought, as she made her way to the kitchen to get those two cans of lager that had been preying on her mind. Positive thinking. Or positive drinking.

CHAPTER NINE

'Now listen, Laura. Mummy's going to go into her bedroom for a little while and I don't want to be disturbed at all. You can watch television if you like or, better still, read a book, and you can have only two biscuits. But just leave me alone for a little while. You can come in when I call you.'

'What are you doing, Mummy?'

Zoë wondered how she could explain this. 'Well, I'm going to do some thinking. No, not thinking. I'm going to give my mind a rest.'

'Can I do it too?'

'Yes, well, you do it in your bedroom, and I'll do it in my bedroom.'

'Why can't I do it in your bedroom?'

'Because I need to concentrate. Why don't you just watch television?'

Laura moved off obligingly in the direction of the TV set, and Zoë went into her bedroom, shutting the door firmly behind her. At last. An opportunity to do some real meditation. Lots of people swore by it, she knew. And what better night than tonight, the third-years' parents' evening. She needed to be calm. Stella had said that meditation would help her become calm and balanced, get in touch with her deepest self, and develop her self-assurance. Perhaps. Stella had lent her a tape, which she said would teach her the basics. And so Zoë lay dutifully on her bed, and inserted the tape into her cassette player.

Strings played softly in the background, music ebbed and flowed like waves, and then a smooth American voice crooned a welcome. On no, thought Zoë, I hate American accents. Hello, murmured the voice. I'm so glad you are listening to this tape, and I feel privileged to come into your home and into your heart. My love is with you, surrounding you, enfolding you, loving you. (Tautology, thought Zoë.) Now first, I want you to relax. Rela–a–ax. And the voice talked Zoë through the routine of contracting and relaxing muscles that was so reminiscent of her ante-natal classes. Except this tape went deeper. Let your tongue relax. Let your mind relax. How do you relax your mind? Mind, relax! Zoë ordered.

It was quiet. Too quiet. What was Laura doing? It was an ominous sort of silence. Was she hurt that her mother had dismissed her so abruptly? Was *she* causing difficulties for Laura in the future?

Now that you are fully relaxed, your body will feel heavy. Oh so heavy. You are now ready to begin your meditation.

The phone rang. Zoë reached sharply over and switched the tape off and listened hard. The phone stopped ringing. A wrong number, as usual. She switched the tape back on and curtly informed her various muscles to resume their former state of relaxedness.

Listen and see if you can feel your heart beating. Feel your breathing. Zoë's was rapid. Now breathe deeply. Let go all your worries, your resentments, your anger. Breathe in love, energy and prosperity.

Prosperity? How can you breathe in prosperity? What sort of materialistic society is it that thinks that you can breathe in prosperity?

And now, in the silence that follows, I want you to rest completely. And listen. Listen to the still, small voice you hear in the very depth of your soul. Now listen.

If I mark the fifth-year comprehensions first thing in the morning I can use my free period for going to the bank and I must ring my mother, I need some more orange juice and to prepare the Cicero and . . . Zoë was asleep, her head now slightly on one side, her breathing deep and regular.

Did you listen? Did you hear the voice? Was it the voice of your conscience, telling you to forgive someone, to love someone just a little bit more? To love yourself just a little bit more?

Zoë slept.

'Mummy!'

Zoë came to consciousness. She heard Laura's soft, insistent voice. Oh no, she thought, I fell asleep. 'Mummy! I want you.' Zoë smiled to herself. She was possessed of no new inner truth, but had enjoyed a very pleasant rest.

'Come in, Laura!'

Laura bounced on to the bed. 'I did the telephone,' she said.

'The telephone?'

'The man on the telephone. I told him your mind was having a sleep.'

'Laura. Who was on the phone?'

'A young man.'

'A young man? How could you tell his age?'

'No, silly Mummy! That was his name.'

'Dr Young! What did you tell him?' Zoë was aghast.

For it was certainly the Head, who often rang his staff at home just to check they weren't slacking on the job.

'He was a nice man, Mummy. I told him you were making your mind go to sleep in the bedroom and you told me to watch *Neighbours* and have some chocolate biscuits and I played tag with Katie and Tina and I ate all of my dinner except the peas and about your new dress and your new make-up and you said I could put some on if I was good and I want a Barbie for my birthday.'

Every muscle in Zoë's body tensed more tightly than it had ever tensed in its life. 'What did he say to you?'

Laura grinned.

'What did he say to you, Laura? Laura!'

'I putted the phone down.'

'Well, Zoë, it's different. I mean, I will like it. No, I do like it. It just takes some getting used to.' Sandra grinned at her friend.

'I've got too much make-up on,' Zoë said, anxious for reassurance.

'No, no. I've seen a lot of people at school wear more than you. It's just that I'm not used to it. I think if you rub off a bit of the blue eyeshadow – the bit under your eyebrow – there!' Sandra took her forefinger and rubbed it off herself. 'And your mascara's smudged below your eyelashes. I'll just get a tissue.'

'Do you like the dress?' Zoë asked.

Zoë's dress was scarlet. It had a row of large black buttons down the front, and black borders to the short sleeves.

'It's dramatic. Kind of sixties, I suppose. Are you wearing it for the parents' evening or are you just showing me?' asked Sandra, doubtfully.

'I thought I might wear it tonight. Stella said that it was important for me to project an assertive image. I went to Boots' in Chisholme for the make-up. Angela suggested the colours.'

Sandra whistled and Zoë laughed. Sandra looked at her friend again. She looked like a painted doll. But that was probably because she had never seen Zoë in make-up before. Stella had a point; Zoë needed to lose her drab, dishevelled image. The door, seemingly of its own accord, opened, and revealed Laura in a long pink nightdress with a colouring book hanging loosely from one hand.

'What do you think of your mummy, Laura?'

'Very pretty.' Laura ran to Zoë and put her arms around her hips and buried her head in her stomach. Suzanne entered the room. Suzanne was the babysitter. She was in the sixth form at Millers'.

'I think Mrs Swann looks really nice tonight. Don't you, Miss Coverdale?'

And as far as Sandra could see, there wasn't a trace of satire in her voice. So, thought Sandra, it's me. I'm not prepared to allow my friend to change. Perhaps it threatens my own security. Sandra had begun to read the articles in the *Guardian* about personal growth and was learning a few things.

'Right!' said Zoë. 'I think I'm ready. Suzanne, remember it's bedtime at quarter to eight; and Laura, Suzanne is only going to read you one story; and Suzanne, make sure it doesn't have witches, wolves or burglars in it otherwise you won't get her to sleep; and Laura, Suzanne will tell me if you've been a good girl or not when I get home.'

Sandra bent down, kissed Laura, and looked at her watch. They were still quite early and would reach school in good time. Travelling together to parents' evenings saved petrol and provided company. Also it enabled them to have a drink afterwards.

'That's the best thing about this diet!' said Sandra. 'I can still eat and drink whatever I want. Are you looking forward to the evening?'

Zoë explained. 'I don't have too many parents to see. The Head allows any second year who wants to drop Latin to do so, and most of them do. I've a class of eighteen third years, and most of those won't take it as a GCSE course. Most of the parents will spend their time justifying their daughter's decision to pack Latin in. But I'm ready for them!'

'What do you mean?'

'Stella's taught me some assertiveness techniques and if I have trouble I'm going to try them out.'

'Oh, go on. What are they?'

'She's shown me a way to deal with confrontation. First you have to describe the situation as it seems to you: that's D – D for "Describe". Then it's E – that's for "Express your feelings about the situation". Then it's S – "State the changes you wish to occur", and then C for "Consequences". You have to say what the consequences will be if there isn't a change. Like this. If I want to get Laura to bed, I would say: "Laura, it seems to me that you are not going to bed. I feel angry that you are not going to bed. I want you to go to bed, and if you don't go to bed I won't read you a story". Yes, that's it.'

'Have you tried it?'

'No. But I thought I might give it a whirl tonight. If I need to.'

'I approve of assertiveness training,' said Sandra, approvingly. 'Lots of us in my women's group at university took assertiveness courses. I think it's good for a woman to know how to stand up for herself and I'm sure this is what you need, Zoë.'

They drove into the school car-park, activating the intruder light as they did so. Sandra joined the line of cars parked edgeways against the wall. The lights of the building blazed out into the darkness.

'It's unnatural,' Sandra said, 'coming to school at night. Imagine how lovely it would be to have an ordinary job that was actually over at five-thirty.'

'Aah, but the long holidays!' Zoë said.

'I get bored,' said Sandra. 'You need the school holidays. You have Laura. But I don't. I don't earn enough money to travel a lot, and I end up spending weeks with my parents, spattered with their disapproval and disappointment. They rang last night. My dad reminded me that the offer's still open. If I do my CPE in law, he'll support me. But that means giving in to them. I can't decide. I, Sandra, find it easy to make decisions. Hi, Fred!'

Sandra winked at the caretaker brewing some tea in his office, and the two women made their way to the staff room. Here Zoë took off her coat and examined herself in the mirror. Who was that woman in the red dress? She was absurd.

'You look lovely!' said Sandra.

'Oh, Zoë! Is that you? Going out somewhere after the parents' meeting? You look so glamorous! New man, is it? You dark horse!' Debra shook her hair in front of the mirror revelling in its glossiness. Sandra watched a smile play around her lips, a cruel smile. She bristled with hatred. A bell rang, to remind staff to assemble in the hall. Zoë and Sandra took their mark books and left the staff room together.

Already the school hall was buzzing with a myriad of voices, the heels of the mothers clicking against the pitted school-hall floor. The Head sat enthroned behind a large table on the stage, nodding seriously at the parents in front of him. Sandra found her place and braced herself.

'Miss Coverdale? I'm Emma's mother.' Sandra looked at the middle-aged, plumpish woman opposite her. The lapel of her coat had fallen over her name badge. Emma's mother. Emma who? Sandra taught four Emmas in her third-year group. Mrs Emma pursed her lips and prepared to listen.

'Well,' said Sandra, 'I'm pleased with her. She's working hard. Her creative writing is promising and she seems to be enjoying reading *Macbeth*.'

'How strange! She told me she found it difficult!'

'Yes, well, they all do. But she is enjoying it all the same. She's happy to answer in class.'

'Last year you told me she was very quiet.'

'She's come out of herself this year.'

Please make her go away, prayed Sandra, feeling hot and tense. Despite this hiccup, she often enjoyed parents' evenings. She liked talking about the girls she taught, and knew that no one appreciated listening to her conversation about the girls more than their parents. But also she felt vulnerable, open to criticism. And yet, she reflected, sometimes the boot was on the other foot.

'I think, Mrs Collier, if Stacey read more fiction, her grammar and spelling would improve.'

'But I do get her books, you know. I take her to the library and we choose books together and I say, you've got to read them you know, Stacey. I've always been a great reader myself –'

As one set of parents rose, shook hands, and left, another took their place. Anxious faces, smiling faces, bashful faces, self-assured faces.

'Mr Parker, Hayley is doing very well . . . Rachel Cassland's mother. I'm very pleased with her . . . Julie Wells . . . Rose Atkinson . . .'

Sandra's head was spinning. After twenty or so sets of parents, she was hardly in control of what she was saying. Occasionally she glimpsed her colleagues, also face to face with assorted parents, talking intensely, laughing at the jokes of the fathers, reassuring the mothers. Sandra didn't have a headache yet, but knew she would not be able to sleep that night, would drink, and would have a hangover in the morning, and that throughout the night fragments of conversations and glimpses of half-remembered faces would litter her dreams. At last, a pause. She looked around her. All these teachers telling all these parents what their daughters were like. As if they didn't know. All this pronouncing on people. Why bother? And yet, Sandra thought,

I love it when Stella turns round and tells me, *you* are obsessive/compulsive, *you* need to overcome your self-defeating negative thought patterns. It's so lovely when Stella tells me what to do. And Sandra could see how she simplified these parents' lives, as Stella simplified hers, telling them what to do with their daughters to ensure success. Read more, practise spelling, improve your handwriting. The easy answers.

Sandra looked around her. There was Zoë on the other side of the hall, with a queue of three sets of parents. Her carefully brushed hair was dishevelled again, her cheeks were hectic. Sandra wondered what was happening.

'Oh she enjoys the Latin well enough – it's just like doing a crossword puzzle, isn't it? – but I'm afraid she'll drop it in the summer. She needs the sciences, you see . . .'

'Can't even do her homework myself, but then, as we say to her, there's not much point doing Latin. Not these days.'

'I'm sure even you agree that French and German are so much more *useful*.'

Zoë pushed her hair back behind her ears in a repeated nervous gesture. She knew it would be like this.

'It's a dead language. So really we were against her taking it in the first place.'

'I'm sorry,' said Zoë.

A bulky red-faced man thrust himself into the seat opposite her, in a cloud of stale cigar smoke. 'Tracey's dad. You're the Latin teacher, aren't you? Not what I expected. She says you have trouble controlling the class. I tell her I'm not surprised, trying to teach them a language nobody speaks any more.'

Zoë wanted to say that the only girl who ever disrupted the class was Tracey, that he was a philistine, they were all –

'Do you remember doing Latin, Charles?' said the well-dressed woman to her well-dressed husband, as they sat facing Zoë. '*Amo, amas, amat*? It's funny to think they still do it.'

Parents, thought Sandra. I've got to see my own parents soon. At half-term probably. Funny facing them, now Stella has taught me so much about them. What can I say to them?

A small woman with protruding eyes perched herself on the edge of the chair opposite her. Sandra's last parent this evening. Her lapel badge read 'Mrs Karen Thomas'.

'Well, Mrs Thomas, I'm sure you know that Karen isn't working quite as hard this year. I think she's discouraged a little too easily. For example, in her creative writing. Rather than just tell a story, she must try to enter into the character's thoughts and feelings a little more . . . Probably she's stronger on the science side; she doesn't seem to want to explore . . .'

'I am surprised to hear you say *that*, Miss Coverdale. She loves English. She spends ages over her homework. That story you gave them last week, about the soldier in the trenches, she thought it was the best thing she's ever done. She came into the kitchen and she told me all about that lesson you had with them. I'm surprised, I am.'

'Oh, yes, that essay on the trenches was good. Oh yes. I mean, sometimes she does show flair.'

Mrs Thomas nodded.

'I mean, she's very sensitive.' What the English teacher says when all else fails, thought Sandra. 'And I know she concentrates in lessons.' Why am I saying all this? thought Sandra. It's rubbish. Why am I agreeing with her? Why can't I stick to any one opinion?

'Well, I'll tell her how nicely you say she's doing, Miss Coverdale.'

'Yes, you do that.'

'You used to need Latin to get into Oxford but they've changed that now, haven't they? So we've advised Rebecca to drop it.'

'You've got to think about the future when you're educating your children, haven't you? That's what we tell Francesca. Can *you* tell us any good reason for taking Latin?'

Not that you would understand, thought Zoë. She said, 'I'm sorry you feel like that.'

'I know she hasn't been keeping up with her homework but it's only Latin.'

I'm going to scream, thought Zoë. Or walk out. No. I must be assertive. D-E-S-C, she told herself.

'In my opinion, an employer won't think much of GCSE Latin.'

D-E-S-C, thought Zoë.

The next parent arrived, a mother on her own, comfortable-looking, in a royal blue coat, the buttons open to reveal a bottle green pullover.

'I'm Kelly's mother. You're her Latin teacher. How's she doing?'

'She is struggling rather with the translation we do. It's the little careless mistakes, I think, that pull her down.'

'Ah well, it's only Latin.'

Zoë cleared her throat. 'It seems to me that you do not regard Latin highly. This makes me feel very angry and upset. I would like you to – ah – change your mind, otherwise I – er –'

'Oh, how interesting! You've been on an assertiveness course! I'm doing one too. It's all part of our training programme in the office. How do you find it? Does it work? I bet it's more interesting than Latin!'

CHAPTER TEN

They sat, at Stella's request, in a circle. We must all
draw in a little, she had told them, now that we all
know each other. So each of them had shifted their
cushions towards the centre of the room. There was
Sandra, her legs tucked beneath her; her friend Zoë
rather stiff, apprehensive; Jim, who seemed to smile
knowingly; Angela; Carol, hunched, cross-legged;
David, his eyes heavy-lidded; and the stately Norah.
Stella reflected with pleasure that no one had left the
group; true, Kevin was not yet quite ready to attend,
but agoraphobia was not an easy condition. She loved
sitting in a circle like this with her group. Circles felt
special to her. Unbreakable bonds, Gill had taught
her. And Stella at the head of this circle, a fountain of
love and serenity – and healing too. She felt herself fill
with energy. If only Roland could see her now.

'I would love,' she said, 'to spend quality time with
each one of you during a meeting, but of course that's
impossible. So I need to know if there is anyone who
especially needs the love and support of the group
tonight – someone who feels in a bad place, or is facing
anything difficult for her – or him. Then we can give
you priority.' She waited for someone to speak. How
easy to be loving, she thought, when you are in love.

Shall I say something? thought Sandra. Because I
am facing something difficult – half-term with my parents. But no, she thought. She didn't wish to dominate

the group, and felt certain that someone was sure to have a worse difficulty than hers. The temptation, however, to pass everything, her whole dilemma, over to the group, to rid herself of the responsibility, was so overwhelming. Perhaps if no one else spoke, for someone had to start the ball rolling; otherwise what was the point of having a meeting at all? She would wait just a few moments longer.

Carol raised a finger, still hunched, her head down. Stella asked her to speak. Damn, thought Sandra. Carol raised her face and Sandra was interested to note that she did look bad; she seemed pale, and her eyes heavy.

'Perhaps I shouldn't have come tonight,' Carol said. 'I don't feel too good. Very strange.'

'No, no, you're in the right place,' murmured Stella encouragingly.

'Shivery,' Carol went on. 'And my limbs are aching and heavy. I'm almost certain I'm coming down with something – a cold, or flu. I recognize the symptoms.' Sandra noticed Angela move away from her slightly. 'But I can't work out what brought this on.'

'Has anyone at your shop been off ill?' asked Sandra, trying to be helpful.

'It's not that,' said Carol. 'It's me. I've let this thing in.'

'But it's not your fault for being ill!' said Sandra. 'You've caught a virus or if it's a bacterial infection you can get antibiotics.'

Now Stella had to interrupt her. 'No, Sandra. Carol is doing some good work here around her illness. She's learning from it. She knows how we can create our own disease and our own remedies. Go on, Carol.'

'I know this group is helping me, and I feel the love and support of you all, but there's just this constant feeling of defeat and depression, which I can't shift.'

'What do you want to do, Carol?' crooned Stella.

'I want to lie here on the floor and not move.'

'What do you want the group to do, Carol?'

'To give me its love. I need the group to hug me.'

'Let's all give Carol a group hug,' said Stella. 'All together. Come on.'

Carol rose. Sandra watched as, one by one, each group member came out and hugged her. Jim first, then Zoë, and Angela, and she herself rose to move over. Only David, she could see, had curled up on his cushion and had gone to sleep. All together they surrounded Carol and hugged. Sandra felt like she was part of a rugby scrum, and was glad to be somewhat on the outside. She accepted that there was a relationship between the mind and illness, but she couldn't rid herself of the suspicion that germs might have something to do with it too. When Stella said so, they all went back to their places.

'I can feel your support,' said Carol. 'But I still have to work on this guilt I feel. I can't be making good progress, can I, if a few weeks into the group I let in this disease?'

'Don't be too hard on yourself, Carol. It's very generous of you to share your illness with the group. It helps us all see the close relationship between mind and body. Our illnesses are often an expression of our inner state. A sore throat can express a desire not to talk; when we are sick there is often literally someone or something we cannot stomach. We must listen to our bodies.'

Sandra interjected. 'I know sometimes when I'm tired I get colds – we all do – but what about things like chicken pox? I had chicken pox when I was a child. Why?'

Stella half closed her eyes, looking wise. 'I can't say, Sandra. But perhaps you were trying to express some sense of corruption inside, your feeling of worthlessness, or your irritation at yourself.'

I caught it off my cousin, Sandra thought. And then she thought, but Stella could be right. I mean, why did it happen then?

'Sometimes,' continued Stella, 'our childhood illnesses can be a cry for attention – a demand to have our needs met.'

Zoë shifted uncomfortably, and guiltily considered Laura's bouts of earache.

'But the last thing we must feel,' said Stella, 'is guilty.'

There was a silence. Sandra's mind raced. How terrifying to be entirely responsible for your own illnesses. Yet Stella and Carol seemed to accept this happily. I'm a nasty old sceptic, thought Sandra. These are negative thoughts. And if I don't watch out, I'll get ill, and that will serve me right.

The silence continued. 'Is there anyone else who needs the group tonight?' Stella asked. 'Zoë?'

Zoë looked up, startled. 'No, no, it's all right. I'll just listen.'

'Jim?'

Jim's story this week involved a visit to his cousin's zoo in Devon, where he was attacked by a macaw, and was stuck for four hours outside Reading when the train he was on had engine failure. Jim said he was working on thinking positively, but things just seemed to happen to him. Stella nodded sagely, but Sandra noticed that Angela did not seem to respond at all.

'Sandra?'

'Me?'

'Do you want to speak to the group?' Stella asked.

Sandra was filled with conflicting emotions. For she had felt subtly put down by Stella, and not for the first time either. On other occasions too, Stella had deftly corrected her, made her feel ever so slightly inferior. Or was that her own intellectual arrogance? Or was Stella frightened of her? Whichever it was, Stella's mild rebukes brought out a resistance in Sandra. For one delicious moment, she contemplated rejecting Stella's request with a toss of her head, demonstrating her hurt. But no. The opportunity to have the group's attention was just too tempting.

'Do you want to speak to the group?' Stella asked.

'Yes,' said Sandra. 'Soon it's half-term and I've arranged to go and stay with my parents for a few days. And I know what they're going to say. My father's always wanted me to study law, and he's offered to finance me through my CPE – you know, to convert my degree to law – and I'm not sure whether I want to or not. Whether to leave teaching. I can't make up my mind. It's my indecision,' Sandra concluded, looking round at the group helplessly.

Stella intervened. 'In therapy sessions with me, Sandra has had to face up to her indecisiveness. This is partly because over-strong parenting has resulted in an under-development of her Adult, and she is in conflict between the conformist part of her and her internal rebel.'

Sandra resented that, resented being described and pigeon-holed in front of the others. She felt immediately like proving otherwise. My rebel, she thought. And saw in her mind's eye some sort of soldier in camouflage with a machine gun and a bandanna. My rebel. She felt quite fond of him really.

'One thing that might help, Sandra, would be to role-play your meeting with your father. You can try to tell him how you feel. Is there anyone in the group who would be Sandra's father?' Stella inquired.

Sandra realized immediately it would have to be Jim. David was fast asleep and, in fact, Jim smiled in his lopsided way, apparently quite happy to perform. He nodded to signify his assent.

'Do you want to do this sitting or standing, Sandra?'

Sandra could not imagine for one moment sitting on the floor with her father, and decided to stand. Jim, in denim shirt and jeans, tonight, his dark hair stiff with mousse, stood opposite her, not looking her directly in the face.

Stella prompted him: 'Tell her you want her to leave teaching.'

Jim cleared his throat. 'Me and your mum would like you to think about giving up teaching and doing law.'

That wasn't her father! Sandra was appalled. Her father never said 'me and your mum' and anyway, he'd never utter the words 'doing law'. A picture of her father rose before her – a tall greying man, muscular and imposing, a contained self-assurance, his firm jawline; and here was Jim, smaller, insinuating, dressed in denims, with his cat-like smile. No! It would never do.

'I'm sorry,' said Sandra. 'This isn't going to work. I can't . . . I can't . . . get into it.'

'Never mind!' said Stella brightly. 'We'll try it another way.' And she went to a corner of the room and retrieved a gaily coloured cushion, obviously bought from some South American emporium, with black tassels and embroidered sequins. 'This can be your father!'

Stella placed the cushion in the centre of the circle where it sat limply, waiting to know what was expected of it. 'Sometimes,' Stella said, 'it's easier to talk to an inanimate object, to tell it what you really feel. Don't hold back, Sandra. Tell your father the truth. If you want to shout, shout. We don't mind.'

Sandra looked at the cushion, frowned at the cushion. This is my father, she thought. I shall tell him the truth. 'Look, Dad, I know you mean well, offering me the chance to do the CPE. But I feel you're forcing my hand. Although there's a lot about school that I don't like, teaching itself I've always enjoyed, and –'

'Tell him how you *feel*, Sandra. Tell him how you feel.'

Stupid, thought Sandra. But she continued. 'I feel pressurized by you. I feel resentful, and I feel angry.' That's what you're supposed to say, isn't it? she thought. 'Don't tell me what to do!' she informed the cushion sternly, wondering what the others were making of this. And then she had a very familiar feeling, which she felt compelled to trace. A feeling of

123

observing herself. The feeling she used to have the first few times she'd had sex, that feeling of dislocation: am I doing it right? Am I feeling the things I'm supposed to feel? What is he thinking of me? Why aren't I losing myself in this thing? The cushion faced her blindly, its sequins glittering sightlessly.

'Oh, I'm sorry, Stella. This still isn't any good.'

Stella was as serene as ever. 'Perhaps it's not working because you're not clear in your own mind what it is you want. Talking to your father comes at a later stage. You need to talk to yourself first.' Stella took two upright chairs from the wall and moved them into the centre of the room. 'This chair,' she said, pointing to one, 'is the part of you that wants to give up teaching, and this –' pointing to the other '– doesn't want to give up teaching. When you sit in the teaching chair, explain why you want to continue teaching, and in the other chair argue for giving it up. This technique, adapted from Gestalt, helps you separate the conflicting parts of your mind, and is very useful for making decisions. Go on, Sandra.'

Sandra sat in the teaching chair. 'Every time I go into the classroom and see the girls sitting there, I get a real buzz. I enjoy explaining things to them – you know, the hard bits of Shakespeare – and I love having discussions and hearing what they've got to say about things, and I think I get on with the girls quite well. I even enjoy marking their books and essays. It's interesting. But that's only half of it. When I go up to the staff room –'

Stella interrupted: 'Move chairs now, Sandra.'

Sandra rose, and sat down heavily on the opposite

124

chair, facing the empty one, which she addressed: 'In the staff room, the atmosphere's quite different. You can be having a conversation with someone, and someone else comes over and hovers over you, because they've got something important to say about something petty, like a girl in your form who's handed in her homework late. All the time there's this atmosphere of earnest urgency and bells going all the time and people bumping into you when you're going to get your coffee. Oh I know every workplace is like that —'

'Move chairs again, Sandra!'

She moved. 'Every workplace is like that, otherwise it wouldn't be work, and you can't expect to find the perfect workplace. It just doesn't exist. But —' This time Sandra moved of her own accord. 'In my school everyone gets together in cliques and each clique talks about the other cliques. There's the lot who moan about how education's in decline and bring back the O levels; and the quiche-making dinner-party set; and the gynaecological set who talk about their bad periods and hysterectomies; and whatever it is that's so exciting in the classroom isn't there the rest of the time. I feel people are watching me and disapproving of me.' Sandra moved. 'But they'd disapprove of you in law school as well, Sandra.' She moved again. 'No, at least you're allowed to be an adult in law school. The trouble with school, is that the teachers treat the other teachers as children!' Sandra moved, and thought to herself, this is like musical chairs, and said, 'But if you go to law school you'll feel you owe your father something and you want to be free of him.' Sandra looked around her. She was absolutely certain that the rest of the group was bored rigid. There she was, sitting in the middle of the circle, talking to an empty chair, or talking to herself, for that was what she had been doing, while they all listened. She was suffused with self-consciousness. She could not go on.

Stella prompted her: 'Is there anything else you need to say?'

'Oh no!'

'Is it clearer now?'

'Oh yes!' Sandra said, knowing she was lying. Actually she felt a lot worse. The whole thing was far more complicated than she realized. She half liked school, and half didn't, which meant she half wanted to accept her father's proposal, and half didn't, so she could never be entirely happy, whatever she did. She looked at Carol and realized why it was Carol was so depressed. Because all the time you kept going round in circles.

'Just stay with your feelings, Sandra,' Stella suggested. 'Then you won't go wrong. Stay with your feelings.'

I feel depressed, thought Sandra. I've got a headache. I want a pint of beer and a packet of peanuts. I, Sandra, love and approve of myself.

'Norah?' Stella continued her way round the circle.

Sandra was intrigued to see Norah hand over a folded piece of paper to Stella, and Stella smiled knowingly, apparently certain of the contents.

She explained to the group: 'Sometimes when we find it difficult to accept part of ourselves, it helps to focus on what positive contribution that part of you makes to the rest of you. For example, if you have difficulty accepting your size' – is that meant for me? thought Sandra – 'you could focus on your body and think of what it does for you, how you can get pleasure from it. Norah has agreed to write a letter to her nose thanking it for all it does for her.' Sandra watched Norah turn scarlet. Stella glanced at the contents. 'This is lovely, Norah! Would you like to read it to the group?' There was no response. 'May I read it to the group?' Norah nodded almost imperceptibly. Stella began. '"Dear Nose, Thank you for letting me breathe. Thank you for letting me smell flowers and perfume and freshly baked bread. Thank you for filtering the impurities from the air I breathe." This is wonderful, Norah! Beautiful! Pin this up in your bedroom.'

And Sandra glanced at Norah and Norah glanced at Sandra and Sandra knew then for a certainty that they both found this whole thing utterly ridiculous and yet here they were, sitting in a circle like infants at story time and subjecting themselves, grown adults, to this drivel, because, because . . . Sandra looked at Stella, radiant tonight, and wondered how it would be to know what one wanted, to assert oneself with calm serenity, not to be a slave to one's appetite; Stella said all this was possible. It must be possible. Look at Stella. Sandra found her rebel crouched behind the thickets of her mind, and with the rapid machine-gun fire of her positive thinking, gunned him down. It *will* work, I *can* be decisive, I *will* be slim. Rat-a-tat-tat.

'Angela?' The group focussed its attention on Angela. Knowing that, she undulated slightly and pursed her lips. There was a pause. The sibilance in Angela's voice was attractive.

'I still seem to have a lot of complications with men. Just now, there's two men who are – ah – pursuing me, and one of them's a poet. A proper poet, who gives readings. And like Sandra, I find it hard to make my mind up too. And I know that the man I had a relationship with before is still interested in me, as well as the man who lives in the flat above me. I'm trying not to commit myself.' Angela ran her tongue round her mouth and Sandra was sure she saw her glance at Zoë. The bitch, she thought. I don't believe any of it. She looked at Angela again and thought, yes, I do. And watched Stella for her response.

Stella paused. Angela had stirred up something murky. But why? For her blossoming relationship with Roland could have nothing to do with Angela's obsessive pursuit of men. And it was impossible to be jealous of Angela's call-girl looks.

Stella spoke: 'Have you thought, Angela, if there are any ways in which you invite this attention?' I must make her see that she is an addict, thought Stella.

'Not really.' Angela shook her hair, which she was wearing loose. 'Men just seem to find me . . . attractive.' She glanced at Jim who winked at her.

'But four men at once is a little unusual and suggests that there is something you are doing to get this attention. What do you think?'

Angela shrugged and Stella sensed her hostility. 'What you could do,' Stella suggested, 'is watch yourself. Watch yourself to see if there is anything you do which attracts men –'

And tell us what it is, thought Zoë. Although, of course, she knew. Zoë examined her fingers, slightly lined now, and her nails, bitten to the quick. She knew she was unattractive. But Stella had told her last week that attractiveness was a state of mind, that maintaining a relationship had ultimately little to do with looks. Zoë knew that made sense, but her problem was that she didn't even have a man to start maintaining a relationship with. She had once, and he was no good. She lacked the courage to start again. And the looks. What was the point of trying? She listened again to Stella.

'Perhaps you give signals to men that you are available, or plan your life so that you meet men.'

Meeting men. That was the problem. There weren't any to speak of at Millers'. How do you meet a man? That would be a start . . . How do you meet a man? How would I meet a man? What if I planned my life so that I met a man? If Angela invites complications with men, why can't I? Perhaps this therapy is working after all, thought Zoë.

CHAPTER ELEVEN

At one corner of the café-bar, dim and smoky now, stood a small stage, forming a quarter-circle against two walls. At the front of it was a tall microphone, leaning slightly, a dilapidated wooden chair, and a round table with a jug of water, an empty glass, and a half-full pint of beer. At the bar, on the opposite side of the room, the crowd was three deep, and Angela watched it idly, as she conversed with Carol. The café-bar they were in was, in fact, owned and financed by the local council. It was known as the Mill Lane Centre, and its function was to provide a venue for artistic events. Upstairs was a small gallery; in the next room was an intimate theatre; Angela and Carol were sitting in the café-bar meeting area, which tonight was the scene of the annual fundraising evening for the LeftWrite poetry group.

Angela had imagined it differently to this. When Spencer had invited her to Mill Lane, and had promised a poetry reading she had pictured to herself something more cultural. Rows of chairs, perhaps, like in the theatre, and real poets in suits and a clever audience that clapped politely. In fact she could see that the Mill Lane Centre was a glorified pub, and that the fundraising was an excuse for a booze-up. The audience sat around small tables, drinking together, smoking heavily; and God knows *what* they are smoking, Angela thought, as she looked at the types of people assembled there. The men were, by and large, quite good-looking, but scruffy, in worn leather jackets and unwashed hair. She had heard of poetic licence and she thought perhaps that gave you the excuse to dress like that. At least Spencer was reasonably tidy, in his Fair Isle sweater and black trousers. There he was near the stage, holding a sheaf of papers, talking to an elderly woman and one of those leather-jacketed men. She looked back to the bar, and could just make out the top of Jim's head, quite noticeable since he'd had his hair permed.

Jim was slacking. Although she had given him a number of opportunities to declare himself, he had done nothing. So she had decided to bring him here to listen to Spencer tonight. Spencer had told her that all the poems he would read were about her; her beauty, her unattainability, his undying love. She thought it would do Jim good to hear them. Spencer himself she did not care for particularly. He was shorter than her for a start; he wore thick-rimmed black glasses and squinted when he took them off; most of the time his hair needed washing, or perhaps it was the Brylcreem he used. But it was sweet the way he idolized her. And so she let him. She realized Carol was rather quiet this evening. It wasn't her flu; she had been over that a week or so; Carol just seemed low-spirited. But then, thought Angela, she always did. Just then, she saw Jim edge his way through the crowds, holding aloft a tray of drinks. She re-crossed her legs and waited for him.

She had barely started her Martini when Spencer approached her. She looked up at him and smiled, with that serene smile that she had seen and admired on Stella, and had resolved to try.

'Hello,' he said.

She smiled again, inscrutable.

'I'm pleased you could come, Angela.' He grinned foolishly. There was a pause. 'Can I introduce you to some of my friends in LeftWrite? I said you might be coming and they're interested to – to see what you're like.'

Lovely, thought Angela. She was glad she had come. To be introduced as the subject of a collection of poems was delightful. One evening, when she stopped to talk to Spencer in the hardware shop he owned, he had explained to her about courtly love, and how poets in the olden times had ladies that they dedicated all their poems to, and she was his lady. She had no doubt she would meet his friends' expectations. She allowed herself to be led towards the stage, and explained to Carol and Jim that she would not be long.

'That's Spencer,' said Carol, in explanation. 'He's the one who writes those poems about Angie.'

'Do you like poetry?' Jim asked, turning his attention to Carol.

'Not much.'

'Why did you come, then?'

'I thought it might be better than staying in. But it's been just another of my mistakes. I thought by getting out I could move away from this feeling of defeat I'm experiencing, but it's with me all the time. There's no escape. In a way it's worse here. All these poets – they can all *do* something – and everybody seems to know everybody else, and here I am, with no achievements, no talents, no friends.'

'I'm your friend,' said Jim, and reached out and took her hand.

'I know, but you're from the group, and I know that the members of the group are more valuable than real friends because they love you all the time no matter where you're at but they're not real friends, not friends you make yourself.' Carol looked up at him, pitiful. Jim moved her hair away from her face.

'Come and have a walk outside,' he said. 'We'll explain to the bloke at the door that we're just going to have some fresh air.'

They walked slowly along Chisholme High Street, past kebab shops and a Pakistani grocer, light and spices spilling out into the night. Jim put his arm around Carol's shoulders, in a companionable way.

'Do you know, Jim, I should feel happy tonight. It's my anniversary.'

'Anniversary? What, your birthday?'

'No, not my birthday. Twelve years ago today I started in therapy.'

'What? With Stella?'

'Oh no! A therapist who worked at Chisholme Health Centre, but I went private with him. I've worked with a number of therapists since then, and learnt such a lot. I ought to be grateful, really, instead of depressed. I suppose it's just the after-effects of the flu. They've all been wonderful, all of my therapists. I don't know how I'd have managed without them. There was the time my dog died; Gerald let me see him four times a week then. And I could have never got that job at the Chisholme council offices without Robert; my self-esteem was so low three years ago I couldn't have even walked in for an interview without intensive counselling. I know I've come a long way.

The therapist I had before Stella was a woman too – Jess. She got me through my relationship with Eric. She suggested I try rebirthing and I think I probably will next. Perhaps that's what I need now. Jess used to say that you have the right to be born as many times as you want.'

They came to the park gates, locked now.

'So you see, I've got a lot to look forward to. Planning my rebirth – and there's a course in Mongolian and Tibetan Overtone Chanting starting up soon – but I feel so defeated by myself.'

Carol stood by the park gates. In fact she felt rather better. It was nice to contemplate her coming rebirth; nicer still to realize that her depression gave her fuel for innumerable more therapy sessions; and even nicer than that, here was Jim who had left Angela and come with her, to listen to her. Not all men were like Eric; not all men preferred Angela. Jim still had his arm around her. He moved closer, and he kissed her. That was nice too. His chest pressed against her.

'We need to talk some more,' he said. Carol suggested 8 Lincoln Grove, and so they moved off, walking more quickly now. Carol linked arms with Jim, making a mental note of how she was feeling, what was occurring. For she would need to analyse it all later. Perhaps with Stella, perhaps not.

'It's good of you to invite me back to your place, Carol. I knew, right from the start, that there was something between us. Know what I mean? There's more about you than most women. It's good this happened tonight. Because I've got nowhere to stay tonight. My mother kicked me out. She came home and

134

found her pet budgie dead in his cage and said I'd poisoned him. Packed my suitcase, she did, and told me I could get lost.'

'I thought you said your mother was in a home? Senile dementia, or something . . .?'

'Oh, she got better. Well, as I said, if there's anywhere in your place where I could kip down . . .'

She had shaken the hands of several poets, and been looked at with interest and admiration. When Spencer suggested she should sit at a table by the front of the stage, so that she could listen properly to his performance, she accepted, enjoying her status as celebrity. He touched her elbow as she sat down; she liked being treated with distinction. This was one of the things that disappointed her about the therapy group. Everyone was supposed to be equal. Angela had to listen to everybody's stories, even boring people like that old schoolteacher and the woman with the huge nose. Sometimes she found it hard to conceal her impatience. But tonight was lovely, tonight was her night.

Spencer ascended the stage and adjusted the microphone. It crackled as he moved it, and Angela watched him pick up his papers with a rustle exaggerated by the microphone; he looked around him foolishly, waiting for something to happen. The people in the café took no notice. Then a younger man with a beard, whom Angela had met earlier, got up on the stage too, and spoke to the audience as the microphone wailed its feedback, telling everyone to belt up now, as they were beginning the second half, and they were kicking off with some love poetry by Spencer Preston.

Spencer looked down at his papers and shuffled them again. His voice, when it came, was nasal and flat. 'I wrote this one after I met her for the first time. Right. Here goes.

> 'You walked into my shop
> And into my life . . .'

Angela listened to the account of their first meeting, when during her lunch-hour she had popped into his shop for some Rawlplugs. He had kept her talking and discovered that she worked in Boots'. He was so charmingly aware of his inferiority to her that he never asked her out, or expressed his feelings, but simply took to buying his lunch in Boots', from the low calorie sandwich counter, his razors in Boots', his aftershave in Boots'. Pathetic really. But sweet.

> 'So I thought it was my duty
> To write about your beauty . . .'

She watched him now, his head bowed, his cheeks tinged with red. He wasn't really very attractive and were it not for the poetry Angela may not have let him pursue her. Every so often he looked up, flushed and dishevelled, and gazed at her. Angela turned around to see if Jim and Carol were watching him. It was difficult to see the table she had shared with them; impossible, in fact. She looked again, not paying much attention to Spencer's next poem. That's where they were sitting, next to the Ladies. Other people were sitting there now. Jim and Carol had gone.

'I brood among the tool kits
Awaiting your return.'

First she was confused, then annoyed, and then absolutely furious. How could they? How could anyone desert her? Anger swelled in her, drowned out the sound of the poetry. They had ruined the evening for her. What should she do? Stella said you should go with your feelings. She felt murderous. And revengeful. She would show them. Somehow. She tossed her head and tried to pull back her concentration. But Spencer had moved closer to the microphone and his words were distorted and unintelligible. She watched him. He might do. The shop was in fact his; he'd told her he had inherited it from his father, and all the goodwill that went with the business. He wouldn't desert her.

How dare they walk out on me, she thought again. Stella had said that everyone in the group had to support everyone else. It serves me right, thought Angela, for going to that silly group in the first place. It hasn't helped at all.

She wondered really why she had put up with it for so long. She had let Carol persuade her that her relationships with men would improve with therapy but instead they had got worse – except for Spencer, and she had met him before she started the group. All that money she had spent and nothing to show for it. She had even seen Stella privately. Angela thought back over her two consultations with Stella. Those had been quite enjoyable, she had to admit. It was fun telling Stella all about her various admirers. In fact, Angela

137

recalled, Stella had had some very interesting things to say about her relationships with men.

Stella had said that the reason she encouraged so many admirers was because she didn't love herself enough. The admiration of men helped to bolster her self-esteem. Stella said that if she learned to love herself, she would need men less. Loving yourself sounded a bit perverted to Angela; at first she wasn't sure quite what Stella was talking about. But then it became clearer. Loving yourself meant being kind to yourself, believing in yourself, and sticking up for yourself, and Stella had said at a meeting that every individual is unique and precious and Angela certainly felt that that applied to her. You are responsible for yourself, Stella had said another time. You must make things happen for you. That was Angela's philosophy too. She liked this whole idea of loving yourself, once she had understood it properly.

So she had accepted that Stella might be right. Maybe she did have a problem after all, and that problem was that she didn't love herself enough. So the answer was simple. She just had to love herself more. She caught a glimpse of her reflection in the mirror that ran along the wall and thought how easy it would be, to love herself more.

> 'You illuminate the world for me
> You fill my world with ecstasy
> You are as perfect as can be.'

Stella had said, one thing you can do to love yourself more is to make a list of all the things you would do for yourself if you thought you really deserved it. Then one by one you had to do those things. Treat yourself as if you deserved love, she said. Angela asked herself what she would most like. Some kind of triumph, she thought, I would like to take part in some kind of triumph.

Most of all, she loved people's admiration. To walk into that stupid therapy group and say something that would shut them all up, or something to prove that she didn't need them. But what? What could she do? She looked at Spencer again, sizing him up. She could just about manage to put up with him. He would do anything she said. She had never married as it had been so impossible to choose the right man, and there was so much fun to be had not being married. But just recently she had begun to wonder. She could have a proper house, and a lovely wedding – everybody watching her as she walked down the aisle.

And it would show them all. It would spite Jim and spite Eric, and make Carol feel even worse about herself. And the whole group would congratulate her. Besides, being married needn't be too constricting. Even if you were married, men could still admire you, couldn't they? Yes, thought Angela, I should like to get married. I think I deserve to get married. She caught Spencer's eye and smiled at him and looked down, shyly.

CHAPTER TWELVE

'How are you doing, Zoë?'

'All right.'

'No, I mean how are you doing. You know, with your' – Sandra lowered her voice slightly – 'personal growth.'

Sandra sat opposite Zoë in the school canteen. Sandra had told her cheese and onion pie, chips and beans in no uncertain terms that they would not make her fat, she was not afraid of them, and that whatever they might think, she loved and approved of herself. With a hearty appetite she dug in.

'Well, it's hard to say . . . how I'm doing,' Zoë said, trimming some gristle off a tough piece of meat.

'I know!' said Sandra. 'It's impossible to measure, isn't it? I was thinking this morning, when I belonged to that slimming club, at least you could get on the scales and you could see what progress you were making. But with personal growth, how can you tell? Do I seem any different to you?'

Zoë looked at Sandra and thought. 'No, I don't think so.'

Sandra's face fell.

'But I suppose it's how you feel inside. Do you feel different?'

'Yes,' Sandra said with decision, 'I do. I feel I have a lot more self-esteem. I think my affirmations are beginning to take effect. I'm beginning to like myself.'

Zoë wondered whether to ask Sandra if she had lost weight, but decided not to.

'I've been using affirmations too. I've been telling myself I'm a worthy person, and that I deserve love and respect.' Zoë swallowed a mouthful of food. 'But nobody gives me any.'

'Ah, but they will! This is how self-esteem works. I've been reading about it. If you value yourself then this affects other people's judgement of you, and everyone will treat you with more respect.'

'Yes, but I say the affirmations and in theory I know I ought to think more of myself, but I look in the mirror and I see the same old face looking out and –' Zoë shrugged. 'I really would love to have self-esteem but I think until I can do something to earn my own self-esteem, I'm simply not going to get it by looking in the mirror and telling myself I'm beautiful and desirable when I'm not. And don't interrupt, Sandra. I know I'm not. Not compared to women like Angela or you –'

'I'm not attractive!'

'I thought you'd said your self-esteem had improved.'

'A bit attractive.'

'But I still don't see how you can get self-esteem just by wanting it. Besides, doesn't it seem rather selfish to you, telling yourself all the time how wonderful you are?'

'Oh, no! You're absolutely wrong! This is the point. When you learn to value yourself, only then can you relate in a healthy way to other people. Your first lesson in love is to love yourself. Then everything else follows. And it's true. Because this is one thing I've noticed since I've been working on my affirmations. I'm getting on better with the rest of the staff. I'm less susceptible to criticism. From my position of strength I can learn to appreciate the qualities of others rather than feel jealous of them. Self-esteem isn't selfish at all. People confuse it with arrogance but it's not arrogance. Arrogance is a cover for people with *low* self-esteem. You know, Zoë, when I say my affirmations to myself – during prayers is a good time, don't you find? – I get a lovely warm glow. Like in the Ready-Brek ad. You know something? I think I *am* doing well. It's the equivalent of losing a stone or two at a slimming club.'

'Yes, but don't you think that the whole concept of self-esteem is an outgrowth of the individualism of the States and western capitalism? It's the justification of the "me" philosophy? I love myself therefore I can give myself everything I want?'

Sandra felt her cheese and onion pie stick in her throat. Could Zoë be right? If self-esteem wasn't politically correct, where did that leave her?

'No, no! That's not it! It's about seeing every individual as unique and precious. No. Self-esteem is valuing all individuals the same. You're wrong, Zoë. Self-esteem –'

Both Sandra and Zoë were aware of a third presence. They looked up and there was Debra.

'May I?' she said, and sat down next to Zoë. Sandra noticed with distaste that she had selected a small salad from the salad bar, which seemed to consist of mostly celery. I bet you chose that on purpose just to spite me, Sandra thought. Debra was hateful.

'Did I interrupt something?' Debra asked sweetly. 'I thought I heard you talking about self-esteem. Why? Are you planning a Personal and Social Education course?'

'It's nothing to do with school,' Sandra said. 'It's something we're studying out of school.'

'I shouldn't think *you* would need self-esteem, Sandra. We all envy your self-esteem.' Debra gave Sandra a maternal smile. Sandra prodded her jam tart and custard viciously. She had forgotten to tell it that it wouldn't make her fat.

'Actually, Debra, what you think is my high self-esteem is an attempt to over-compensate for low self-esteem by talking a lot and playing the fool. My therapist said so.'

'Your therapist? Are you in therapy?' Debra lowered her voice. Sandra felt her interest and bitterly regretted having mentioned it. She looked helplessly at Zoë. Debra continued, 'And you too, Zoë? So you're also in therapy! What a good idea! I'll tell the Head. He will be pleased.'

Sandra stopped eating her tart. She had betrayed her friend. It was one thing to let the cat out of the bag about herself, but to let her indiscretion harm a friend! I hate myself, Sandra thought, I hate myself, I hate myself.

'*I*'ve never had cause to dabble in that kind of thing,' Debra went on, 'but I do think a sympathetic counsellor can do the world of good. That's what's so lovely about Justin, my husband. He's always ready to listen to me when I have little difficulties, and he's so good at restoring things to proportion. I think –'

'Debra, I'd prefer it if you didn't say anything about this to anyone. I didn't really mean to tell you this.'

143

'You know you can trust me. Is it working, Zoë? Are you feeling any better about yourself now?'

'It seems to me,' said Zoë, 'that you are trying to put me down.' That was D for 'Describe'. Now E for 'Express . . .' 'That makes me feel angry. I want you to . . . stop it. Or,' Zoë glanced around her, 'or we'll move tables.'

There was a silence. A silence so palpable that it could be heard above the clatter of plates and shrieks of girls.

'You *are* touchy today, Zoë!' Debra looked at Sandra and raised her eyebrows. 'Anyway, there's Anne Palmer and I need to talk to her about next week's inservice training.' Debra rose, frostily, and walked away.

'Zoë, you were wonderful!' Sandra breathed. 'You stuck up for yourself.'

Zoë's head was spinning. It was true, she had sent Debra Wentworth away. Just now she felt she could not get up from the chair even if she had to; her knees were weak with tension, her heart was pumping rapidly.

'I was assertive, wasn't I?'

'Well done, Zoë! And I'm so sorry. It was all my fault. I don't know when to keep my mouth shut, and I never think. I could kill myself. Or kill her. "Corpse of Senior Teacher found in leftovers bin in school canteen". But it was my fault. Zoë, I'm sorry.'

'Do you know, I feel rather good now. Full of adrenalin.'

'It's funny. You just said you didn't have any self-esteem, and look at you. Come on. Let's go and get some coffee.'

*

144

The second years looked up when Mrs Swann walked into their form room. She seemed to sparkle. She looked round the class and smiled before she replied *'Salvete, puellae'* to their ragged chorus of *'Salve, magistra!'*

I did it, she thought, as she wrote out the conjugation of *amo* on the blackboard. I stood up for myself. And yet, she had to admit that mixed with her sense of achievement was something akin to terror. Even now she half-imagined that Debra and the Head would march into her lesson and take her away to a Kafka-like trial. *'Amo, amas, amat,'* she chanted with her class, *'amamus, amatis, amant.'*

She needed to think of something different. So she addressed the class, who were looking at her with interest. 'Let's have a rest from the Latin language today. We'll do some Roman background. Find the chapter in your text books about the gladiators!'

She knew that the second years had a rather blood-thirsty streak, and would appreciate the details of gladiatorial combat, and the class was bound to become vociferous as they read about the slaughter of the wild animals. Who said Latin was dull? To find out about other cultures, other ways of doing things – that gave you the ability to examine your own culture objectively, to be fair and balanced. She imagined herself saying that to the Head. She doubted he could understand.

'Right, girls. In twos I want you to design a poster for a gladiatorial show. Remember to do the writing in Latin, and make the whole thing as attractive as you can!'

The girls set to it with some enthusiasm. Zoë watched

them, waiting for the first inquiries and requests for help. Her excitement was subsiding. What, if anything, had changed? She had been rude to Debra and Debra had been taken aback. Little had been gained. Meanwhile Debra was still going to Greece, Dr Young was still savaging the Latin teaching; and still, when Laura had gone to bed, and she sat by the television with the one glass of sherry she allowed herself, she was alone. While Debra billed and cooed with Justin. She wasn't exactly jealous – well, yes, she was jealous. Very jealous. Debra would go home tonight and tell her spouse about that old bat from the Latin department, who was obviously suffering from an early menopause, who snapped at her over dinner. And Zoë would go home tonight to no adult conversation at all. Unless she invited Sandra round. True, Sandra was alone. But Sandra was still young. All of Zoë's earlier euphoria had evaporated; back came that dragging depression that settled at the pit of her stomach. The bell rang.

'You can finish that for homework, girls.'

'But we've been doing it in pairs, we can't!'

'Oh, well, in that case, learn the conjugation of *amo*.'

'We learnt that last week.'

'No, don't tell her that!'

'Well, learn it for a test on Friday!'

Zoë watched the girls depart, immediately breaking into lively conversation, as if the whole lesson had been some sort of unwelcome interruption to their real lives. *Amo, amas, amat*. I love, you love, he loves. He loves me not. Perhaps, Zoë ruminated sadly, it *was* an early menopause.

★

Perdita had actually managed to get into bed with Laura, and the duvet half-covered the cat as well as the sleeping child. Zoë removed the cat carefully. Perdita half opened her eyes and lay fatly in Zoë's arms, awaiting transportation to another warm spot. She deserves to be thrown out, Zoë thought. She knows the bed is out of bounds. But the temperatures that night were predicted to be below zero, and Perdita was getting on for fifteen now. Zoë decided to prepare a litter tray instead. She took the cat with her back into the living room where Sandra was sitting in front of the gas fire, her hands cupping a glass of wine.

'This is nice, Zoë. If only we didn't have school tomorrow.'

Zoë smiled.

'I like your house, you know. I like your taste in furniture and that South American vase you bought and your big poster of Pompeii. You're lucky, having this lovely house and little Laura.'

Zoë half smiled.

'I bet you're pleased really that you've got your independence now. I mean, now that you've got over Mike and everything.'

Zoë didn't smile.

'Oh, come on, Zoë. You know you have got over him. He was a heel. You know that.'

'I know. But –' she shrugged. She was a little wary of explaining to Sandra how badly she wanted some sort of relationship again. She had loved being married. It suited her. Those were her happiest days. And if she said this to Sandra, she would be told again that her desire for male companionship was a product of brainwashing by a society that overrated the nuclear family, that independence was often preferable for a woman than wifedom, and that there was no God-given rule that children had to be brought up by couples.

It surprised her, therefore, when Sandra said, 'I feel lonely sometimes.'

'So do I,' Zoë said, quickly.

'That's why I'm half looking forward to going to my parents at half-term.' She laughed. 'Well, only half.'

'If you were me,' said Zoë, encouraged by Sandra's softer mood, 'how would you go about meeting a man?'

Sandra looked up and raised her eyebrows. Oh dear, thought Zoë.

'It's hard, isn't it?' Sandra said. 'There's no one at school. Four male members of staff, not including the Head of course, because he barely qualifies as human, and all of them spoken for. Can't you go to evening classes or something? Shall I open the next bottle?'

Sandra pulled hard at the corkscrew and the cork freed itself with a little pop. She filled both glasses again. The wine seemed to brighten Zoë's spirits.

'I don't have the time for evening classes, do I? Once I did go to an extra-mural class on English liter-ature and they were all women – librarians, history teachers, that sort of thing.'

'All right then! Are there clubs or something you could join? Are there night clubs for people of your age?'

'Even if there was,' said Zoë, 'I couldn't imagine developing sufficient courage to go. I'm just not that type. You saw how pathetic my attempts were at make-up.'

'The Ramblers' Association? Greenpeace? Amnesty?'

'I could never bring myself to join something I wasn't committed to just in order to meet a man. It's hopeless. Look, Sandra, you've had too much to drink tonight and I'm not letting you drive home. We both need to sober up a bit. I'll put the kettle on and prepare the cat's litter tray.'

It was true. Zoë did feel slightly tipsy as she made her way into the kitchen. If only, she thought, there was a way of meeting a man that didn't actually involve meeting a man. If only a man could just arrive on the doorstep. The litter poured out in a steady stream and made a little pile in the tray. Zoë shook the tray to distribute it evenly. She took Saturday's *Guardian* from the pile of old newspapers on the kitchen chair and spread out a double sheet on the floor. 'The Noticeboard', it said. She knelt down. The left-hand column was entitled 'Lonely Hearts'. She read on. 'Environmentally aware woman, 40s, into blues, Greek Islands and good conversation, seeks tall, wise man, any age. Coventry area.' 'Intelligent Socialist male, attractive if pot-bellied, is looking for similar, slimmer female for ongoing fun.' Zoë picked up the paper and went back to Sandra. 'Look at this!' she said.

'Oh, I know,' said Sandra. 'They're in every week now. What? You mean, for you? Well, it is the *Guardian*, I suppose. It's not such a bad idea!'

Zoë knew it was partly the wine, and partly the result of a very odd day, but also, she dared to think, also the result of her therapy. To place an ad in a newspaper for a male friend – even if it *was* the *Guardian* – that was progress. It was like Angela said – creating opportunities. It was a positive, assertive step. It was the true way to self-esteem – to do something, to take action. And you had to use a box number and if you didn't like the sound of the man who wrote back you could always decline to meet him, and even though she had no confidence in her cosmetic skills, writing a literate description of herself was something she was quite equal to. And no one need know it was her. Quickly, thought Zoë. I've got to do this quickly, before I change my mind.

'Go on, Zoë, get some paper. How would you describe yourself? Now remember to be positive! Attractive, erudite woman? Lovable, attractive, erudite woman?'

'Something plainer, I think. Professional woman, forty, seeks caring male friend, north-west.'

'No! Be more original else you won't attract attention. Can you make it funny?'

'I say, I say, I say! Professional woman –'

'No, don't be silly. Let's think.'

Zoë stopped the car at the post box on the corner of the street. The morning was bitterly cold and the pavement sparkled with frost. Sandra and Laura watched her as she dropped the envelope into the post box and paused for a moment, waiting to hear the gentle thud as the letter reached the bottom. Zoë Swann, the attractive, intelligent, humorous woman, just turned forty, interested in theatre, literature, cats and personal growth, who wants a loving, witty man to grow with.

CHAPTER THIRTEEN

Sandra saw the net curtains twitch and knew that some-one had been waiting for her. She knew by the time she reached the front door, it would be open; one or both of her parents would be standing there, wreathed in smiles, taking her bags from her, ushering her in, hugging and fussing and kissing. Sandra knew that sitting there in the car she was being observed, and so could not pause and recollect herself before her entry. So she got out of the car and went to the boot for her luggage.

This is how Sandra felt. As if she had been unfaithful to her parents. As if she was returning to a fond doting husband after a night with a lover. Here she was coming home to her parents having exposed all their character, all their faults to Stella, and worse, to Zoë, to Angela, to Carol, to Jim, to David, to Norah. Sandra's mother was over-protective, a perfectionist, making the decisions for her daughter that Sandra should have learnt to make herself; she overfed her, teaching her that food equalled love; she set her imposs-ible standards. While Sandra's father, authoritarian, demanding and reactionary, caused Sandra's rebellion, her resistance to conformity. Now she knew all this, how could she face them? How could she accept their love, when she knew how it had been misapplied? Stella had told her that the end of therapy was to forgive your parents; they, in their turn, had parents that had failed them; but Sandra was not at the end of her course yet, and had not reached forgiveness. She might get to that by the summer. Meanwhile, here she was, outside her front door – her parents' front door. There was the neat lawn, the row of miniature conifers, rusty with brown now, the red-tiled garden path, the whole house a picture of substantial Yorkshire affluence.

The door opened.

'Sandra! We expected you an hour ago! Was it the M62? Those road works outside Leeds? Never mind, darling. At least you're safe and sound. Give me your bag – Sandra, you ought to get yourself a proper suitcase – and come into the front room and we'll have a drink.' Margaret Coverdale was alive with excitement. She had still not quite got used to losing the girls. True, Sandra had been over in Manchester for more than seven years, and Sheila was in her final year at Newcastle, but it was such a short time ago that they had been a proper family all living together. Her best times were when the girls visited, and this weekend, not only was Sandra coming, but Sheila too was arriving tomorrow morning – they would meet her at the station – as it was Betty's silver wedding and she was having a family party. And as wonderful as the party would be, Margaret felt that the best part was having both girls to herself for a whole weekend. For now she was happy to let Ron look after Sandra, take her coat – she noticed it was missing two buttons – and hang it in the cupboard under the stairs, and she watched her husband grinning at his daughter with proud affection.

'Sandra! Now what can I get you? Are you hungry yet? Or would you just like a cup of tea? Or coffee? It's a little too early for sherry – what do you think, Ron?' Margaret stood at the door of the lounge and looked at her daughter. Sandra seemed larger somehow. Either because she still expected Sandra the little girl to come home, and had never quite got used to her adult daughter, or because she'd put weight on. She took after Ron in that way. Last week she'd let out a number of his trousers. At my age, he'd told her, it's not worth the effort. She'd chaffed him. She made a point of going to Rita's aerobic class on a Wednesday and it did her the world of good. Ron said he only ever cared for football, and his footballing days were well and truly over. At Ron's suggestion she opened the drinks cabinet in the wall unit, and got out the decanter of sherry. Why not? For it was a real treat to have Sandra with them.

Good, thought Sandra. I can do with something stronger than tea. Though Mum's sherries wouldn't even make a mouse tipsy. And look at her. Checking that each glass is exactly the same. She watched her mother take one glass, and pour a drop from that into another. She's making sure that everybody has exactly the same amount. Doing everything perfectly. The curse of my life. Be more careful.

I must be careful, thought Margaret. I've known a sherry to trigger off a hot flush. I'll just give a drop of mine to Ron, and we'll all have small ones as we'll be drinking later this evening. She took the small silver tray from its display position on the unit and placed the glasses on it. The sherry sparkled through the cut glass.

'Guess what, Sandra? Dad's booked us a table at the Elgin Arms tonight. To save me the cooking. It's our treat. We'll dress up and make an evening of it. Do you remember the Elgin Arms?'

Sandra did. It was a large pub several miles out in the country. Proper, substantial, real food. Steak and chips, loin of pork and roast beef – good English fare. Dad's choice. Typical. He's a caricature of himself, Sandra thought. However, her spirits did rise at the prospect of a meal out. It would be fun. A little more luxury than a teacher's salary could afford. Why not?

'That'll be nice,' Sandra conceded.

'Sheila will miss it,' said her father, 'as she can't come until tomorrow morning. Some friend of hers is having a twenty-first and she doesn't care to miss that. An independent madam, is Sheila.'

Sheila was five years younger than Sandra. From childhood Sandra had resented the fact that she had fought all Sheila's battles. Sheila had had a much easier ride than she did – no wonder she was now so much more together than her older sister. Sandra had *begged* her mother to reveal the facts of life; when she had done so Sheila had stationed herself behind the settee and had heard everything, taking it all in with that air of cool detachment that characterized her even at that age. Not surprisingly Sheila turned out to be a scientist; she was taking a degree in chemistry and was doing very well. But it would be lovely to see her tomorrow. There were all sorts of things she could say to her that she would not tell her parents; that had always been the case.

Sandra sipped at her sherry, trying to make it last;

she regarded her parents. Her father was greying now, but he retained his square good looks; that was his bone structure, her mother was in the habit of saying. His firm jaw line, his regular features. There were little creases, Sandra noticed, around his eyes, and around his mouth too. Sandra's mother was as elegant as ever. This afternoon she wore a navy box-pleat skirt and a pale blue embroidered blouse, which looked strangely familiar. It bothered Sandra. Then it clicked: Anne Palmer, the Deputy Head, had one just the same. Marks & Spencer, no doubt. For a horrible moment Sandra's mother merged into Anne Palmer. Yes, Sandra thought, my mother would have made a wonderful Deputy Head. Poor me.

'How's school?' her mother asked.

'Don't ask!' said Sandra. There was an uncomfortable pause. She shot a look at her father. 'It's fine actually. Just working hard, that's all.'

'That's what I tell Joan and George,' said Margaret. 'No one knows how hard teachers work. People think of all those long holidays and the short hours but I tell them it's not like that. And it's getting worse, isn't it, with all these new tests?'

Sandra watched her father. He stroked his chin.

'I read an article in *Good Housekeeping* about stress, Sandra. Did you know that teachers suffer some of the highest stress levels of any profession? All the different pressures on them, and keeping the classes in control. You would tell us if it got you down, wouldn't you? Stress can lead to all sorts of things.'

Ron Coverdale looked at his daughter. It was hard for him to articulate his emotions, he knew; it was hard for all men. But it was so lovely to have her in the house, even if it was only for a few days. A first daughter's always special. He winked at her; that would have to do.

Oh! thought Sandra. I know your game. Playing 'I told you so'. He never wanted me to take up teaching. And now, just a little wink to remind me of his offer. I'm only home half an hour and he's starting. I, Sandra, love and approve of myself. Sandra remembered when she had insisted on going out with a boy whom her father disapproved of – Christopher. He was on the dole and rode a motorcycle. When he packed her in after two weeks her father was jubilant. And he actually said those words – I told you so. I know a thing or two, Sandra, lass.

Stella had said that her parents had never let her make her own mistakes and so she was making some now in order to give herself lots of learning experiences. It was a fascinating idea, and one that Sandra kept returning to.

'Do you want to unpack, dear?' said her mother. 'Otherwise your dress will get creased. You have brought a dress for the party? Aunty Betty did say posh frocks. Oh good. But it will be rather creased in that sports bag. Would you like me to iron it for you? It won't take a moment. Did you bring that skirt that needed a zip replacing?' Sandra nodded. It's lovely to be needed, thought Margaret.

Sewing is my mother's way of getting control, Sandra knew. And really she would have preferred to mend her skirt herself, except she had other more important things to do like marking and, of course, her therapy. Ought she to tell her parents? Ought they to know?

'Come upstairs with me, love, now you've finished your drink, and leave Dad to put on the sports results. We'll unpack together and I'll tell you about Aunty Janet's home. She's coming tomorrow, you know. Uncle George is bringing her. Come on, love. The carpet's a bit loose on the stair. I don't want you to trip. Do be careful.'

The restaurant was up an open flight of stairs that led from the middle of the pub to a mezzanine floor with windows on all sides. The table that the waiter guided them to adjoined the window, and looked out over a large waterwheel, which was now still, but floodlit, as was the lawn, and multicoloured fairy lights hung in the trees.

'I don't remember it quite like this,' Sandra said.

'They renovated it last year,' Ron Coverdale explained. 'It's gone more upmarket. But they still do a decent rib of beef. I took your mother here on her birthday and we had a grand meal.'

Sandra settled back in her plush velvet chair and considered her father's choice of words. 'I took your mother here.' Typical. Dad had to do the arranging; Margaret was a passive entity; and she was defined by her role – 'your mother'. Sandra picked up the menu. Imagine eating roast beef and Yorkshire pudding on a Saturday night. Or if she didn't want that there was loin of pork, or lamb cutlets in rosemary, or a steak and kidney pie, with vegetables of the day. She looked at her father and his ruddy meat-eating cheeks.

immediately Sandra felt like a vegetarian alternative. And indeed, the restaurant offered a vegetable lasagne. She thought. Vegetable lasagne, and vegetables of the day. Was it worth eating all those vegetables to prove a point? Probably not. So she compromised and ordered the poached salmon, as did her mother.

In fact Sandra loved the preliminaries of a restaurant meal. The tantalizing suspense of wondering precisely what the meal would be like, how much there would be – how rich was the hollandaise sauce? – all that, and the delicious wait, knowing that there was, at the end of it, the certainty of a surfeit of food. The nice thing about going out with her parents was that they believed in feasting too. Her father often said, 'What's it all about, if you can't have a good time?' and this attitude, she admitted, had rubbed off on her. She knew too that the white Bordeaux her father ordered would only be the first bottle; poor Margaret had to drive home, but then, she was never really a drinker. That's because she doesn't like to lose control, Sandra thought. Control of herself or any of us.

'Oh, this is nice!' Margaret said. She looked at Sandra opposite her and thought how lovely life was, how lovely it was to have daughters and see them grow up and not to lose contact. She enjoyed listening to their news, and knew she had the capacity to recreate fully in her own mind all they told of their lives. She wanted to encourage Sandra to talk to her now, but she had to admit that Sandra had been a little reticent tonight. Margaret hoped her job was not getting her down.

'I hope your job's not getting you down,' she said.

It's started, thought Sandra. You can do better for

yourself than teaching. There's no need for you to persevere with a job you don't like. You know there's the money if you need to study again.

Her father came in, 'You know there's the money if you need to study again.'

'I know.'

'There's no need for you to persevere with a job you don't like. You can do better for yourself than teaching. You only have to say the word and we'll send you down to London to do your CPE.' Ron spoke convincingly, he hoped. He'd suspected for some time that Sandra wasn't entirely happy at Millers'. She was tired in the holidays, always marking when he rang her up. And although he had been temporarily convinced when she took her teachers' training course that it could all lead somewhere, he was no longer so sure. He had never quite given up the idea of a solicitor, or even a barrister, in the family. He would have liked Sheila to do medicine too, but she chose chemistry. What was wrong in wanting the best for your daughters?

The starters arrived. Ron had chosen pâté and so had Sandra. Margaret nodded when the waiter brought the prawn cocktail. Sandra buttered her strips of toast generously, as she loved butter. Especially salty butter, that set up a craving for more. Thick salty butter, contrasted with crisp toast that yielded to the pressure of the teeth. Her father's voice interrupted the anticipated pleasure of her first mouthful of toast and pâté and butter.

'You'd make a smashing barrister. You're the persuasive member of the family. I'd hate to have you prosecute me!'

Sandra laughed and ate her strip of toast in one, hardly tasting it.

'Look, Dad, I haven't made up my mind yet. I don't know what I'm going to do in the future. I know teaching isn't financially rewarding, and it's low status too, but I like the kids, I like what I teach; I'm just not really sure.'

'She was telling me before, Ron, about the women she works with. That Debra sounded awful. I never realized teachers were so career-minded. I don't think you need be ashamed if you decide to move on, dear.'

'Mum, please don't push me. I need time. If I say yes to your offer now, I'll always feel you've pushed me into it. That was the case throughout my childhood. Do you remember when you pushed me into taking tap-dancing lessons, and how I cried before I had to go?'

'But when I knew you hated it I stopped you going!' said Margaret, feeling a rush of guilt. 'I thought you would enjoy it.'

Sandra filled her second glass of wine. 'That was because you always liked to make decisions for me. Dad too, of course. You were the ones who decided I should go to a single-sex school rather than the co-ed and I remember feeling kind of powerless. You never seemed to trust me enough to let me make my own mistakes.'

Her parents looked at her, puzzled.

'Much of my rebellion is a reaction to your domination, and I have a difficulty now in making up my own mind as I had no grounding in this when I was an infant.'

'When you were an infant?' Margaret felt she was being attacked and could not understand why. Besides, what decisions do infants take?

Sandra licked her finger and ran it round the plate of pâté, which was good, if a little rich. She swallowed more wine. It was surprisingly easy to explain to her parents what she had discovered about herself. Perhaps they would learn something from it too. She felt a rush of love for them. Perhaps this was the beginning of forgiveness. Perhaps she was a quick learner and would be the star of the therapy group. Perhaps she was rather drunk. She and her father had stolen a sherry before they had left, and she had drunk another in the bar before the meal. Still, what the hell.

Sandra poured her father some wine, and refilled her own glass.

'Do you know what I've done this term? You know my friend Zoë, the Latin teacher?'

'Yes,' her mother said, dubiously.

'We've joined a therapy group. I'm in therapy now.' I wonder if I should have said that, thought Sandra, but I'm glad I did.

'Therapy?' said her father. 'Isn't that for people with nervous breakdowns? Therapy?'

'It can be,' said Sandra, ambiguously.

Margaret's head was swimming, and she'd had very little wine. 'But Sandra, there's nothing wrong with you!'

Sandra was amazed at her mother's ignorance. 'There's a lot wrong with me!' she said, outraged. The waiter arrived with three warm plates, which one by one he placed in front of them. Not in front of the servants, thought Sandra, noticing her parents' silence. Two waitresses followed and slowly and self-consciously served the vegetables: carrots with parsley; cauliflower in a thin cheese sauce; roast and boiled potatoes. No one spoke. When the waitresses had retreated, Sandra picked up her knife and fork to eat. Before doing so, she glanced at her mother, and saw the pain and distress written there. She felt she had to explain, had to make her mother see that therapy was necessary, that although she had caused Sandra's problems, it wasn't her fault.

'What it is, Mum, is that I wanted to find a solution to my eating disorder and I need to learn to be more decisive and just . . . just *grow*. It's a sort of personal growth experience.' She forked some salmon, dipped it in the hollandaise sauce, and swallowed it. 'By working through the imbalances in my childhood, I can reject the old decisions I made that didn't work for me, and make some new ones. You've got to understand the past in order to move forward into the future. That's what my therapist says.'

'But you were a lovely little girl,' Margaret said.

'And what's wrong with liking your food?' demanded Ron, cutting up his steak.

Sandra felt herself growing down and down, like Alice in Wonderland. She had a dim awareness that she had been talking nonsense; had learnt little more than jargon from Stella; that her parents' common sense was infinitely more valuable. If her father knew how much it had all cost . . .

'I just thought I'd try therapy,' said Sandra, defensively. 'Besides, I thought it would help me deal with the kids at school, and Zoë wouldn't go on her own and she needed it more than me.'

'Oh!' said Margaret, relieved. 'You did it for your friend.'

'Sort of,' said Sandra, feeling safer now. She did not want to upset her parents – she loved them – and besides, sitting now in the Elgin Arms, everything felt different. She was in her parents' comfortable world, and she did not need to be in therapy. She was a lovely little girl with a big appetite.

She flicked the rubber band that she was wearing round her wrist. She was falling into the old trap, letting her parents make up her mind for her. Thinking like them, and not thinking for herself. Or were her parents right? It was all impossible! She resolved to ask Sheila what she thought. Sheila was always so objective about everything. It was the scientist in her. But for now she could do no better than enjoy her food.

Sandra smiled at her parents. 'The salmon's lovely! And won't it be fun at Aunty Betty's tomorrow?'

The right word to describe Aunty Betty was resplendent. It was the green and gold brocade dress she was wearing, or perhaps her over-large earrings, like little diamond chandeliers. Aunty Betty was every bit as substantial as the old stone house she lived in with Uncle Jack and Philip. She was a little flushed, but her hairdo was holding up well; every wave, every curl was in place. Sandra hugged her with enthusiasm. Her face, the house, even the smell was comfortably familiar. She hugged Uncle Jack too and let him take her coat, and joined in all the excited praise that the various members of the family bestowed on each other.

'Margaret – you do look well!' from Uncle Jack.

'You're not doing so bad yourself!'

'Betty – you look good enough to eat! You're a lucky man, Jack!'

'Look at the girls! Aren't they gorgeous!'

'Aunty – you look wonderful.'

Sandra thought to herself that this was a form of positive thinking too. She peered into the lounge, and spotted her Aunty Joan – the youngest of the three sisters – talking to an older woman, and a little way away from them her two cousins Katie and Claire, both still at school. Impulsively she ran in and hugged them all, closely followed by Sheila. It was lovely to be in the midst of her mother's family like this. There were people from Jack's side too, whom Sandra dimly remembered. What with them, and some neighbours and friends whom she did not recognize, the room was quite full. Uncle Jack thrust a glass of something bubbly into her hand and Sandra obligingly drank it, and looked around her with unfeigned pleasure. She stood close to Sheila.

'How do you feel, Sheil, back with all the family again?'

'Weird. As if I've never really grown up at all. No one seems to have got any older except for Katie and Claire.'

'I feel different,' said Sandra. She felt as if she was in fact the only one who had changed, the only member of her family who had a life outside that room. She knew of course that was an illusion.

She didn't know who she preferred being – Miss Coverdale of Millers' Grammar School; Sandra in the therapy group; or Sandra, Margaret's girl. Which one was she really? She glanced at her sister. She knew that Sheila would soon spot someone she just *had* to talk to, and would dart away. Normally Sandra would do that too, but today she felt differently. It was as if her therapy had helped her see everything more clearly; as if it gave her a sort of X-ray vision that let her understand how her whole family articulated. She stood by a bowl of peanuts and helped herself, just watching.

There was cousin Philip. He was in his mid twenties like her and still lived at home. Sandra could see now there was a possessive streak that her Aunty Betty shared with her mother. She was certain Aunty Betty wanted to *keep* Philip, as her mother had wanted to keep her. Would Philip ever be able to form a relationship with a woman? Interesting. Or perhaps he was gay. Even more interesting. That would throw the cat among the pigeons. Uncle Jack would be outraged. Just look at Philip now – the quick way he responded to his mother's signal from across the room. An Oedipus complex if ever I saw one, thought Sandra.

Then look at Katie and Claire. They were heterosexual – no doubt about that. Both were dressed in bottom-hugging short black skirts and sheer black tights. Sandra had a momentary shock. They were her baby cousins; she even remembered being allowed to push Katie in her pram. But Katie must be sixteen now, and Claire just a little younger. Both looked horribly precocious, heavily made up, with brilliant red lipstick. Interesting that Aunty Joan and Uncle George had allowed it. Either Aunty Joan was vicariously living through a second adolescence as she had married Uncle George far too early, or had no interest in her daughters now they were no longer children. So, starved of maternal love in this crucial stage of their life, they were attempting to attract sexual attention as compensation. Poor things.

And there was Rita, the aerobics teacher. Rita was Aunty Betty's neighbour's daughter. She was Sandra's age, and Sandra had played with her when they were younger. She'd never liked her much. It wasn't surprising *she*'d turned out to be an aerobics teacher. Father belonged to the Territorial Army, and Mrs Bowen, Rita's mum, was a strangely submissive sort of woman, always very quiet and willing to follow Aunty Betty in everything. Sandra supposed Mr and Mrs Bowen had a sort of sado-masochistic relationship – Mr Bowen enjoying inflicting pain, and Mrs Bowen quite liking it, and poor Rita a result of all that, enjoying inflicting pain on others in the stifling conventionality of the keep-fit class.

Through the kitchen hatch she caught a glimpse of her father talking to Uncle Derek, Uncle Jack's brother. Now he was interesting. He –

'Sandra! How lovely to see you! Why aren't you talking to anyone? You gave me a kiss and then you walked off!' Aunty Joan smacked Sandra on the cheek with gusto, leaving a sticky red brand-mark of lipstick. 'So there's another one. And now tell me all about what you're doing.'

Sandra's account of school, her flat, her friends was interrupted by a commotion at the front door.

'That'll be our George with Aunty Janet.'

Aunty Janet was the oldest member of the family – the family antique, thought Sandra, with amusement. She was in fact her mother's aunt – Sandra's great aunt, in her eighties now, and in a home, since her arthritis meant that she had great difficulty walking. Uncle George wheeled her in now, and Sandra looked at her with a rush of affection. She was the first at the wheelchair. She knelt down and took Aunty Janet's hand, swollen and gnarled. Aunty Janet seemed completely composed, unaffected by the buzz of conversation and clink of glasses around her. She smiled benignly at Sandra.

'It's Margaret's girl, isn't it? Sheila.'

'No, Sandra, Aunty.'

She nodded, as if she knew all along. Sandra questioned her about the home, about her health, and noticed with interest how Aunty Janet, unlike her other relations, did not wish to interrogate her about her teaching, her life in Manchester. Aunty Janet's main topic of interest was Aunty Janet.

'They wheel me into the television lounge sometimes but they do put it on a bit loud. That's because of the ones that are hard of hearing. On a Saturday they give us chicken. They gave us all apricot pie once. I can't abide apricots.'

Sandra listened affectionately. If you couldn't take a lively interest in food when you were over eighty, when could you? Sandra was joined by her mother, who pecked Aunty Janet on the cheek, and pulled up a chair to talk to her.

'Aye, it's Margaret,' said Aunty Janet. 'She's a fine lass, your Sheila.'

'Sandra,' said Sandra and her mother.

Three generations, thought Sandra. Her own grandmother had died when she was very little, and she never really knew her. Aunty Janet – her grandmother's sister – was the nearest she had to a grandmother. She rarely saw her now. Aunty Janet had never married, and assumed a proprietorial air over the three sisters, Margaret, Betty and Joan. Margaret had stayed for a week with Aunty Janet when Betty was born; Margaret and Betty stayed with her together when Joan was born, as her mother had never tired of telling her. Aunty Janet knew the girls well. Sandra recollected that old people had good long-term memories. She wondered how vividly Janet remembered the sisters. Sandra knew, for Stella had told her, that the human personality was more or less fixed at six. From questioning Aunty Janet, she wondered what more information she could glean. Margaret, as controlling as ever, was asking Janet what she wanted to eat, to drink. Tea? Without sugar? And some cake? There was Aunty Joan, the scatterbrain, shrieking in the corner with some man. And Aunty Betty, the middle sister, was standing with her arm around Philip, smiling and hectic. The three weird sisters, Sandra thought. She had been teaching *Macbeth* to the third years. 'The Weird Sisters, hand in hand –'

'Your mother does look well,' Aunty Janet said. 'And who'd have thought it? She was such a tearaway when she was younger. Bessie called her the little rebel.'

'*My* mother? Don't you mean Aunty Joan? Aunty Joan would have been the rebel.'

'Oh no. Joanie you could always rely on. She was the good one. She always did as she was told. And Betty was the scatterbrain. That's what Bessie said. Left everything lying about.'

'Are you sure you're not confusing them?'

Sandra's mother came back with a cup of tea in Betty's best china.

'Don't be cheeky! My legs have gone but I've still got a brain. You were a trial to your mother, Margaret.'

Margaret laughed as she attached a tray to the wheel-chair.

'And Betty was the scatterbrain and we always said Joanie would make a good little mother.' Janet nodded in confirmation of her own opinions. Margaret laughed again.

'I remember Mum saying that! You two had us all typecast from the start!' Both women chuckled and Sandra felt excluded.

I can't be wrong, she thought. People don't change that much. Or do they? Or –? My head hurts. It's drinking in the afternoon that does it, especially on top of last night's wine. The noise and laughter oppressed her suddenly, and she decided to go upstairs for a visit to the bathroom. When she got there the door was locked, and so she stood a small way away from the locked door, waiting.

Sandra was troubled. An idea was growing within her, an idea she really did not wish to admit to herself. She fixed her eyes opposite on a framed tapestry Aunty Betty had hung on the landing. It vexed her. The cross-stitch annoyed her. She felt like kicking something. She felt like she did when she was small. Once she opened the door of the washing machine and all the water cascaded on to the floor. Her mother was livid, but assumed Sheila had done it. Sheila was smacked. And Sandra felt murderous until she had gone up to her mother and admitted it was her. It was surprisingly easy to confess – such a relief. She felt so much better afterwards. The bathroom door opened and someone she did not know came out, and smiled at her. Sandra went into the bathroom and sat on the edge of the bath and thought.

It's easy, said a stern interior voice – who she recognized as the same voice that confessed to opening the washing-machine door – to judge people, and look back, and interpret all their behaviour in a way that suits you. But human beings aren't that simple. There's more to your mother and aunts than your analysis allows. Think how complex you are. Do you deny them the same complexity? Sandra, what have you been doing?

But if you can't analyse and label your parents' behaviour, said an anxious Sandra to herself, mentally moving to another chair, then how can you be sure that any psychoanalysis is accurate? How can I carry on with my therapy? She thought of how lovely it was to be in Stella's room with Stella, seeing simple solutions to complex problems, what fun to expose oneself to the group, getting their sympathy. Unconditional positive regard. Sandra, said the stern voice, you're wrong about your mother and father. And Sandra, it continued, you've been in the bathroom far too long so go downstairs and join the others.

When Sandra re-entered the lounge, the hubbub had increased. There was a thumping beat, and in one corner a middle-aged couple were attempting to disco-dance. They joggled around on the spot, grinning and sweaty. Rita and Philip joined them, Rita bouncing athletically. Ludicrous, thought Sandra. And there was Aunty Betty and Uncle Jack now, doing a form of half-remembered rock and roll. Around them spectators started to clap. Sandra poured herself another drink. Just as she was about to sip at it, she felt someone pulling at her arm. It was Sheila.

'Where have you been, Sandra? They've started dancing now. Come on, let's show them how it's done!' Sheila pulled her into the middle of the dancers and Sandra had no option but to join in.

She was unhappy. She wasn't a good dancer and she knew it. Besides, she had an aversion to this sort of pop music from the early sixties. It all sounded like syncopated nursery rhymes. Curiously tame now, she thought, detaching herself. Suitable for ageing uncles and aunts.

But Sheila seemed to be joining in with gusto. Sandra envied her sister. Sheila gave her a wink of complicity. Looking at Sheila only, it was easy to start to dance. Sandra began to move her feet, and then her waist. In fact, it was fun. The movement cheered her up. And there was her mother, watching them. Sheila beckoned repeatedly and she joined them too. Sandra was surprised at her mother's sense of rhythm. The three of them seemed to fit together so well. And then, dancing in the middle of all her family, she was filled with a sense of exultation. This *was* fun. It didn't matter what you looked like – everybody looked ridiculous really, if you thought about it, but it didn't matter, it was the family. So what if she was over-mothered? So what if her father was hopelessly old-fashioned? Who's perfect? And Sandra rejoiced that she wasn't too.

Sheila came to talk to Sandra as she was getting ready for bed. It was delicious to compare notes about the party, to conjecture about Philip's relationship with Rita, to laugh at their parents' behaviour. But it was strange, too, to hear Sheila talk of her life in Newcastle. That was another sister; a stranger-sister, who had broken away from them all, and had the temerity to lead her own life. When she glanced at Sheila, sitting on the edge of the bed wearing a dressing-gown she had owned since school, but with her hair cropped short, she looked like a troubling mixture of the old and the new. Sandra felt Sheila's eyes upon her as she lifted her arms and removed her slip. To Sheila it was no secret that Sandra worried about her weight, and she knew that Sheila would be looking with a dispassionate eye at her swelling body. She felt hugely self-conscious, and decided to forestall any comment.

'I've put a bit on again, haven't I?'

'I don't remember. What do the scales say?'

'I don't know. I don't have any in my flat.'

'Have you weighed yourself on Mum's?'

Stop it, thought Sandra. Don't interfere. She loathed her sister for having the presumption to think she could ask such direct questions.

'No,' Sandra said, defensively.

'Oh, don't be so prickly. Find out whether you've put weight on and then if you have, you can do something about it,' said Sheila, airily.

'I *am* doing something about it.'

'You've not joined another slimming group, have you?'

'Certainly not. I'm trying . . . something different, that's all.'

A horrible realization dawned on Sandra. She could never, never tell her sister, her rational, well-balanced, sensible sister, about *The Love Yourself Diet*. Never.

'Go on. What are you trying? An exercise programme?'

'No, nothing like that.'

'What then? What else can you do? Are you dieting?'

'Sort of.'

'But you were eating a lot today.'

Like a wave rushing up on her, Sandra felt again that overwhelming urge to confess, to tell all, and to be judged. Besides, Sheila might be impressed, and if Sheila approved, that would really give her impetus. She tested the water.

'I can . . . eat a lot – on this diet. It's not really about controlling your food intake.'

'Oh?'

'It's your thinking. It's a thinking diet. If you think slim, you can be slim.'

'You mean, like you think of yourself as somebody who is slim, and imagine the healthy food that person would eat, and eat like that?'

'No. You think that the food you eat won't make

you fat. Because thoughts create results. And if you love yourself you can let go of all the blocked energy that creates fat. So you think positively about yourself and food. Everything I eat turns to health and beauty. Am I making myself clear?'

'No.'

'In this book it says that food will only make you fat if you think it will.'

'So if you eat some chocolate, and you *think*,' Sheila paused, 'it hasn't got any calories, it won't have.'

'Sort of.'

'Sandra. You're mad.'

Sandra looked down at herself, at her swelling stomach, her dimpled knees. If *The Love Yourself Diet* worked, she would have lost weight by now. But she hadn't. She had slowly got bigger and bigger. It hadn't worked. The realization filled Sandra's limbs with lead, and she sat down by the dressing-table, defeated.

'Where did you get that book from?' asked Sheila.

'Just a bookshop. Illuminations. In Chisholme.' She may as well tell all. 'I'm in therapy. I've joined a therapy group. To help me with my weight problem. And my personal growth. And my therapist suggested it.'

'You're in *therapy*?'

Sandra nodded glumly.

'But –' started Sheila.

'I thought if I understood why I overate and I could never make up my mind, it would help me. Help me to change. It's a good idea,' Sandra said, lamely.

'If it works,' said Sheila.

'If it works,' echoed Sandra.

There was a silence. Sandra turned her back to her sister as she removed her bra and pulled her nightdress over her head. She wriggled so it fell over her hips and to her feet. Sheila held her counsel.

'But the problem is,' said Sandra, eagerly, 'I go with a friend, a good friend – Zoë Swann, the only friend I've got at school – and it's working for her, and I don't want to let her down by stopping going, so I feel I'll have to carry on a little bit longer. I don't think it will do me any more harm.'

'You're mad,' Sheila repeated. 'That's why I love you.'

CHAPTER FOURTEEN

The young girl at the reception desk had assumed, of
course, that they were married. Stella explained that
she had simply travelled down with Mr Temple, as
she called him, and Mr Temple would sign himself in
when he had returned from getting the luggage from
the boot of her car. She watched the girl check her
name against a typewritten list, and she repeated 'Stella
Martin' when she found it.

Everything was wonderful. Everything. This small
hotel, the White House, situated on a little prominence
overlooking a rolling landscape of mist-covered hills,
was perfect. Its entrance hall, with its wood panelling
and faded tapestries, was intense and atmospheric.
Stella was wild to explore the hotel itself, dying to see
her room, and wondered how close it would be to . . .
Roland joined her, a suitcase in each hand. His glasses
had slipped a little on his nose.

When he had signed in, the girl took them both
up the red-carpeted stairs to the top corridor,
through several fire doors, and stopped outside room
number nine. She opened the door for Stella to enter.
Roland stood in the corridor. For one moment Stella,
noticing the bed was a double bed, thought, they've
confused the booking – they've put us together – in
the same bed – but then the girl explained that all
delegates had been given single rooms, and some did
have double beds, as she saw Stella's confusion.

Blushing, Stella entered and shut the door behind her.

It was perfect. Her bed had a white-lace counterpane; the wide window looked out over a large lawn with a shrubbery at the far end; everything had an air of genteel elegance. Stella stood by the window and saw a man and a woman walking near the shrubbery. She wondered if those could be the course facilitators. She had read about them in the course literature she had been sent after forwarding her deposit. Herbert Schumansky and Mina Thomas. Both were American. This was their first workshop in the British Isles, and Stella was glad and excited to be part of it. Since booking for the course she had heard some mention of 'Modern Myth and Mickey Mouse', and all of it had been favourable. There, on the dressing table, was the programme for the weekend. She picked it up eagerly. After the evening meal, there was an informal get-together. Work proper was not to begin until Saturday morning, when Herbert and Mina would explain their main techniques. Most of the rest of the day involved screenings of the relevant films, and small workshops to facilitate self-discovery. Stella loved self-discovery.

The figures she had seen disappeared into the shrubbery and she turned and looked at her room again. Now, she lay on the bed to see if it was hard enough, for she liked a hard mattress. It was a little springy. She bounced slightly and frowned. If she couldn't sleep, she thought, she could always try the floor. She put her suitcase on the bed and opened it, hung up her clothes, took her various toiletries to the sink – it had a slight hairline crack near the plug, which she winced at – and finding the packet of incense sticks she had placed at the bottom of her suitcase, she extracted one and lit it. The familiar hint of sandalwood in the air assured Stella the room was at least temporarily hers. She paced around the room, unable to settle.

It was lovely, she thought, to look out over the hills as evening fell. But she felt alien too. She knew she ought to love being close to nature, but Stella had spent all her life in cities; first London, then Manchester; she approved of the countryside – she did not love it. Herefordshire – where she was now – she did not know at all. Carol had told her to be sure to visit Glastonbury on Sunday, which was not far, and her client Graeme Grant had mentioned Hay-on-Wye and the bookshops. Stella was sure she ought to feel interested in that. But just now, alone, she felt a stranger. And she was very much alone. Her husband, she remembered with pleasure, was six thousand miles away.

She lay on the floor on her back, her knees bent, her palms upwards and she breathed deeply. I, Stella Martin, love and approve of myself. Now the interesting thing about Richard was that she had received a letter from him that very morning, and in it he had said that he had been contacted by Gill Goldstein! Just as Stella had suggested! Gill needed an accountant, and Richard had visited the TransFormation Foundation and had been very impressed by its facilities and Gill's plans for its future development. He had arranged to spend a week there living on site to assess its work, and had decided to undergo some psychoanalysis and personal growth work to see how it all went. Purely as an experiment, he'd said. Gill herself would work with him. Stella was delighted. Mostly delighted. She had always wanted Richard to go into therapy. She knew he needed it badly; he needed to look outside himself, and into himself. No one better to help him than Gill. But at the same time, there was Roland. Most of the time she forgot Richard existed. If, through personal growth, he should wish to become closer to her again, she would need to deal with her feelings for Roland. Just now, she wanted to feel wronged by Richard. So she hoped his therapy would be a slow process; certainly, *she* knew he had a long way to go!

And Stella wasn't going to think bad, negative thoughts today. This was a special, magic weekend. *Her* weekend. She knew she gave so much emotional and psychic energy to her clients, to her group especially, and this weekend was for her to get back in touch with her inner self, to receive from others, to grow, to learn, to relax, to live. And . . . And there was something else which she was deliberately not thinking about, because when she did it would be so delicious and so delightful and it was almost more fun not thinking about it. Stella's weekend. So you're going away for a weekend! her mother had said, a few days ago, when she rang her. Very nice too. I could do with a holiday. Stella had said, no this was not a holiday, this was a course; she was learning things, things to help her with her work. What things? New developments in psychoanalytic techniques. You learn that in a *hotel*? her mother had said.

A hotel. There was only one worry Stella had. In a

hotel, she would not be in charge of the food. It was impossible to tell what she would be expected to eat. Or tempted to eat. There might be a sweet trolley! Stella felt her heart pounding. Best not to think about that. She would think about something else now. Something else. The other thing.

Stella sat up and clutched her knees and was suddenly tense, tense as a bowstring. If anything happened, it would happen this weekend. To the best of Stella's knowledge, no one else they knew from Manchester was coming down to the White House for 'Modern Myth and Mickey Mouse'. So they were effectively alone. And in the intimate atmosphere engendered by such a course anything could happen. Till now, their communication had been one way; Stella told Roland, her therapist, about herself. Here, in a group, he would speak of himself. On the journey down, he had been reticent. Much of their conversation, as they sped down the M6, concerned the connection between homoeopathy and psychotherapy, which was very interesting but impersonal. They spoke of their expectations of the course. They stopped and had coffee at an awful service station and discussed the curse of the motor car, and the soullessness of city life. And all the time Stella had a dreadful secret.

Now the sky was darkening outside and Stella's room fell into shadow. Now she could think about her secret. It was awful. She had had a dream. Now, Stella was a little sceptical about dream interpretation, although really she had an open mind. But as for this dream! In this dream, she was lying on a couch, a brown leather couch, in a consulting room, and there was a blanket over her, and she was speaking to someone, and she became aware that the person was Roland. She didn't see him in the dream but knew absolutely that it was him. And he lifted the blanket and beneath it she was completely naked. And they embraced and she actually dreamed they . . . and it was almost impossible to look him in the face this morning when he met her at the Quays! It seemed impossible for him not to know what she had dreamt.

Stella was disgusted and delighted with herself. Yet the long journey down here had dissipated the intensity of the dream. It was, in fact, only a dream. And she did not yet know whether the lovely warmth she felt when she was with him was reciprocated, or whether it was only part of their professional relationship. Love me! she ordered him. You, Roland Temple, love and approve of me, Stella Martin. There was a soft rap on the door. If it's him, thought Stella, he does love me – it's a sign! If it's someone else, she thought, as she rose and went to the door, he still loves me because it's silly to be superstitious and I know I must never set up win-lose situations for myself, only win-win situations. She opened the door.

'Have you settled in?' asked Roland.

Stella was pleased she had met everybody informally last night as she felt so much easier this morning, beginning the course with people she could already put names to. There was Lynne from Ealing – a tiny, blonde woman with roughly cropped hair – Dan from Sussex, for example, and of course, Herbie and Mina themselves. Stella entered the hotel lounge, carrying a mug of black coffee which had been provided, cradling it in her hands for warmth.

There was Herbie. He stood and greeted her, putting his arms out for a hug. Stella put down her coffee and hugged him. He was wearing bright red trousers with two large white buttons on the front. And there were his hands. On those he had white gloves. Mina, sitting by him, wore a red and white spotted dress. She guessed they must be Minnie and Mickey. She appreciated the effort they were making. It was good to know she was in the hands of facilitators who took their work seriously.

Very quickly the others arrived and settled in the scattered easy chairs. She smiled as Roland came to join her, a clipboard in his hand. Soon the room felt full. Through the french windows Stella could see a still pond, a leafless tree by it. She paid it scant attention. Herbie was beginning. He had in his lap a large, leather-bound book, certainly an antique, which he opened with loving care. He read from it.

'Once upon a time, many years ago, there lived a young psychoanalyst called Herbert. Our story begins when he had a revelation so profound that he knew it would change the course of pyschoanalytical theory.' Herbert gently closed the book, and leaning forward slightly, continued to address the group.

'For some time my own analysis had reached an impasse. My analyst had failed to come up with any model of my story that I could relate to, that I could feel was *me*. There seemed to be no archetypal pattern that fitted my behaviour. Yet my story wasn't very different from many men. I had problems with my father. His expectations of me had always been incredibly high. A brain surgeon, at least.' The class laughed gently. 'And I rebelled in the usual way. I decided instead to go on the stage. I met his questioning about my life with lies. And my lies were so careless, it was as if I *wanted* him to discover my deceptions.' Roland nodded. 'I turned to drugs too. I had a friend. We did drugs together. He had a bad trip one night, and died. It scared me. It saved me. It was then I went into analysis. And I reached this impasse.

'Then one night, I had a dream. In it I was with my analyst; I spoke, and in reply, he whistled. When I looked at him, he was some kind of insect. I freaked out. The next afternoon, I took my kid brother to the movies. We saw *Pinocchio*. I just took one look at Jiminy Cricket, and knew. He was my analyst. And as I watched the film, it all fell into place. Geppetto was *my* father. He made me, but wood wasn't good enough for him, oh no; I had to be a real, human boy. Pinocchio goes on the stage as a stringless puppet – like the bit parts I was taking. The fox and the cat that kidnapped Pinocchio – the drugs. And that kid who was changed into a donkey – my friend who died. Guys, I *was* Pinocchio. My analyst was Jiminy Cricket, my conscience. You can guess the rest.

'Together Jiminy and I realized that for modern western culture, the old archetypes of human behaviour – taken from Greek and Roman myth, from East European folklore – were unknown to most of us. No way could we pattern ourselves on stories and heroes we none of us knew. But what do we know? What do all western kids watch and believe in? Who has created our creative imagination? Walt Disney! It was so simple, and so brilliant. As our work spread, we ran courses, started cartoon character analysis together, and then, when my father's business collapsed and he was in debt for thousands of dollars, *I* was able to redeem him, saved him from the belly of the whale. It works.'

Stella breathed in deeply. This was incredible. It was the most interesting idea she had heard for months, for years. It was so obviously true. For she too had seen all the Disney films. As a child she was never a great reader, but had been taken to the cinema. Mina spoke now.

'I was one of Herb's first clients. It worked for me too, guys. Looking at me now you wouldn't guess I was eaten up with resentment. I had three older sisters, all of them gifted in some way. One was musical, one was beautiful, one was brilliantly clever. Yet I seemed to project the hatred I felt for them on to others. I was never able to maintain a relationship with a man. Somehow I would poison it, maybe through sheer wickedness, or talk and talk so that I sent them to sleep.

'Herb made me see who I was: Maleficent. The evil fairy from *The Sleeping Beauty*. My sisters were the three good fairies; I was the fairy who was not invited to the ball. I had carried that resentment for sixteen years. Once I saw that, I could let it go.'

This is wonderful, thought Stella. Who am I?

'Mina's right,' Herbert continued. 'That sudden, felt identification with a Disney archetype can release you from old behaviour patterns as suddenly as the prince's kiss wakes the sleeping princess. Your inner child, all

184

those years ago, saw the film, made the connection, and kept it locked in your psyche. This weekend we'll unlock it. OK, guys?

'This is how we proceed. During the whole of the day, you must go to as many of the Disney screenings as you can. We've printed out flyers giving details of locations and films. Then we'll meet in small workshops for you to discuss your response and make the connections. I know what you're thinking: how do you *know* when it's the right one for you? Sometimes it's just gut reaction; other times that feeling just grows. So Mina and me have this box of stuff' – Herbie stood and went over to a large cardboard box Stella had not noticed before – 'that you can use to get the feeling.' He drew out some Mickey ears. 'Here are things you can wear to make you feel the part. It can be really cathartic to *be* the character. I like to get you to act it out. Act out your role, get in touch with those feelings, and release them. Right, you guys. I'm ready!'

Stella wriggled in her seat with anticipation. There were so many films to see that it was hard to know which ones to choose; there were simultaneous screenings. She wondered whether to simply follow Roland, but she knew that she ought to listen to her inner promptings and view the films that spoke to her. For that reason she selected *Dumbo*, followed by *Alice in Wonderland*; Roland opted for *Peter Pan* and *Cinderella*. Did she imagine that lost look on his face as she announced her decision? She was sure he would have liked her to stay with him. But that was not to be. She moved off to Conference Room 2 for the first screening.

Herbie turned the lights off, and the video rolled. Stella knew, knew absolutely, that this would work for her. The Disney music was so familiar, so comforting. The clear lines of the cartoon characters, the simple, colourful, predictable world of Disney; that castle soaring to the sky, the perfection of it all. How could she have not realized its importance? Why were the most simple discoveries the most significant? And there was Mrs Jumbo, looking skyward, awaiting the delivery of her new baby. Perhaps, just perhaps, Mrs Jumbo was her mother. Stella was an only child, and her mother was a large woman. But no, Mrs Jumbo cared for Dumbo, despite his deformity, and Stella's mother made her grow up too quickly, and besides, Stella certainly had no deformity. She felt her small, shell-like ears. *Dumbo* was a wonderful film, and so moving at the end, but it was not for her.

Stella thought perhaps she looked somewhat like Alice. Something about the eyes. Herbie had said last night, when he was talking to her informally, that a physical characteristic can be a clue. She watched Alice with interest. And yes! Alice drank from a bottle entitled 'DRINK ME' and shrank. Stella remembered her dieting days. She ate the cookie labelled 'EAT ME' and grew again, grew to a giant. Those binges she had. But as Alice's adventures developed, again Stella felt she was on a cold trail. Who were the twins? The White Rabbit? No, it wasn't this one either. She regretted not having followed Roland. She might have been Wendy or Tinkerbell, or Cinderella to Roland's Prince Charming. She felt cheated. *Alice in Wonderland* wasn't really such a good film after all.

Stella bit greedily into her sandwiches at lunchtime, realized what she was doing, and put them to one side. Emotional eating. Still, it was easier not to eat when Roland joined her.

'How have you got on?' she asked eagerly.

He smiled warmly at her. 'This is good, very good. I'm close to something here; I felt some kind of identification with John Darling – the spectacles, you know. The Lost Boy.'

Oh, you poor thing, thought Stella.

'But that only lasted a moment. I lacked his sense of adventure. And you, Stella?'

Stella shook her head. 'Not yet,' she said. 'But there's plenty more to see.'

'It's a pity there's not a screening of *Mary Poppins*,' said Roland, looking at Stella.

'Why?' she asked, very curious.

'Mary Poppins,' he said. 'Practically perfect in every way.'

Stella shivered with delight. He meant her. And she saw the justice of his comment. She was about to reply in some way, when their conversation was riven by a loud gulping sob. They both turned, and there was Dan, crying. Herbie and Mina both ran to him, held him as the sobs came.

'I can't face it!' Stella heard him say.

There was some muffled conversation. Then Herbie stood up.

'Listen, you guys. Dan here has made an identification.' Stella was wildly jealous. 'He wants to work this one through with you.' Herbie paused. 'He's Dumbo.' Stella looked at him and thought, yes, yes, he *is*

Dumbo! They filed into the lounge and Herbie strode to the box, brought out some large grey ears and some face paints. He set to work with gusto. He painted the tip of Dan's nose pink, gave him two red eyebrows, and a rattle to hold.

'OK, Dumbo. You're the baby. You're at the top of the burning house. You've got to jump. Cheer him everyone!'

They all cheered. Dan stepped on to a chair.

'I don't want to! I don't want to! I'm scared!'

'How do you feel, Dumbo?'

'I'm scared. You all hate me. They hate me.'

'You've got to jump, Dumbo. Jump!'

Dan landed in a heap. 'It's sticky!' he wailed. And sobbed.

The group gathered round and held him. In a broken voice, Dan explained.

'I was bullied at school. I was a fat boy. And I was so fat my chest was – it looked like breasts. They called me names. It was that ridicule. I knew it again when I saw it on the screen. I'm Dumbo.'

Mina urged, 'You can fly, Dumbo!'

'You can fly!' crooned Herbie.

'I can fly,' echoed Dan.

Stella was deeply moved. Dan would be able to see now that he could move on from that old destructive pattern. He would be free to fly. To spread his wings. She would use this method with her group. Roland reached out and squeezed her hand and she squeezed it back, and then realized it was his hand, his lovely hand, and held it just for a moment.

They both decided to see *Lady and the Tramp*; Stella

then preferred *Snow White*; Roland, *101 Dalmatians*. She settled again in front of the screen; how beautiful it all was, the snow-covered boulevards of *Lady and the Tramp*. But no, these dogs were not herself and Roland; Stella was not a dog, even a pretty dog. As a child, she knew, she was afraid of dogs. And yet, something answered in her as Lady and her mongrel boyfriend shared a dinner. She glanced at Roland, who smiled softly.

She parted from him as he moved off to view *101 Dalmatians*. She was tired now. Her attention had wandered from the film once or twice. Often, watching the screen, Stella felt her eyes grow heavy, shut. She willed herself to stay awake for *Snow White*.

Funny, she hadn't noticed. Snow White too had heavily-lidded eyes, almost as if she were asleep as well. Stella watched her sing to herself by the water, and there was the prince, as if in a dream. A dream, thought Stella. Magic Mirror, on the wall, who is the fairest of them all? She watched the Stepmother's anger. Her mother's temper. Her mother would shout at her, Stella remembered, and then afterwards apologize and make up, as if she was two mothers, a beautiful mother, and a witch mother. Poor Snow White alone in the forest. Stella felt her fear.

But those eyes. They were nothing to be afraid of. For they belonged to the animals of the forest, Snow White's friends. The spirits of nature, affirming goodness. Her affirmations. Stella entered the low cottage with the animals. How untidy the cottage was! She set to work to scrub it clean, making it all perfect. And here they all were. Stella's children. Her dwarfs. Her therapy group. Here was Sleepy – that was David – and Sneezy – Norah – and Sandra was Doc and Zoë was Bashful and Carol was Dopey and . . . Grumpy. Who was Grumpy? Richard was Grumpy. Perhaps.

Stella made all the dwarfs wash before dinner. Cleansed them. And no, here was the poisoned apple! Food! For her, all food was poisoned. Of course. It's a wishing apple, says the wicked witch. All your dreams will come true. All my dreams *will* come true, thought Snow White. And she falls to the ground. Dead. But not quite. And her group put her in a glass coffin. Which is my frigidity, thought Stella. And I need a kiss to wake me. Here comes Roland. And I wake, and we are all so glad, and I cry with happiness. And Snow White felt the tears running down her cheeks.

'I'm Snow White,' Stella whispered. 'I'm Snow White,' she said, rather more loudly, so the others in the room might hear her. 'I'm Snow White.'

'Hey!' said Mina. 'That's great! Hey, listen everybody, we've got Snow White!'

'I'm Snow White!' she told Roland as they sat down opposite each other at the dining table. 'It was overwhelming – the identification I felt. More and more, as I think about the film, areas of my own life come into focus. When I first –' Stella stopped. No one knew better than her the protocol of the therapist–client relationship. Since Roland was her therapist he would need to hear the details of this identification; they would have to work through it at some stage, perhaps back in Manchester. Besides, she had things she wanted to ask him.

'What about you? How were your viewings?'

'Good. It was good. I . . .'

Stella held her breath.

'I felt fleeting kinships with most characters. But I knew Cruella de Vil.' Roland began to drink his soup. He said no more.

'Was she your mother?' Stella asked, in her most professional tone. She paused and watched him swallow his soup.

'No. A woman I knew.' He shook his head and smiled. 'But it doesn't matter now.' He replaced the spoon very tidily in the bowl. Stella said nothing, hoping by her silence to encourage more talking. But the silence simply increased their awareness of each other. They sat alone to eat as the hotel dining room was composed of a number of small tables; all the course students sat at separate tables in twos and threes. Some wore props; there was Peter Pan with a little green hat; Lynne wore a leather collar with a dog licence. She had made a strong identification with Lady during *Lady and the Tramp*, she had told Stella. The film had provided a model for her fear of abandonment.

Stella stole a glance at Roland. His face was becoming familiar to her. She noticed that his lips were well-shaped, almost girlish. But his other features were straight, regular, accentuated by his cropped hair. She wondered what he looked like without his glasses. As she re-crossed her legs under the table her foot brushed his. He did not seem to respond.

As his soup bowl was removed – Stella had skipped the soup – her stomach lurched, as she entertained the idea that perhaps he did not feel for her as she felt for him; that his kindness, his concern, his interest, were all purely professional. That he came away with her this weekend because he was genuinely interested in the course – which was interesting, very interesting, but . . . That he accepted a lift because he was hard up. That this Cruella de Vil woman was still around. Stella filled with tears.

The waiter brought the main course; spaghetti bolognese, heavy on the meatballs, as it said in the handwritten menu that Herbie had provided. The waiter brought it in a steaming tureen, and gave warm plates to Stella and Roland. She didn't have the energy to start.

Then Roland grinned at her. With his spoon and fork he lifted some spaghetti. 'Come here!' he said. 'Let's do it like they do in the movies!' She helped him separate a strand of spaghetti, and they sucked the strand from each end, like Lady and her Tramp. 'Bravo!' cried Herbie, who had noticed them. And of course, their mouths met, and Roland kissed her, and their friends cheered, and Stella's misery dissolved, and she was elated. He loved her. But how strange it was, to kiss someone, and to have food in your mouth.

Roland now served the spaghetti and Stella sat, demure, expectant. He had kissed her on the lips. Which really one's therapist ought not to do. But she was very happy. It was seven o'clock. Herbie had arranged one more screening – *The Sleeping Beauty* – which they were all to see, and he would happily work with anyone, he said, who needed to do stuff around that film. But the rest, he had said, were welcome to

192

relax in the bar, but to beware what happened to Dumbo!

Am I Sleeping Beauty too? wondered Stella, watching her singing in the forest on the eve of her sixteenth birthday. Sleeping Beauty had a dream about a prince – she glanced at Roland, whose chin was propped on his hands – and her dream came true. If you dream a thing more than once, they said, it's sure to come true. In fact, Stella knew, that was how visualization worked. Stella remembered her own dream, and now that she was more tired it returned to her with increasing clarity. She was lying on a couch. Roland came to her.

No! Perhaps she was all of the three good fairies. There was something familiar in the way they worked magic for other people. She looked at Roland again and hoped he didn't notice how frequently she looked at him. Yes, there *was* a resemblance between him and the prince. Did he see it? He appeared deep in concentration. Together they watched the princess's enchantment, the prince's battle against the witch-dragon, and then, her awakening. My awakening, thought Stella. Then Roland whispered to her, 'I just love happy endings!'

Before Stella could reply, the lights were turned on, and the group dispersed. Stella and Roland made their way to the bar with Mina, Dan and his magic feather. Herbie and Mina had suggested he keep it with him for a while to give him confidence. They formed a group together and the conversation was intense. Stella willed Roland to stay, dreaded him rising, saying he needed an early night. She drank red wine – she didn't notice how much – and chose to speak little, but to frown in concentration.

It was past eleven before Dan and Mina left them. Roland and Stella sat in armchairs by a low table. Neither had quite finished their wine. Stella knew she was not breathing properly. Her breaths were shallow, her pulse raced.

'How do you feel?' Roland asked her, with concern. 'It's been an intense day for you.'

She loved the way he talked to her about her.

'I feel as if I've made progress. I'm not at all tired. I have so much to think about and work through.'

'Good,' he said.

'It's so interesting to realize that we owe as much to Walt Disney as we do to Freud and Jung and Berne and Perls.'

Roland nodded.

'Because he has created the world both as it really is and as we want it to be. I can see that now. My dreams are there in those films.'

'And our nightmares too,' Roland said.

Daringly, Stella suggested, 'Your nightmare. You were telling me before about Cruella de Vil.'

'Cruella,' he said, ruminatively. 'Did you notice her hair was white and black? Two sides to her? She made fur coats from Dalmatian skins. She used their skins for fur coats.'

'Did you know her well?'

'I loved her.'

Stella was struck dumb. She did not want to hear that. But the past tense was encouraging. She may as well know the worst.

'Can you talk about her?'

'She used my skin for her fur coat. She used me, Stella. It was as bad finding that out, as discovering what sort of woman she was. I couldn't ride that. Love turned into casual disregard. She taught me how to cry –' He stopped and shook his head. Timidly Stella reached out and held his hand. He clasped it with his other. She moved nearer to him.

'Don't cry now,' Stella said. She thought he would.

'No,' he said. 'It was all over some time ago. And besides, there's –'

He can't make the first move, thought Stella, because his professional reputation would be at stake. I can't make the first move, because ... because I can't. She watched Roland finish his wine. She spoke with decision.

'It's too late now to do some work with Herbie or Mina. It's a shame. I've done no re-enactment tonight, but there's one scene I feel would help a lot in the area I have difficulty with.'

'Tell me,' he said.

'The Snow White thing – you know, that glass coffin – and Sleeping Beauty too. The glass coffin – and the circle of thorns surrounding the castle – these are archetypes of my repressed sexuality. If I could try a re-enactment to break through that –'

'Do you want to try?'

'In my room?'

'Let's go.'

Up the stairs, through the fire doors, to Stella's room. When she turned on the light she realized the curtains were still open. As she went to close them she heard some howling from the shrubbery. Roland came up behind her. 'That's Phil. I spoke to him earlier. He's re-enacting Pongo.'

She closed the curtains. 'Do you think I should just lie on the bed, or cover myself, or what? What do you think?'

'We must try to make it as authentic as possible. We need the seven dwarfs to stand guard over your coffin, I think.'

'We can use my pillows, look, and the standard lamp can be a dwarf!'

'And the trouser-press can do for several.'

'Roland. Do you think I'm dressed correctly? Will the jeans spoil it?'

'They might do.' He stroked his chin.

'Look. I know! I could change into my nightdress!'

'Yes. You do that.'

Stella took her nightdress and disappeared into her small bathroom. A few moments later she emerged in a lacy gown.

'You look lovely,' he said. 'Just the part.'

Stella lit an incense stick and blew it so it smouldered. She climbed on to the bed and lay there.

'I don't feel right yet, Roland.'

'Get off, and we'll put the counterpane over you.'

'Right.'

Soon it was done. Stella lay on her bed, the counterpane laying softly over her. Roland moved over to the door and turned off the light. The moonlight stealing in through the curtains and the light from the bathroom provided soft illumination. In the distance they heard a door slam.

Roland spoke softly. 'The dwarfs knelt by Snow White's tomb, each one wishing deep in his heart that she would wake up. Then they heard the sound of hoofbeats, and Snow White's handsome prince rode up to the coffin. He approached it' – Roland approached the bed – 'and gently kissed her beautiful lips –' Roland knelt by the bed and kissed her, kissed her long and tenderly. Somewhere out in the garden a dog howled. Stella sat up, Roland's arms around her.

'It works,' she said, wonderingly. 'Kiss me again.' This time she kissed him back. She removed the counterpane and he rolled on to the bed with her. He was so tall, he felt so different to Richard. There was nothing of Richard's calm assumption that he could have her at will. Roland treated her like a princess. He lay lightly on her – he was so slim – there was almost nothing of him, nothing at all, except for – Stella could not think of a word for it in her mind . . . except . . . for his personal growth . . .

They walked through the garden hand in hand. Yes, there were birds singing in the trees. Stella realized with surprise that it was almost spring. There were crocuses just starting to bloom: yellow, lilac and white – a whole mass of them, just in front of her. She could see the beginnings of daffodils too – fresh tall green stalks, as bright as if someone had painted them, some with their tops swelling; others had slender green heads hanging down, the yellow petals peeping through. This was the sort of morning, thought Stella, where one could almost expect music to strike up, strings, possibly, to serenade them like in the films. She squeezed Roland's hand.

197

This morning they did not need to talk. They were both a little tired; they had stayed up most of the night, talking, and Roland had explained how he had felt for some time that Stella was his soul mate; how impossible it was to let her know, as he feared risking her displeasure, knew that as her therapist he had no right. Of course, Stella knew that the therapeutic relationship had to be over. But – and this was the most wonderful thing – she didn't *need* a therapist any more! Not now she had Roland. When you are in love with the right man – who is a therapist anyway – why have another therapist? She had thought this all out while Roland lay asleep beside her in the early hours of the morning. She had lost nothing, gained everything. This was perfection.

She saw something lithe and nimble run across their path. 'Oh, Roland! A rabbit!'

But the animal darted up a tree.

'I think it was a squirrel,' Roland said, and stopped to kiss her again.

Stella never imagined it could be so wonderful. She had never felt so in harmony with a man. Roland was so tender too, so careful not to hurt her, so desirous of her pleasure. But it wasn't just that. It was the knowledge that he thought as she did; they shared philosophies, lifestyles, professions – so much. One thing now was blindingly obvious to Stella. They were destined for each other. In this way she could see that the prince–princess motif in Disney films reflected the attainable ideal of male–female relationships – and this she had achieved. It was the crowning moment of her life.

There was a purity about Roland. And an innocence too. Stella loved that innocence. The other men she had slept with – and there were only two – had taken her as if they were embarrassed about their own sexual needs. It was quick and brutal and messy. But Roland was so different. He wanted to give her pleasure, and he worshipped her – yes, he worshipped her. It was almost as if he'd never made love to a woman before. He made her feel so special. He was careless of his own pleasure. So unselfish. She was so lucky.

They found an old sundial, moss-covered, and stopped by it, trying to work out how it told the time, but unable to decide. Roland took her by both hands.

'I love you, Stella,' he said, again. 'But right now I feel guilty, much as I know that guilt is a wasted emotion.'

'There's nothing to feel guilty about!'

'You're married.'

Stella wanted to reply, 'No, I'm not!' because in her mind she wasn't. Richard had gone. Roland was the only man who was real to her now. Richard was a very long way away. And yet, standing there, suddenly feeling cold, Stella began to think. If this weekend was not going to be all they shared, if their relationship was to continue – and it *must* continue – other people would be affected. Primarily, Richard. And in her love for Roland she suddenly felt tender towards Richard. It would destroy him. Utterly destroy him. Still, she would do everything she could to soften the blow. Before he returned to England she would arrange for him to see a good therapist; she would ask Roland for some recommendations. She looked up at Roland.

'We'll have to deal with that; that's for later. I love you too, Roland.' Which was hitting the right note. Responsible, yet passionate.

They walked on. They had in fact skipped the farewell session of 'Modern Myth and Mickey Mouse', entitled, 'That's All, Folks!' They had explained together to Herbie and Mina what had happened to them; how the course had helped them to realize they were made for each other. Mina had actually cried with pleasure for them. To Stella it had felt like a sort of wedding. In a way, she felt as if she was now married to two men.

Later they would drive back to Manchester. They did not need to think about the immediate future, and indeed, Roland had suggested to Stella that she spend the night in the Quays. Then perhaps, she thought, he could spend time in her house, in her room. And at the weekend . . .

Next weekend, Stella remembered, her parents were coming to stay.

She glanced up at Roland. What would her mother think? Of him? Of the situation? What would he think of her mother? No, it was impossible. She could not, should not, bring them together. And yet, Stella knew had been taught by Gill – that she was a grown woman now. That her mother had no power over her. That if she was to relate freely and openly to her mother, she ought to be honest about Roland. If she felt no shame about what had occurred, she ought to feel free from shame in introducing him to her mother and father. She had read a book about shame. Unhealthy shame caused so many ills: addiction problems, low self-esteem. One had to fight to get free of shame. I, Stella Martin, feel no unhealthy shame. She would introduce Roland to her parents; she had nothing to fear. Fear and shame had gone from her life. Fear and shame and Richard had gone from her life. Her parents ought to know that. Stella mentally congratulated herself on the clear way she was making decisions. Praise yourself, Gill had told her. Give yourself credit for what you can do.

Gill! She must tell Gill! She would be so thrilled! For in fact it was Gill who had effectively introduced them. She would write as soon as she had a moment to herself. Be grateful, Gill had told her. Thank you, Gill, she said inwardly, thank you.

The back of the hotel rose in front of them, the bare branches of the trees surrounding it looking odd against the almost summery blue sky. Thank you, hotel, she said. Thank you, Mickey Mouse. Thank you, thank you.

CHAPTER FIFTEEN

Stella said, 'I want you all to lie on the floor. On your backs.'

Sandra wondered whether there would be room for them all to stretch out. She ached with self-consciousness. She slid forward, her feet pointing to the centre of the room, and watched Zoë do the same. She knew she ought to shut her eyes but to do so would be some kind of submission. Sandra noticed there was a faint crack in the plaster wandering aimlessly along the ceiling. She focussed on that.

Stella said, 'Tonight I want you to do some creative visualization with me. A guided fantasy. First you need to relax.'

Sandra listened and Stella took them through the familiar procedure of contracting muscles, and letting them go. Sandra made a half-hearted attempt to follow the instructions. Her mind was racing. Here she was again lying on the floor with a bunch of people she didn't really care about, hardly knew – with one exception – all of them trying to achieve some miraculous change the easy way, lying on the floor, letting Stella do all the talking. Sandra was tense with resistance. She heard Zoë's deep breaths beside her, and felt half-envious. The faint snorts from her left were no doubt from David, who had almost certainly fallen asleep.

Stella said they were to breathe deeply, into their abdomen.

Sandra lifted her stomach up and down so Stella wouldn't guess that she was deliberately resisting. But since her visit home everything had been different. She had lost her faith. What good was it going to do, this accusing her parents, labelling their shortcomings, examining and licking her wounds? And this overeating problem. Unless she stopped overeating, she had realized, she wasn't going to lose weight. And her indecision. Well, she had made a start. She had decided that this therapy business wasn't for her. For it was a business. Sandra had so far spent nearly £200 on her personal growth. And yet, here she was, lying on the floor at 8 Lincoln Grove, breathing deeply under Stella's guidance, because . . .

Because of Zoë, came the glib reply. There was little doubt that Zoë was benefiting in some way from it all. Zoë now had hope. It was fun sending that letter to the *Guardian*, fun waiting for a reply. She couldn't let Zoë down. But this was the odd thing. Sandra had other reasons for not giving up, and these included Stella. For when she had examined her feelings towards Stella, it was odd, but she did not feel resentment, resentment for being taken for a ride, resentment for being exploited. She felt sorry for Stella. This was against all reason. She thought that if she was to explain to Stella why precisely she was giving it all up, Stella would in some way crumble. Would realize too how silly and self-defeating the whole business was. She couldn't do that. But also, Sandra knew, there was something else. She couldn't give it up, not yet. It felt too nice. Being listened to, coming here after school and lying on the floor and being told to daydream, for that was what they were doing now.

Stella said, 'I want you to imagine that it's a beautiful, sunny morning in early spring. You are going for a walk in the country. You walk down a path and come to a stile. You know that once you cross over this stile, you will be apart from all your worries and problems. Here you will be entirely safe.

'You have crossed over the stile. You look around you and there are crocuses: lilac, yellow and white. The daffodils are just about to blossom. A squirrel runs in front of you and climbs a tree. You hear birds singing and you feel a deep sense of contentment and peace. You could almost sing yourself.'

This sounds like a Disney film, thought Sandra. This isn't my fantasy. She wondered quickly where she would most like to be. At a party, perhaps, with all her friends and all her family, celebrating something.

Stella said, 'You walk past a sundial, and stop there, feeling the warm sun on your skin. You feel so peaceful that you hardly want to move on, but the gentle sound of running water entices you a little further. There, in front of you, is a small stream, its clear water running over tiny pebbles. You dabble your fingers in the water. Then you turn. Underneath an old oak tree you see a dark shape. It is a chest, an antique chest. Curious, you move over to it. You lift the rusty lid, and look inside. And inside, is the thing you have always wanted. It is yours, and you can have it for ever. What is it? An object, something abstract? What is it you desire most?'

What is it, thought Sandra, that women desire most? Beauty? To be slim? Love? To be successful? Rich? What did she want?

Stella was silent. She shut her own eyes and thought of Roland, Roland holding both her hands and looking at her and saying that he loved her. Zoë saw a letter on the mat in an unknown hand, and a large group of schoolgirls eager to understand Catullus. Angela saw her engagement ring, resplendent with diamonds, saw herself going down the aisle, all eyes upon her. Carol saw a golden effulgence, a radiance, so dazzling it concealed what was in there. But yet she had not lost the consciousness that Jim was not there tonight, had unaccountably missed the meeting.

I don't know what I want, thought Sandra. I know really if I was slim I still wouldn't be perfectly happy. And if I was calm and decisive, I wouldn't be me any more. Sandra wondered about the others in the group; she turned her head slightly and saw Zoë's face creased in concentration, and a smile playing on Angela's lips. She saw Norah too. Did she want a new nose? Was that what she saw in the chest? A little, tip-tilted, or snub nose? Sandra thought it would make a rather effective surreal painting – a nose in a chest. What do I want, Sandra asked herself urgently. I want to be happy most of the time – and healthy. You can't find that in a box under a tree.

Stella said, 'Now take it. Take whatever it is you found under that tree. If it is an object, pick it up and put it in your pocket. If it is abstract, breathe it in. Whatever it is, you can take it with you. It's yours. Take it with you when you go back across the field, back across the stile. It will be with you even now, in this room.'

Sandra felt cheated. She had come back with

nothing. But possibly, she told herself, there was nothing you really wanted, or nothing that was yours to give yourself. And how did she know what she really wanted anyway? Do we always know what's best for us?

'Good!' said Stella. 'Now, when you feel ready, you can sit up slowly, and if you feel it would help, you can share with the group what it was you found in the box.'

But the group was silent. After a time, it was only Carol who was prepared to share her vision of a golden effulgence. You're hedging your bets, thought Sandra. She listened to Carol speak, and felt a mixture of contempt and affection. She had heard Carol speak many times about her 'block'. She wondered whether in fact Carol was really quite fond of her block. If you want to do something, thought Sandra, you might as well just go out and do it. And she remembered her over-eating and felt guilty.

Stella then asked the group if anyone knew what was wrong with Jim. Carol and Angela exchanged glances, neutrally, inquisitively. Stella murmured that she was sure he would contact her. She explained, too, that Kevin was making good progress with his agoraphobia and hoped to join them soon.

'Would anyone like to use the time remaining to explore and resolve anything that has come up for them during the week?'

There was the usual silence. Then Angela spoke. 'I have some news,' she said, rather coyly. Everyone turned to look at her. 'I'm getting married,' she said.

Excepting the fact that Jim was not there, the reaction was all she could have wished for. Everyone stared. Stella rushed over and took her hand and said how happy she was. But Angela could read in the expressions of the others a certain degree of envy. That was what she was after. It was immensely satisfying.

'Who?' asked Sandra. 'I mean, who is he?'

Looking at her, Angela replied, 'He's a poet.'

Sandra was unwillingly impressed. 'Anyone we'd have heard of?'

'I doubt it,' Angela replied. 'His name's Spencer Preston.'

Sandra thought hard. No, she'd never heard of him.

'Do you make much money from poetry?' Stella asked. This was a subject she knew little about.

'Oh,' said Angela, 'he has his own business too. And the other thing I wanted to say was, I would like you all to come and celebrate with us. We're having an engagement party – a disco – upstairs at the Jolly Waggoners in Chisholme High Street. You're all invited. Jim too,' she added, looking at Carol. 'And please bring anyone you want to.' She looked at Zoë and smiled kindly.

'How do you feel about all this?' asked Stella. 'It must be a sudden decision for you.'

'I feel wonderful,' said Angela.

Carol sat hunched and cross-legged. She raised her hand. 'Stella,' she said dully.

The group turned its attention to her.

'I think I have a problem with this. I can't quite ... It's not ... It's not that I feel envy. I mean, I've met Spencer, and he's not ... he's not my type, if you know what I mean. It's not that. Nor do I want to get married. I think that independence is too precious a thing to lose for a woman. Marriage is still a subservient state. But this development of Angela's has made me confront yet again my lack of achievement – although I feel that marriage is hardly an achievement – I feel as if I am nothing inside. And I feel betrayed. Dreadfully betrayed. I feel that Angela would know my difficulties with this issue and that she would have let me know before the meeting, and I feel as her friend, she should have told me. I feel relegated, made to seem unworthy in front of the group. As if my friendship for her is devalued in a significant way. But worst of all is this nothingness, this emptiness . . .'

And to Sandra's astonishment Carol began to scream. She yelped like a wounded animal with a mixture of sobs and shrieks. Sandra was alarmed. Stella ran over to comfort her. In between yelps, Carol continued talking.

'She – knew this – would happen! She hates me! She – despises me. She wants to destroy me!'

'Yes, yes,' crooned Stella, rocking her in her arms. 'Just let it out. Deal with this now.'

Angela watched Carol, watched the concern of the group focussed on her. How dare she! she thought. My triumphant moment, my announcement of my wedding, and she stages this. The bitch. Angela breathed deeply and stood up.

'I can't take it!' she screamed. 'I was so scared to tell you all this – it took me so much courage to agree to his proposal – with my problems about men – and I thought you would all support me. I can't cope. Oh God!' That should do it, she thought.

Stella looked at her, and for a moment was lost.

'She hates me!' screamed Carol.

'I don't! You hate me!' screamed back Angela.

'It's OK to feel that way,' said Stella. 'This is a difficult time for both of you.' She had one arm round Carol, who was still crying noisily. She was afraid that Angela would leave the room, and was glad when Sandra got up and tried to calm her. Stella felt a mild panic rising. She hated conflict, hated emotion she could not control. This was a situation – this naked hostility between the women – she had not bargained for.

'I need her to apologize to me,' blurted Carol.

'She hates me!' insisted Angela.

So much for unconditional positive regard, thought Sandra. She wondered what Stella ought to do now. She couldn't have them both expressing their feelings like that. It just wouldn't do. What if somebody else in the group started? Even David had woken up. If this had happened in the classroom, Sandra would have separated them, and spoken to each individually, and kept them apart afterwards for as long as possible.

'OK, OK,' said Stella. 'Both of you need to do some work around this. Can you face each other now and talk about this with your Adult? If one of you sits here' – she pointed to a cushion – 'and the other, there, you could use this opportunity to have a meaning-ful dialogue. Come on, Carol.' She led Carol to a cush-ion, left her, hugged Angela, and got her to sit down too. Sandra noticed that Carol was red-eyed with weep-ing; Angela's anger was white hot and tearless. 'Go on, Carol. Remember you're speaking from your Adult.'

'From when we were children, she's used my inadequacy as a foil. She's paraded her men in front of me, forced me to watch her successes with men, and although I know she's sick, and I know I ought to pity her, I feel tonight she's intended to publicly humiliate me. I know that. But, wait. I think I feel something new here. Some new strength. Maybe from the chest, from that gold light. I'm strong. I can get through this one. I do pity you, Angela, and I forgive you. Yes, I forgive you. I can do that. Oh, thank you, Stella. Thank you for helping me see that.'

'Well done, Carol,' Stella breathed. 'Angela, do you want to say anything to Carol – from your Adult?'

'Yes. I know jealousy is hard to suppress, isn't it? But I don't think a man ought to come between us. I can see now it is hard for Carol to accept that I'm getting married before her. I didn't mean to hurt her by telling her in front of the group; I thought she had got on well in her therapy and would be able to feel happy for me. But I can see that I was wrong and I'm sorry, Carol.' Angela got up and hugged her.

Silly bitch, thought Angela. No wonder no one wants her, not even Jim. Carol hugged her back. You are the sickest person I know, Angela, she thought. Sick and twisted and evil. I'm glad I'm not you. The two women sobbed as they hugged.

'Well done!' said Stella. 'We've seen some really courageous work done here this evening. We're all privileged. I admire both of you. We've all learnt a lot.'

Stella felt exhausted but justified, very justified. She made these women face up to their feelings. It will have done them no end of good. Honesty, she decided, that was the thing. Honesty. And she would be honest too.

Sandra and Zoë were too embarrassed to talk much on their way out. Honesty, thought Sandra. That's something you can have too much of.

CHAPTER SIXTEEN

There was one more thing Angela needed to do before her engagement party and that was to sever her links with the therapy group. She knew she had never needed therapy. It had all been Carol's idea – Carol's revenge. Angela knew there was absolutely nothing wrong with her at all; she had known that all along. Spencer had put it rather nicely when she had told him about the group. He had said that there was nothing wrong with her; she was perfect; if anything, she should lead the group, to show them what it was like to be perfect. Then she had let him kiss her. Still, oddly enough she had shaken off her annoyance with Eric, which was what she had joined for in the first place, and in that way it had worked for her. This was why Spencer was driving her up to Greenfield this afternoon. She was to see Stella. She had booked a private session and it was her intention to explain to Stella that she was leaving the group.

Angela felt quite gentle towards Stella. In many ways, Stella had given her good advice. It *is* important to think well of yourself, and it *is* important to take the things you need. Angela had often wondered about Stella; wondered what *her* love life was like? Was she married? Angela didn't know. She was quite pretty and no doubt had some man in her life. Greenfield, she knew, was quite an exclusive area, and when she and Spencer located Stella's house, she was pleased to see how well appointed it was, and regretted just for a moment her decision to give up therapy. Had all the meetings been in *this* house, she might have stayed a little longer.

'This is where my therapist lives,' said Angela. 'You can leave me here and come back in about half an hour. Or you could just wait outside. I won't be long.'

'I'll wait,' said Spencer.

Angela rang the doorbell. The door was opened by a very tall man with very short hair and one earring. Angela wondered if this could be Mr Martin. He looked down at her.

'Stella will only be a moment. Would you like to wait in here?' He ushered her into a room at the front of the house and left her there alone. She stood and looked around her with curiosity. There was a large flat-screen television with a video beneath it. The pale fabric three-piece suite must have cost a fair amount, and the heavy mirror over the fireplace looked like an antique. The gold carpet looked of a good quality too. Angela resolved to have one like it when she set up her new home. There on the mantelpiece was a photograph of Stella on her wedding day. Angela moved over to look closely at it. Stella had longer hair then, although it was raised in a bun. Very elegant. And Mr Martin looked a lot shorter and had a lot more hair. Angela looked again. That wasn't Mr Martin. That was somebody else! Either Stella had divorced and the tall man was her new husband – but then why keep her old wedding photograph? – or this tall man was some sort of lover, or – Stella opened the door.

'I'm ready now, Angela. I'll see you upstairs.'

Angela walked upstairs, eaten by curiosity, determined to solve the mystery. 'Your husband's very nice,' she said.

'My husband?' said Stella, confused. 'My husband's in California. Oh! You mean Roland.' And she blushed. Angela noticed that. Ah! she thought. You're at it too. In some ways, now, she liked Stella more.

She was taken into a small room at the back of the upper floor, a room with a hint of jasmine incense. Angela sat down and waited until Stella took a seat by the table.

'Do you feel better now, Angela? Thursday night was traumatic for you, I know. But you did well to acknowledge your feelings.'

'I'm fine now,' said Angela.

'Good, good. What do you want to work on today? Do you want to talk about your decision? Because it represents real progress for you, you know, to be able to settle for one man. I'm proud of you.'

Well, it's more than you can do, thought Angela. She smiled to herself.

'Yes, I have made progress,' Angela conceded. 'That is what I wanted to talk to you about. I think I'm better now. I can see the advantages of marrying. I'm going to leave the group.'

'Sorry?'

'I said I'm going to leave the group.'

'Oh.' Stella was taken aback. She wanted to play for time. 'Is it because of Thursday night? I can see it must have been painful for you. But I think we resolved all the issues, didn't we?'

'No, it's not that. I knew Carol would find that hard

to cope with and I know how neurotic she is,' Angela said gaily. 'But I don't need a therapist any more. Not now I'm getting married. *You* know what I mean,' she added confidentially. 'When you've got a man to talk to, it's better, isn't it?'

'I don't want you to rush this, Angela,' said Stella. 'I would suggest that even if you do wish to leave the group, you do it gradually, over a few weeks or so. To suddenly remove yourself from a means of support over what will be an emotionally demanding time for you could be very dangerous.'

'Dangerous? What do you mean?'

'What if you have difficulties with your fiancé?'

'Oh, I can manage *him*!'

'What if you find you become interested in other men? This is a problem for you, you know.'

Not just for me, thought Angela. In a way, it pleased her that Stella should play the same game. All us women are the same, she thought. Only some are more successful at it than others. The failures go into therapy, she deduced. And she couldn't blame Stella wanting to make a living out of therapy.

'I'm better now,' said Angela. 'Anyway, if I have a problem, I'll know where to come.'

'Absolutely,' said Stella.

'I've always felt you understood me.'

Stella smiled to herself. That was her gift. That ready empathy with people who suffer. It was sad that Angela felt she had to leave, sad that at the moment she was blinded by her love for this new man into thinking she could survive without help, but this would certainly only be a short phase. Stella had decided to

215

give up therapy too, but then, her man was a therapist. Angela's man was only a poet.

'I've always felt you understood me,' continued Angela, 'because we are so alike.'

Transference, thought Stella.

'You're a one for the men as well.'

Stella was dumbfounded.

'Is that your lover downstairs?'

'No!' Stella countered, angrily. 'He's my therapist. I mean, he was my therapist. I've . . . I've stopped –'

'Therapist is a new word for it!' But Angela was not shocked. She was delighted. She could not understand why Stella seemed so upset. She thought they could have a nice chat about their men; could become friends, even; Angela needed a replacement for Carol. But Stella avoided looking at her and seemed angry.

'In a therapy session,' Stella said levelly, 'we confine the discussion to the client and the client's growth. Do you think you may be avoiding an issue by trying to deflect the talk in this way? Are you perhaps not wanting to confront your real reasons for wanting to leave the group?'

'No,' said Angela. 'I want to leave the group because I don't need it any more, whatever you say. I just wanted to have a friendly chat with you. *I'm* not avoiding anything.'

You're embarrassed, thought Angela, being caught at it. It's you who needs the help. Angela was vastly amused. 'Anyway, there's little point us talking further. I've made up my mind. To show you've not got any bad feelings, do come to my party on Friday. Bring your bloke – or your husband if he's back. Or both – I don't mind.' Angela opened her handbag to write out the cheque. 'Do I pay any extra for giving in my notice like this?'

'No, no,' said Stella.

'Right, well here's your money. I'll look forward to seeing you on Friday. Bye, Stella.'

Stella stood at the door of her room and watched her go down the stairs and out through the hall. Never had she felt so insulted. Angela was disgusting. Stella could see that she had in fact made no progress at all; Angela had not understood her own problem; Stella had failed. But it wasn't that. In some way she felt tainted by Angela. Fancy suggesting that what she felt for her poet was anything like what she felt for Roland. Angela had an illness, a personality disorder; Stella was properly in love, and it just so happened she was married to the wrong man. How dare she suggest that there was any connection between the two. How shallow Angela was! How glad Stella was that she was leaving the group! There's little you can do for a woman like that. Suggesting she had a lover living with her illicitly while her husband was away! Roland had only stayed the one night.

Still, the good thing about him being there was that he would help her to get over that silly woman's suggestions. He would listen to her and make her feel better. He still said to her, 'Stella, you're practically perfect in every way!' She loved him saying that; he would make her feel better.

And then, she thought, as she put Angela's cheque away in the drawer, ready to be banked with the others tomorrow, she would feel serene again. Then she could take the decision about Angela's engagement party. Her first impulse was not to go. A disco in a pub! But perhaps if she arrived late, and just put in a brief appearance, it would demonstrate that she was above taking offence, was giving Angela her blessing, but was not really part of it all. And she would bring Roland. It would be nice for him to see her group, to see the people she had been helping. Nice for them too, to see him. She called him up from the kitchen where he said he would do some reading for his book.

'Roland!'

'Have you finished? I'll come up.'

She looked in her mirror to brush her hair. She loved him so much. Since that wonderful weekend they had hardly been apart, except for work. They had talked continuously. She had told him everything about her, about her parents, most of which he knew already, which was the lovely thing about falling in love with your therapist, and about her other men, and even about her days at Slim-Plicity. He had told her about his boyhood, his experiences at university and once, once had asked her if she wanted to know more about Cruella. Stella thought, and had said no. She could not bear to hear now that Roland had ever loved anyone else, even if it was over. She made him promise it was quite over, and said that was enough. Then that evening they had gone down to the video shop at the corner, and hired *The Sleeping Beauty*, and watching it again had been so arousing, and they had kissed and caressed, and then made love while it was on. Roland came up to her now and she went up to him and put her head against his chest. He hugged her. She had lost a client, she thought, but who cared, having Roland?

Later, in the kitchen, sharing some decaffeinated Earl Grey tea, she spoke of what had happened.

'Does it bother you,' he asked her, 'having Angela know about me?'

'Oh no! It was more that, she thought I was like her, having two men. But it's not like that. Richard is gone.' And she looked up at her calendar. Soon he would be coming back. Fear grasped her. How could she face him? How would she cope, if he went to pieces? Would Roland feel guilty too? Would it destroy what they had? Roland followed her glance to the calendar and read her mind. They were silent.

'Perhaps you should write to him first,' Roland suggested. 'It might be easier for him that way.'

'Yes,' mused Stella.

She imagined him receiving the letter, his shock, his disbelief. Richard, having that calm exterior, might not show much on the surface, but things ran deep within him. She knew that. He might do something drastic. She would write to Gill too, just in case. He would probably fly home, trying to save their marriage. It would be so hard. He would beg her; she would have to be kind but firm. He might ring her parents and beg them to intercede on his behalf. He might demand to see Roland. There would be the most ugly scene. Would Roland be able to stand it? No! She must think positively. Richard will read the letter and of course he will be devastated, but he will come to accept it, after a long time.

And he will let her go, Stella, the great love of his life. He will be a changed man, she thought. But it will probably do him good.

'I'll write to him,' said Stella. 'Soon.'

They held hands over the breakfast bar. I'll write soon, thought Stella. For she had suspected that Roland was finding it hard to cope with the deceit. Since their weekend in Herefordshire, despite spending all their time together, despite Stella's willingness to make love, he had held back. Except during *The Sleeping Beauty* video. On one hand, it was lovely not to feel *used*, in the way she did with Richard. But on the other hand . . . Yes! It was almost certainly guilt. She would write as soon as she could.

'Will you feel better when I've written?' she asked him.

'Yes,' he said, and squeezed her hand.

CHAPTER SEVENTEEN

Sandra wasn't in the mood for a disco and particularly not Angela's. But curiosity had driven her to accept the invitation; that, and an opportunity to go out on a Friday night. Zoë was coming too, and it was just as well. She had not received any response to her lonely hearts letter, which did not surprise Sandra. She remembered reading that older women fare badly when looking for mates; single men of their age, given the choice, prefer younger women. Zoë's disappointment, which she shared, and her own gnawing irritation over something that had happened at school that afternoon, had conspired to make her feel mulish and antisocial.

But now she had to go, because there was in fact something she was rather looking forward to. Angela had rung her a couple of nights ago; had asked her, as an English teacher, to help her to write a poem for Spencer, for the party. Sandra explained that you couldn't just teach people how to write poetry and that it was hard to write poetry if you weren't used to it, but not liking to disappoint her, suggested that she write out a poem by someone else. Angela readily assented to this, and last night at the group meeting Sandra had given her a copy of Christopher Marlowe's 'Come live with me and be my Love'. Its romantic idealism seemed appropriate somehow. She was sure Spencer would be delighted to receive it.

What to wear? Sandra examined the contents of her

wardrobe and found an old black tasselled skirt she wore when she was a student. That would have to do. It still fitted; that was because the waistband was elasticated. Sandra knew she had put on weight since then. A tie-dyed T-shirt completed the ensemble. And plenty of eye make-up so no one would notice her figure.

I've got to decide, thought Sandra, whether I want to stay fat and carry on overeating, or diet and get slimmer. The phone rang, and Sandra went to answer it.

'Sandra, it's me!' said Zoë. 'I've had a letter!'

'What does it say? What does he sound like? Read it out!' Sandra was thrilled. She heard the rustling of paper.

'It doesn't say my name – that's because I didn't give it. There isn't a photo either – but I didn't ask for one. Listen. "I've never answered a lonely hearts advertisement before, but there was something about your few words that appealed to me. I think I could be the man you're looking for. I see you're interested in personal growth, and I think I know what you mean. Shall we discuss it? I can understand if you're reluctant to commit yourself to meeting a stranger. I shall be in the bar of the Players Theatre at 8.30 on Friday 13th. If you're not superstitious, come and take a look at me. I shall be wearing a yellow rose." Sandra, this is so exciting. What shall I do?'

'You've got a week to decide.'

'Do you think he sounds my type?'

'It's a bit cryptic, but I bet he's trying to keep you interested.' Sandra wondered. She didn't really trust men; this letter was rather brief. But how could she dampen Zoë's enthusiasm?

'Shall we talk about it at the disco?'

'Yes, let's.'

Well, thought Sandra, as she applied yet another layer of mascara, there's no harm in her going to have a look at him. As long as she doesn't do anything silly. Perhaps she might suggest to Zoë that she went with her, to see him – and to be there, just in case of trouble. Yes! That was sensible – and besides, she could find out what he looked like too. Sandra applied the rest of her make-up with gusto.

She regarded herself in the mirror. What was it she had been thinking before the phone rang? It felt important. She couldn't remember. If it was really important, she told herself, it will come back.

The Jolly Waggoners was a large pub on the corner of Chisholme High Street and Wellington Road. It had several doors, and Sandra wasn't sure which one to choose. She entered through the main door and was glad to get in out of the rain, which had been falling relentlessly all evening. It had made a mess of her hair, but then, it was a mess to begin with, which was the advantage of not having a hair-style as such. Sandra found herself in a very large pub, with the bar in the centre of the drinking area. There was no sign of any stairs, or of anyone from the group. She decided she had better ask if she was in the right place. A waiter passed her, and she soon established that for private parties you had to go out again, and go in through two doors down and up the stairs. Back into the rain again.

Once inside for the second time, she shook herself down and regained her composure. Here she was, at a therapy group party. She assumed Angela would have other friends there too, of course, but, she reflected, this was the first time she had actually been out with anyone from the group. Odd, as in some ways they knew each other so well. Normally, in real life, you only got to know the surface of people, and their problems, their hopes, their fears remained, for the most part, a mystery. But in the group, Sandra knew the insides of people, knew of Angela's difficulties with men, Carol's block, Jim's dramas, Norah's hatred of her nose, but she knew nothing else. Where did they all work, live? Where did they do their shopping? And Stella too? What was her life really like?

This was not the first time Sandra had wondered that, for Stella fascinated her. Partly it was a feeling of kinship – they shared the secret agonies of dieters. But partly it was this; if it worked, if all this therapy, if this positive thinking really worked, then it should be Stella, its chief practitioner and teacher, whose life should be close to perfection. And from the evidence of the group sessions, Sandra had come to believe that might be the case. Perhaps. She could not decide.

Sandra could hear the music thumping as she went up the stairs, and there, by the entrance to the disco, were a number of coats and dripping umbrellas. Sandra added hers. Then she opened the double doors to the disco proper, hoping Zoë was there before her.

She didn't seem to be, although it was hard to make out figures distinctly in the dim lighting. Sandra looked over to the small bar at the back of the room and did not recognize any of the people standing there. No one was dancing yet; small groups stood around talking, or trying to talk, for the indistinguishable pounding of the music muffled all human conversation. It was uncomfortably loud. Not only that, but the lights from the console changing from blue to red to green dazzled the would-be dancers, and Sandra was alarmed to see smoke eddying from the disco equipment. She realized that this was intentional; part of the DJ's box of tricks.

She sat down and watched. No Zoë. No Stella. But there, in a corner talking to some women she did not recognize, was Angela. Her body language was vivid, self-conscious; she threw her head back to laugh, she touched her friends as she talked to them. She looked beautiful. She wore a dress of crushed red velvet that hugged the contours of her body. Sandra ached with envy. Her shoulders were bare, and glittered. Sandra wondered if she had put something on them. But where was Spencer, this poet? Sandra expected someone with a distant, romantic, intense expression – someone like Ted Hughes, perhaps. But then, real poets didn't have discos for engagement parties. Or did they? Angela seemed to be without a man, and it was impossible for Sandra to work out who Spencer must be.

Just as she was deciding to get herself a drink at the bar, the door opened and Zoë came in. They greeted each other with enthusiasm and went to the bar together. What conversation they had was shouted above the music. Yes, Zoë had brought the letter; yes, she would let Sandra look at it soon; no, where was Angela?

So Sandra and Zoë watched the others. With a sinking feeling Sandra realized she shouldn't have come. No one else from the group had arrived; there was no one else here she had the slightest desire to talk to; she had nothing in common with Angela anyway. She felt depressed, alienated. She didn't even want to dance. Besides, look at Angela's friends. They were all so immaculate and flashy. Short satin dresses, hair stiffly permed and set, men in suits with coloured braces, everyone looking good and conscious of it. Sandra looked down at herself in dismay.

But the odd thing was, she didn't have the slightest desire to be like Angela and her friends. It was this world of conventional glamour and fashion imperatives that she was to be rescued from by therapy and its alternative philosophy. And yet it was the therapy group that brought her by a circuitous route to the sort of disco she wouldn't normally be seen dead in. It was all very strange.

The high-pitched gabble of the DJ was absurd, and made her want to laugh. It was all so silly. People bouncing up and down to music. And it was silly too, people who lay on the floor in groups and tried to work out the meaning of life, she told herself.

She watched the dancers shake and bounce on the floor, their eyes unfocussed. Women moved their heads from side to side jerkily, as if they were counting. Men held their hands in front of them like the paws of upright four-footed animals. 'The only way is up!' Dancers jerked their arms into the air in ragged unison. These aren't my people, thought Sandra. I'd better cut my losses. But before she could suggest to Zoë that they make an early departure, she sensed the presence of a third party.

It must be Jim. Although he had a short back and sides now, and wore a tie-dyed T-shirt over his jeans. Yes, it was Jim. She was delighted. It was someone she knew, and she felt a rush of warmth towards him. Then she remembered he had seemed interested himself in Angela once. How was he feeling? As a fellow member of the therapy group, she felt obliged to inquire.

'How are you?' she shouted above the level of the music.

'I'm OK. How are you?' he shouted back.

'OK! Come outside!' Sandra realized it was impossible to have a proper conversation and led Zoë and Jim out of the room. Outside, once more, she repeated her question.

'Are you all right, Jim?'

He shrugged. 'I'm surviving. It's not been too easy recently. I shouldn't be telling you this, but I need to talk about it. I've been out of the country. In the Middle East. Doing some work . . . for a certain country, know what I mean? Very hush-hush.' He lowered his voice. 'Espionage.' He looked around quickly. 'I think they're off my tracks now. But earlier this evening I was being followed. The problem is, I reckon they've spiked my food. Not poison, but some sort of mind-drug. Like I have these strange dreams and wake up screaming.' Sandra listened, alarmed. 'If I think to myself what I know, they can read my thoughts and they'll be on to me. But I heard about this party and I reckon I'm safe here. D'you want to dance?'

Sandra and Zoë declined. He's mad, thought Sandra. Or he's having us on.

''Scuse me,' he said, and moved off in the direction of the Gents. A small man came out as he went in; a small man, with thick glasses, and a faintly anxious expression. Sandra felt his attention momentarily fix on them, and he frowned, as if trying to remember who they were.

'Are you friends of Angela's?' he inquired.

'Yes,' Sandra said. 'From the –' and stopped. Because Angela might not like it spread, about her therapy.

'I'm Spencer,' he said. 'I'm glad you could come.' He shook both their hands in turn and re-entered the disco. A blast of music escaped as he opened the door. Sandra and Zoë exchanged glances. There was no accounting for taste. Sandra was surprised to experience an overpowering desire to giggle. He was so –!

'Zoë, I can't go back inside. Why don't we go and have a drink in the main bar. I know where it is.'

Sandra felt much more comfortable in an ordinary pub, surrounded with the din of drinkers and the less intrusive rhythms of the juke box. Zoë got out her letter and handed it to Sandra with pride. To Sandra's disappointment it was typed, and the signature was printed clearly, John. There was little to be gleaned from the letter. She explained her fears to Zoë – no woman ought to meet an entirely strange man alone – and suggested her presence as a discreet third party. Zoë's face lit with eagerness.

'Of course, Sandra! That's so sensible. He won't know who I am until I approach him, and if we think

228

he's odd or something, we just go away. And you could wait somewhere, couldn't you, while I introduce myself, and –' Zoë broke off, coloured. 'No. It's a silly idea. I'm not going.'

'Why not?'

Zoë shrugged. 'I couldn't do it. I couldn't go up to a man and introduce myself, with him knowing I'd put a lonely hearts ad in a newspaper.'

'But *he* answered it!'

'I know. But . . .'

'Zoë. I'll be there. Whatever happens, it'll be a laugh. Nothing could possibly go wrong.'

'He may not like me,' Zoë said simply.

Sandra looked at Zoë. It seemed absurd to her that anyone could fail to like her. Zoë's face, lined as it was, had a soft wisdom, a vulnerability; it was the sort of face that was pleasant to rest one's eyes on; it was comfortable.

'I like you,' Sandra said.

Zoë laughed, ironically.

'Anyway,' continued Sandra, '*you* love and approve of yourself, so what does it matter? Do it, Zoë. What have you got to lose?'

'You'll come?'

'Of course. My second night out in a row.'

'Where are you off to on Thursday then?'

Sandra flooded with irritation, and assembled the facts in her mind to relate them to Zoë. She wanted to be as concise as possible. She hated talking about school on Friday night, although sometimes it was difficult not to; school affairs had a habit of repeating on her, like something indigestible. Stray memories of what people had said and done, things she had forgotten to do, remarks in the staff room, all these whirled in her head in the brief weekends, and settled slowly to the bottom of her mind by Sunday evening, and then Monday morning stirred them all up again, like the shaking of the snowstorm in a bottle that she had when she was a child. But today's grievance was specific and really needed to be aired.

'It's a public speaking competition.' Sandra raised her eyebrows in exasperation.

'But Anne Palmer is doing the public speaking.'

'Yes, but the Head is sending her to a conference in his place as he wants to be in school for some visitors connected with some new education initiative and they might be the source of some sponsorship money. And money is what it's all about.' Sandra knew she had fallen into the typical schoolteacher whinge, but didn't bother to change her tone. 'So Anne suggested it would be a valuable experience for me to train the girls and take them to the competition. In less than a week!' Sandra said, her voice rising. 'So every lunch hour now and after school I'll be training them, and then it's off to the Town Hall on Thursday. I mean, I don't really mind doing it, and the kids are great, but it's the way these things are thrown at you. Oh, I'm sorry for talking shop. And of course it means I miss the group meeting!'

'Would you like me to come with you, Sandra?'

'No. You'll need the meeting. Perhaps Stella will let you role-play your encounter with the mysterious John. I wish I could be there.'

'No, no. I can't possibly tell the group what I've done!'

'I would if I were you. Get yourself used to the idea of meeting him.'

Zoë gave a small laugh, and lifted her glass of tonic water to her lips. Sandra realized swiftly that for Zoë, who was beleaguered at school, who had such few friends at home, the therapy group could provide a valuable source of support. Imperfect support, but support nonetheless. Joining a group was another way of making friends – at best. If you needed them. It was a bit like answering a lonely hearts ad, making a deliberate attempt to get your needs met. What was wrong with that?

'Hello! Can we join you?' Sandra and Zoë looked up. There was Carol. She looked strikingly oriental tonight, a band tied round her head, and kohl along her eyes. Sandra was surprised to see her. She immediately assumed she had come for Angela's party – why else would she be here? – and yet, after the scene at the previous meeting, she had assumed that the two women would never wish to be in the same room together again. With Carol, Sandra saw, was an older, distinguished-looking man, who had a hand protectively placed on her shoulder.

'This is Eric,' said Carol, as she drew up a stool. 'Eric owns 8 Lincoln Grove. It's his house.'

'Hello!' said Sandra. Eric's dark trench coat seemed dated; Sandra looked at him with interest.

'Are you here for Angela's party?' asked Carol.

'Mmm,' Sandra replied. 'But it's not really our scene. We thought we'd escape for a drink.'

'I had to come,' murmured Carol, sadly.

'Why?' Sandra was puzzled.

'The only way out is through.' Carol bit her lip anxiously. 'For my own sake, I've got to face her again. This is part of my growth, you see. That resentment can clog me up, I can't deal with it. I have to be there tonight and wish her well. Your own kind words embrace you like loving arms!'

'So you don't feel bitter?'

'I've let it go,' Carol said. 'I spent two hours with Stella today. We worked through it. She told me to come here tonight. Eric's here to support me.' She reached out and squeezed his hand. 'Angela's screwed up Eric too. You've been a victim, haven't you?' She looked at him with wide eyes.

'I wouldn't say a victim. I was entangled with her for a while.'

'What's so tragic,' continued Carol, 'is that Angela's finished her therapy, and she's by no means better. She needs help badly but can't see it. I pity her husband-to-be.'

Sandra listened, her initial sympathy laced with incomprehension. For she knew, if she disliked someone, she would spend as little time as possible with them. What was this obsessive fascination that these two women had with one another?

Their drinks finished, Carol and Eric rose. 'We must go upstairs now,' Carol explained. 'We have a present for Angela and Spencer. The act of giving will be an act of release for me. We'll see you up there. Oh look, isn't that Norah?'

It was, Sandra saw. Norah was, of course, unmistakable. Her nose was so ugly it was beautiful. She had a man with her, who Sandra guessed must be Mr Norah, as she had often spoken of her husband. Sandra looked again. He was a little squashed man with button-like features, a grotesque too in his own right. The shoulders of his fawn overcoat were wet with rain. He looked up at his wife with a trusting affection. Sandra watched them. Norah saw her and smiled, indicating she would join them. With her husband, she seemed more relaxed. They took the stools vacated by Carol and Eric.

'We thought we would stop by briefly,' Norah said. 'This is my husband, Dick.' Sandra and Zoë shook hands with him. 'Sandra, Zoë. Sandra and Zoë are teachers,' she explained to her husband. 'Dick is an ENT specialist.' Zoë frowned. 'Ear, Nose and Throat.' Sandra dug her nails hard into her hands. That's why he loves her, she thought. He picked the best one he could find!

When Stella and Roland entered the Jolly Waggoners it was quite full, so they stayed standing near the bar, close to each other, bodies touching.

'How do you feel now?' Roland asked her anxiously.

'Much better. I've used the affirmation you suggested – I, Stella Martin, do not take responsibility for other people. I wrote it out thirty times before I began the letter. Like you said, I wrote, rather than typed it – so that it really came from me – and yes, it's a relief to send it off. How about you? How do you feel?'

'I'm glad we can be open. I find it easier like that, I think. Stella!' He said her name with a little whimper. Stella's knees went weak. There was no further need to talk and they each sipped their Aqua Libra, oblivious of the noise and fumes of beer from the pub.

Stella *did* feel better. In a few days, Richard would

know the worst. Stella was resigned to the storm that would follow. She had prepared some little speeches that she could use when he confronted her. This was a good one: 'You know, Richard, that what has happened now does not negate the love I once had for you. You are precious to me still, but we must all move on.' That one protected his self-esteem. She would write it down and learn it. She felt no regret, for Roland now seemed as necessary to her as water to fishes. She did not know how she had lived before; if she was, latterly, practically perfect, she had now achieved perfection, with the perfect man. Once she had written to Richard, she treated herself to the luxury of writing to Gill. That was an easy letter to write, deliciously easy. She dwelt on every detail, the course, the weekend, her developing feelings, even their consummation, as Gill, who understood everything, would understand that. But warned her, of course, not to tell Richard. And then, with admirable resolve, she had telephoned her mother to make final arrangements. She had said that she would be introducing her to a friend. Stella's mother was suddenly alert, interested. A friend? Which friend? Have you told me about her? No, Stella had said, ducking out of the issue. She was late and did not have time to explain. But the die had been cast.

'Look, Roland, over there. They haven't seen us. That's Sandra, my overeater, and Zoë, the very non-assertive one. Poor Zoë. *She* needs a man. And the lady with them, the one with the . . . man with the fawn coat, that's Norah.'

Roland peered and studied the group.

*

'Do you know Angela well?' Sandra inquired politely.

'No more than you do, but Stella suggested that it was therapeutic for me to enter public places. I thought I would make a brief appearance.'

'We've been up already. It's pretty dire. Carol's there.'

'We'll join her,' continued Norah. 'We don't want to stay too long.' And they departed.

'What shall we do, Zoë? Have another drink or – look! There's Stella. With a man!'

Both women turned to view her. Having done that, it was difficult to remove their gaze. For there was no doubt that Stella and her companion made an arresting couple. His height was remarkable, and Sandra noticed how very thin he was. Painfully thin. But interesting-looking, with John Lennon glasses. And Stella looked radiant. She had a black cape slung over her shoulders; but it was her eyes, something about her eyes. Sandra wished they could join her, but wondered, can one join one's therapist for a drink? Was it like the student–teacher relationship? If she was in a pub, and a member of the upper sixth, who was eighteen and therefore had a perfect right to be there, saw her, would she go up to her and suggest they drink together? No. No sixth former would be seen dead drinking with a teacher. Would it be intrusive if she joined them? She desperately desired to find out what this man was like. So she continued to look at them, hoping Stella would notice her.

'I think what we'll do, Roland, is visit Angela upstairs just for a few moments. I've bought her a present, I'll give it to her, and then we'll go. Besides, I need to check if Carol has come. This is a significant evening for her.'

'What have you bought Angela?'

'A book of affirmations for married life. It's beautiful. They're joint, you see. We, Angela and Spencer, live together in peace and harmony. That sort of thing.'

Stella glanced again at Sandra and Zoë, feeling their attention on her. She was glad. She talked with a pleased self-consciousness, moulding herself into the therapist they knew, demonstrating also her closeness to Roland. And then felt guilty. For poor Zoë might feel inadequate. So she looked over at them and gave a little wave of friendship. She saw, then, with a twinge of discomfort, that they took that as a sign. They were coming over to join them. Zoë she did not mind; Zoë was innocuous enough. But Sandra; always she felt slightly uneasy with Sandra. Something to do, perhaps, with their shared past. It was a feeling Stella had, that Sandra knew more than she should. Stella always felt the need to prove to Sandra that she was in control.

'Hi!' Sandra said.

Stella made the introductions, without explaining who Roland was. They spoke of Angela, of the pub, of the rain. Then what? thought Sandra. What do you say to a therapist to make small talk? She felt awkward, and was certain that Stella was picking up on that awkwardness, and would confront her with it at the next group meeting. But then, with rising spirits, she realized that in some way, since she had been home, it was over. She did not mind what Stella thought. It

236

was up to Sandra whether she invited Stella into her mind or not. She would talk to her as an equal.

'I saw Jim upstairs, you know. I didn't think he seemed very well. He was going on about someone following him.'

Stella immediately looked concerned.

'This wedding of Angela's will have affected him too. I thought perhaps he was keen on her for a while. I dare say it's activated his persecution complex. If he's still there later, I'll speak to him.' Sandra noticed that having finished speaking, she glanced up at Roland, as if to check he was still there. Obviously he was a new man, Sandra deduced. One didn't behave like that with husbands. Roland then whispered something to her, and asked the others to excuse him, and moved off towards the Gents. Stella followed him with her eyes.

More than anything Sandra wanted Stella to speak about herself. She wanted to know how she had become a therapist, she wanted to know all about *her* childhood – for surely, in a real friendship, both sides share. It had always galled her that her conversations with Stella were so one-sided; she felt, somehow, when she had finished a therapy session, that she had been indiscreet, as her confidences were never returned. Now, here was her opportunity.

'How do you feel about Angela's wedding, Stella?'

'Delighted,' Stella said.

'Are you married?'

'Yes,' said Stella, with a coolness that Sandra found disconcerting. It stopped her. She reached over to a bowl of peanuts that had been placed on the bar for the drinkers, and offered it to Stella. 'Have a nut!'

Stella pursed her lips and shook her head rapidly, almost as if Sandra had made an obscene suggestion. And in her eyes there was something unexpected. Was it fear?

Sandra asked, 'Why not? We eat anything, don't we?'

Stella coloured. 'I . . . I won't eat nuts.' She looked in the direction of the Gents.

Ha! Sandra thought, she's terrified of the nuts.

Stella dared to look at the nuts again. She was feeling empty. The emotion of writing the letters had prevented her from eating earlier, and now she was ravenous. But she could never eat a peanut. Because if she had one, she would have another, and then another, and then she would be stuffing handfuls into her mouth, and then . . . She tried to remember their salty taste, the way that nuts yielded as you bit into them, the firm roundness of the nut against the tongue. She watched Sandra take a few and munch them, and felt Sandra's eyes upon her; that was the worst of all. Oh, hurry up, Roland.

'I can't come to next week's meeting, Stella,' Sandra said, as she swallowed the nuts. 'A school commitment.'

'What a pity,' Stella said. 'We were going to do some different work. Around Disney archetypes – how they affect our perceptions of our self.' Stella looked for Roland. He was a long time. She glanced at Sandra fearfully.

'Disney?'

'Yes. I attended a course.'

Sandra thought perhaps she had misheard Stella.

238

The background noise made it hard to distinguish individual words. Roland threaded his way back through the press of people. Once by her side, Sandra noticed, Stella felt free to glance at the nuts again, like a child peeping at something terrifying from the safety of a parent's lap.

Sandra took some more nuts and felt as if she was stealing them. She almost felt the need to justify herself. Then it came back to her, what she had been thinking earlier. About choosing. Choosing whether to overeat or not. Being slim or not. If she could reach a decision, her head would clear. There would be a solution. But first she needed more information.

'Stella. What did *you* do to resolve your eating problem?'

'I went into therapy.'

'And you're better now?'

'Yes,' said Stella, very quickly.

Sandra was silent. Because she had seen enough to convince her that Stella's problems with food remained. That Stella might be slim, and she might be fat, but that they were, in a sense, sisters. But Stella was lying. And either she knew she was lying, which was decidedly unprofessional, or she didn't know she was lying, which, Sandra thought, was probably true. She wanted to hug her.

Stella did not understand why she was feeling so uncomfortable. Sandra's questions were innocent enough. It was not Sandra, she decided. She felt uncomfortable because she had still not yet gone upstairs to give Angela her good wishes. She must do that immediately. A therapy group engagement was a lovely thing. Sandra was probably eating so many nuts because she was jealous of Angela, Stella realized. Of course. And she was feeling defensive and neurotic as a result. So her questioning of Stella was an indirect way of expressing this neurotic jealousy.

'Roland, I think I'd like to go up now,' Stella said, looking lovingly at him.

'We'll come with you!' said Sandra. 'Just to say goodbye. Is that OK with you, Zoë?'

'Shall we just go to the Ladies first?' suggested Zoë, to Stella's relief. Just now she felt she wanted to be on her own, on her own with Roland. Away from Sandra.

'I'll see you later, then,' she said, and moved towards the exit.

Sandra knew she was feeling rather drunk. She had that familiar faint euphoria, that desire to laugh, and her mind crowded with ideas, glib, rapid ideas, all hitting her with the force of great truths. Me and Stella are as bad as each other. We both want the same things. We both love food. We both want things to be perfect. Sandra reached for the toilet paper which was coiled tightly inside a huge plastic container. She wants the perfect figure and so do I. I want life to be perfect. She wants life to be perfect. But life isn't perfect. Sandra pulled down her T-shirt so it wouldn't make a ridge under her skirt. Life isn't perfect. It's messy and you have to do things like going to the toilet and going to work and – She opened the door of the cubicle to join Zoë, who was washing her hands.

'Zoë,' she began. 'It's like, we all want to be perfect, and nobody is perfect . . .' She trailed away. It sounded trite. She thought just then she'd had a revelation and she'd only had a cliché. Sandra the philosopher trying to find the meaning of life in the Ladies at the Jolly Waggoners. She laughed and decided she might as well have another drink. Perhaps booze was the only answer.

This time when they pushed open the door of the disco, it seemed to Sandra that the noise and lights weren't so oppressive. This was partly the effect of the drink, she knew. She found a table along the wall and she and Zoë sat there with their glasses. Sandra was quite happy to watch. She guessed Zoë had much to think about on her own account. There was Angela, dancing sinuously with two female friends, one short podgy one, the other obviously middle-aged. Appearing to her best advantage, Sandra thought. But where was Spencer? Penning an ode in a corner, Sandra guessed. She looked on the crowded dance floor, looked along the tables of drinkers. There he was! By the bar, alone, with half a pint of lager, watching his wife-to-be forlornly. What a strange engagement party, Sandra thought.

There, opposite her, were Carol, that man Eric, and Jim too. They were deep in conversation. Sandra envied them, felt for a moment excluded. She was supposed to be part of their group. But they had not seen her. Their conversation was too engrossing. Carol only looked up occasionally, and that was to glance unconcernedly at Angela.

Stella and Roland were dancing, holding each other close, oblivious to their situation, and to the rhythm of the music. Sandra wondered again who Roland *was*. He held Stella protectively and tenderly, with a delicacy that Sandra found strange in a man. He held her as if she was a fragile doll. Or as if she was his first-ever girlfriend. She was mesmerized by them and did not notice when the music died away and the dancers stopped. Nor did Stella and Roland. They continued to move slowly in a close circle, and only came to a halt when the DJ announced that Angie wanted to say a few words. Then they turned, and looked towards the front of the room.

Angela had extricated herself from her friends and now stood in front of a speaker, her face aglow, a paper in her hand. Sandra recognized it as the photo-copy of the Marlowe poem she had given her. Angela looked towards the DJ, whose voice now boomed out, 'Be quiet for Angie!'

'First, everybody, I want to say thank you all for coming. This is a very important day for me, and Spencer, and it's lovely to be surrounded by all my friends. So this is my thank-you speech.' Angela paused, breathing it all in.

'The first thank you must go to Spencer of course. And tonight I want to say what I feel in a poem that I've written.' Oh, Sandra thought with interest. She's not going to use the Marlowe after all. She's written something of her own.

'Here it is:

Come live with me and be my Love,
And we will all the pleasures prove . . .'

Sandra looked around the room. Not one of them had noticed. They listened, impressed. Spencer was

still at the bar, mute with admiration. Only Zoë shot
Sandra a quizzical look.

> 'If these delights thy mind may move,
> Then live with me and be my Love.'

The applause was deafening. Angela called for Spencer and embraced him, then sent him back to the side,
where he was dwarfed by the huge lights' console, and
was swallowed by the puffs of smoke that continued to
be emitted.

'I also want to thank everyone who's come to be
with me tonight. I haven't written a poem for you,
though! Thanks to all the girls from Boots', and from
the Health Club, all my friends from home and any of
Spencer's friends who are here.'

She's left out the therapy group, thought Sandra,
feeling irrationally aggrieved.

'And a special thank you to my very oldest friend
who I know has suffered a great deal so she can be
here tonight, Carol!'

Angela had singled her out and now, in a grand
gesture, invited Carol to join her. Sandra watched,
spellbound. Carol, as if hypnotized, rose and moved
towards her. Angela put an arm round her shoulder
and they stood together.

'Carol and I have been friends since we were at
school together. I know she feels bad about losing me,
and I've just brought her here to thank her for being
such a special friend, and to promise her that my marriage won't make any difference to us.'

Carol disengaged herself from Angela's grasp.

'I want to say something too. It's a sort of surprise for you, Angela.' Carol turned and looked into the crowd, speaking with a steady determination. 'It's a kind of coincidence, what I'm going to announce. Angela told me before that she is having a honeymoon in Istanbul.' Angela moved aside, annoyed at this indiscretion. 'Well, it might even be that we'll be travelling out on the same plane! I'm leaving the country too – and travelling to Turkey – to start an experimental inner-growth commune with Eric and Jim – yes, Eric *and* Jim –' she addressed Angela, 'so perhaps we'll all meet over there.' She moved over towards Angela. The two women embraced, in a death-hug. There was a spattering of applause from the audience.

Sandra felt glad they would continue to see each other. For in some dim way she could see that they were necessary to each other; that they lived off each other; that they shared something: something that the therapy made worse rather than better; something to do with self, with selfishness. Sandra was just about to understand precisely what it was when Zoë interrupted her thoughts, stating her desire to go.

'Yes, yes. We'll say goodbye now.'

Sandra stumbled as she rose. She really had drunk too much. She would regret it in the morning. But at least she had the weekend to recover. And then, she thought brokenly, as she made her way downstairs, it would be school again on Monday. Again.

CHAPTER EIGHTEEN

'Again!'

'One of the most important issues involving us in this century can be said to be what energy choices we choose as we come to the end of the century and whether nuclear energy or the other alternative ones –'.

'No, no, stop, Lucy. It's not right. Did Mrs Palmer tell you that it's better not to read aloud, because it stops you making eye contact with the audience? She didn't. Right. And you're tending to run words into each other. You said "nuclenergy", for example. Start again. No, don't. Come here and we'll talk about it.'

Sandra called over the public-speaking team and they joined her at the back of the form room. Sandra's limbs were heavy with despair.

I must be encouraging, thought Sandra.

'Right, girls, at least you've got your subject, and that's a start. There are really only two things you've got to do now; one is rewrite your speeches completely and put them in note form on cards, and the second thing is to practise your delivery.' The girls listened to her nervously. 'For example, all of you are a little low in volume, and I think it's quite important to be distinct, so the judges can hear you.' At the mention of the word 'judges', Sandra saw them tremble with fear. 'Look,' she said, 'let me see your speeches, and I'll think what we can do.' She saw the girls look at the clock. 'Yes, you can go and get your dinner now. I'll look at these and we'll meet again after school. Oh, there's hockey practice. In the morning, before school? Lunchtime again?'

Three days to the competition. Four days to Zoë's meeting. Sandra had a habit of living in the future. It was somehow more exciting than the monotony of the present. She heard the Junior Orchestra begin *The Blue Danube* in a dirge-like rhythm. Well, Sandra, she berated herself, is this how you're going to spend the rest of your life? Never, she admitted to herself, had her father's offer seemed more attractive. But did she want to leave Manchester? And what about the therapy group? Was she going to leave that? And if she did, what would she do about her eating next? Thoughts buzzed in her head like circling flies.

'Sorry I'm late, Miss Coverdale! It was the lunch queue. Catherine and Caroline are just seeing Mrs Palmer but they'll be here soon.'

'That's OK.'

'Miss Coverdale – do I have to do this?'

'I think so – now.'

'I'm dreadful, aren't I?'

'Well, I wouldn't say dreadful.'

Sandra filled with pity for the girl. But pity wouldn't achieve anything, nor would despair. What we need, thought Sandra, is hard work – and positive thinking. Subconsciously assuming Stella's mode, she looked at Lucy directly in the eyes, with concern.

'How do you *feel* when you deliver your speech?'

'It's awful. I hear my voice echoing around the room so I don't listen properly to it and just get it over and

done with as quickly as possible, sort of,' said Lucy
breathlessly.

'Isn't that a rather negative attitude?'

Lucy hung her head.

'In a way, you see, Lucy, your being late for this
rehearsal, and the fact that Catherine and Caroline are
late too, is a subconscious rebellion against having to
do this. You all have a no-win mentality about the
competition, and it's affecting the way you perform.
If you really believed in your ability to win, you'd be
winners.'

As Sandra said this, she believed it. Her voice gained
in intensity.

'You are a precious and unique individual, Lucy,
with an original message to deliver to the judges on
Friday. You're the best person to put across that message. No one else can do it for you. Keep telling yourself that you can do it.'

Lucy looked at Sandra with that characteristic
expression of the schoolgirl being taught: a bemused
vacancy. Hard to tell what impression was being
conveyed. But Sandra persisted.

'Say to yourself, I, Lucy, am an excellent public
speaker. Think that to yourself before beginning your
speech. Don't you want to win on Friday?'

'Oh yes.'

'Think winner, then. Think about boxers and fight-
ers. They train hard, yes, but it's also psychological.
It's a matter of attitude. Success starts in the head.'

Sandra was enjoying herself. She had not realized
how much she had learnt from Stella. Enjoying the
rhetoric, she felt determined to give the whole

philosophy one last chance. She would teach these girls to believe in themselves. She felt her own adrenalin surge. It was a challenge. She would meet it. A faint knock at the door heralded Catherine and Caroline. Expecting Miss Coverdale's wrath, they were surprised to discover their teacher welcoming, excited. And Sandra repeated what she had told Lucy.

The girls had enjoyed it. Sandra was convinced that she had taken the right approach. She had got them all to write down on a sheet of school file paper why they thought they would fail. Sandra had proved to them that these reasons were fallacious; she had got them finally to tear up the sheets of paper and put them in the classroom's waste-paper bin along with the discarded tissues and chocolate wrappers. It did not matter that they did not have time to practise the speeches. That would come later. More importantly, the girls had begun to enjoy it. They had begun to feel that they had a chance. Sandra felt better too. She felt like she did when she had first begun her teacher training. Those dreams had returned; dreams of transformation, inspiration. Having a class looking up at her with the thrill of intellectual discovery. The power of the teacher to develop potential. And here, with these three girls, she could do it. At last. They had left her excited, smiling. Very different from when they had come in. All of them, she felt sure, were actually looking forward to the next rehearsal. Sandra didn't feel tired any more. She strode into the staff room, humming *Eye of the Tiger*.

★

'Lucy, you must slow down. Separate each word. Every little word counts. Now, again, and louder, and separate every word.'

'Choosing the right source of energy for our future-needsisone of the most –'

'Slower!'

'One of the most important decisions . . .'

Sandra watched the hands move round her watch. Since she had improved the grammar of Lucy's speech it certainly sounded more professional. But still Sandra found that what the girl had to say did not keep her interest. She knew that one minute into the speech her attention wandered. What could it be? Lucy's delivery had improved. She used cards, looked at the audience. No; it was the speech itself. The speech was mind-numbingly boring.

'The potential of renewable energy sources can be much improved by suitable energy-storage systems. These may be via pumped water storage (from low to high level), compressed air . . .'

'No, no, stop, Lucy. This sounds as if it all came out of a text book.' Lucy nodded. 'Yes, I thought so. But the point of making a speech is that you've got to have an opinion. How do you think we ought to provide for our energy needs?' Lucy glanced at her friends for an answer. There was an uncomfortable silence.

'Do you agree with nuclear power?' A silence. 'Or do you think it's dangerous? Lucy, say something.'

'Well, I can't really decide.'

'You *must* decide.' At this moment, that seemed very important to Sandra.

Catherine volunteered an opinion. 'Don't you think

it would be a good idea if the government put more money into alternative energy sources to see if they worked because they seem safer than nuclear energy really?'

'Good!' said Sandra. 'Do you agree with that, Lucy?' Lucy nodded. 'Right! Now you must make your speech argue that point of view. It doesn't matter if you can't wholly believe it. In public speaking you've got to sound convinced. Anyway, there are no right answers to complicated problems – you've just got to pretend there are! Again!'

'No, Caroline, keep still. You're shifting from leg to leg! And watch your eyes. You're still addressing the ceiling. Also, you have a habit of tossing your hair so that it falls back on your face and covers half of it. Tie it back on the night. But it's a lot better.'

Sandra sat back on her chair so that it balanced on its back legs. She swung to and fro. Something was still missing. The girls were audible now. Sometimes they even smiled. Lucy had come out firmly against nuclear power and Sandra hoped that Anne Palmer would not think she had been interfering with the politics of the speech. She'd got the girls breathing deeply before their presentation, and she'd given each affirmations to practise. And yet when Sandra listened to them she had this sinking feeling. The speech was still indescribably dull. She covered her face with her hands and thought, while the girls watched her. Miss Coverdale was clearly about to come out with another idea.

'Look, girls.' Sandra still had her forehead cupped

in her hands. 'Somehow when I listen to you speak, I don't feel it's you I'm listening to. It's just a mass of words, like on a dull radio broadcast. You're only seventeen. Try being yourselves. Just say what you really feel. What do you really feel? What do you feel about the whole issue of energy?' She looked up at them appealingly.

Lucy spoke. 'It's boring really.'

'Well, say that then! And say why it's boring. And then go on to say what a pity it is that you think it's boring when it's such an important issue. Tell the truth! Yes! Try telling the truth! Do it now. Stand there, Lucy, and tell me what you really think.'

Lucy reddened. 'What, really?'

'Really.'

'OK. All the time in school, in debate lessons and in physics too when the teacher wants to have a discussion, we have to talk about nuclear energy. And we're all fed up. And we listen to all different people's opinions about it and 'cause we're young we just get easily affected by what people say. But we went to Sellafield and it was dead spooky. Like all the security around it. And it just gave you a weird feeling.'

'Good! That sounds like you. Try not to use words like "spooky" and "weird", but otherwise, that's miles better. Let's look at the speech again . . .'

Anne Palmer had let them have the dress rehearsal in the physics lab. The girls stood behind the demonstration bench and Sandra, feeling very out of place among cupboards full of electrical circuits and batteries, sat at the back, with a few members of the sixth form who had come along to listen to their friends. Zoë, too, was sitting in a corner, waiting with optimism to listen to the results of Sandra's training. Sandra smiled at her girls, deliberately trying to infect them with her determination. But already they looked different, as if they knew what they were doing. Only the very faintest quiver was detectable in Catherine's voice. And her introduction now sounded so much more natural.

'Good evening. I'm Catherine McDonald and I'm in the sixth form at Millers' Girls School. I'm very pleased to be here tonight, and I want to introduce you to the rest of the team . . .'

Zoë smiled at Sandra in encouragement. Sandra's spirits soared. Now it was Lucy's turn.

'Ladies and Gentlemen. Last term I went on a school trip to Sellafield. To be frank, we were all pleased at the idea only because it meant a day off school. We'd heard so much about the nuclear energy debate we were fed up with the whole thing. We sat in the back of the coach and listened to our Walkmans. Or is it Walkmen?' (Sandra put in that little joke.) 'But when we first saw the plant squatting in beautiful countryside, we were surprised at how strongly we felt . . .'

Sandra listened, and knew it was good. Very good. There were still little faults, slight grammatical lapses, words swallowed, clumsy transitions. But it was interesting. And the girls seemed to know what they were doing. Sandra stole another glance at Zoë to see what she thought. She was listening intently.

'. . . which is why we all feel that the government must start taking renewable sources seriously! And I invite you to show your appreciation in the usual manner.'

All the sixth formers clapped. Lucy, Catherine and Caroline looked flushed and happy.

'You were brill!' said one voice. 'Hey, they're really good! You're really good, Lucy!'

Zoë moved over to Sandra. 'You've achieved miracles, Sandra. They sound wonderful. I wish I could come with you tonight.'

'No. You go to the meeting. You need it. Not long before your big night!' Sandra said teasingly to her friend. Zoë's mouth tightened and then dissolved into a smile.

'You ought to train me in what to say.'

Sandra was flattered at the suggestion. 'No, you go to the group tonight and speak to Stella. Tell her what's going to happen. Do a role-play or something. All right, girls,' she said, addressing the sixth formers, 'you can go now. I'll meet you outside the Town Hall at seven. Don't be late.'

Sandra would not let herself fantasize about winning. But they must, they must win. It felt right, and just, that they should win. They had worked so hard. She had worked so hard. And it was her little experiment too. She had made these girls believe in themselves. She had told them all to wear elastic bands around their wrists. And to flick them sharply against their skin if they began to feel negatively about tonight. Their public victory would be a triumph for positive thinking! The thought amused Sandra.

She thought she would have a coffee before the next lesson. She went into the staff kitchen, a little cubbyhole full of flowery mugs and jars of Nescafé. As she switched on the kettle she reflected that she had not thought of getting herself something to eat. She had been so absorbed in the competition that she had momentarily lost her obsession with food. Or replaced it with something else. Interesting.

Now when she thought of food, she thought of Stella. How she would love to talk to Stella – really talk – about the food question. More and more she was convinced that she and Stella shared a problem. She thought back. In those Slim-Plicity days, she had made friends with Helen. But Helen only dabbled in dieting and gave it up, and remained sane. And there was the Fat Women's Support Group. Those women didn't mind being fat. Sandra admired them tremendously, but realized in the end she was not one of them. She knew she was alone with her problem. Until she got to know Stella.

Had she remembered to tell the girls to meet her at the side door of the Town Hall? Damn! She had better see them after lessons this afternoon and make sure they knew. There were to be no hiccups before their performance. And she had also better tell them to pour the water out of the jug before they started to speak, in case they got dry and needed a drink. No. She would not wait until after school. She would find them now. She made a very cool cup of coffee and downed it very quickly. She set off for the physics lab.

In the cracks of the paving stones the snow seemed to be settling. In the road in front of her the tyre treads of the cars were visible as trails in the slush. Sandra did not think, however, that the girls would have any difficulty being on time. All of them lived fairly close to the school, and they had said that their parents would be bringing them. Sandra was early. She was early because she preferred to wait here outside the Town Hall than in her own flat. It suited her mood better. It was impossible for her to relax. She might as well be here. She knew the caretaker in the lobby was eyeing her curiously and with a mild temporary regret Sandra realized that she probably did not look like the stereotype of a teacher with her elderly duffle coat, and messy hair. Sandra rather wished she had arranged to meet the girls inside the building. She had not guessed the March weather could be so bitter. She had been seduced by the crocuses and daffodils into thinking that spring had arrived; it hadn't. She pulled down her glove and lifted her coat sleeve to look at her watch. Five to seven. Two adults and three teenagers brushed past her into the Town Hall. Some of the opposition, no doubt. Sandra felt irrationally hostile; as she watched them unbutton their coats in the lobby, they seemed alien to her. Thus she did not notice when Catherine and Lucy arrived together with their mothers. They shook hands, discussed where Caroline was. Two minutes of doubt and hesitation. Then swiftly around a corner came Caroline and her father. Together they entered the Town Hall.

They were directed up a side staircase. Sandra led the way, ill at ease, not knowing the girls' parents, feeling as gauche as the girls. Except that the girls didn't appear to be particularly nervous; they laughed, expressed admiration for the debating chamber of the Town Hall, chatted and giggled as they always did.

Sandra felt tremendously proud of them, immensely loyal. They had been through so much together. She watched them go over to the rows of seats reserved for the competitors, and felt momentarily bereft as they left her. She took a seat herself.

Lucy's mother took the place by Sandra. She was a nondescript kind of woman, with short, untidy hair, and a face thrown into relief by a large pair of glasses.

'Shall we join you?' she asked Sandra, a little hesitantly.

'Yes, please.' Sandra sat up brightly.

'I must thank you for all the work you've done with Lucy,' she said. 'She has come on a lot. Frankly I never thought she'd be able to speak in front of an audience but I've heard her practise at home and she's not bad.'

Sandra tingled with pleasure. 'She's super, isn't she? Lucy has real character, I think.'

Lucy's mother smiled warmly at Sandra. Each felt how pleasant, how perceptive the other was. Lucy's mother opened the programme that had been lying on her seat when she arrived and, at that cue, Sandra read hers.

The four participating schools were listed with the titles of their speeches. There were her girls, Catherine McDonald, Lucy Parker, Caroline Lord. Sandra surveyed them with pride. Their names seemed so much more substantial than the others. 'Energy for the 1990s and beyond'. The title was Anne's and Sandra had not been able to alter it. Lucy's mother had now been joined by Catherine's mother, and they spoke of domestic matters. Sandra looked around her again.

The chamber was filling rapidly. An official was now talking to the competitors about procedure; he was a tall, greying man, with his back to Sandra. Behind the seats milled other members of the audience. There were parents, of course, their eyes straying to their offspring; teachers, deliberately taking a low profile, keeping themselves to themselves; and a number of men in suits, looking decidedly cheerful, clapping each other on the shoulders, bustling around with a corporate air of importance. These, Sandra assumed, were the Lions. She knew, of course, that the Lions were just a group of local businessmen who promoted no end of local good causes, but she persisted in her mind in thinking of them as golden-maned and ferocious. Thus these rather soberly dressed middle-aged men disappointed her. They seemed at home in the debating chamber – this world of formality, self-importance, decision-making.

The greying man turned from the competitors to address the audience, and asked them to be silent. The competition was about to commence. Sandra felt every muscle tighten. She had become more conscious of this since Stella had taught her relaxation. So she commanded her muscles to relax. She uncrossed her ankles and let her feet drop. She attempted to breathe deeply, let her shoulders relax. But once she had dropped her shoulders, her ankles crossed again and her legs were clenched tightly together. It was no use. It was easy to relax on the floor of 8 Lincoln Grove; impossible here, in the Council's debating chamber, surrounded by parents and Lions.

It was eight o'clock. Still the Chairperson was

introducing the various officials: the timekeeper; the Lord Mayor and the Lady Mayoress, who were gracing this competition with their august presence; the secretary of the Lions' social committee; and the judges. Sandra listened with interest. The Chairperson of the judges was a portly red-faced gentleman, a magistrate apparently, a Justice of the Peace, very used to public speaking. His colleagues consisted of a terrifyingly smart woman, a local solicitor, and a smoothly good-looking young man who taught at the polytechnic – British Constitution, apparently. They all oppressed her. Still she was sure they couldn't fail to admire her girls; but the very fact that they were judges, that they looked so dauntingly official, so unexceptional, so self-assured, worried Sandra. Yes, she found them faceless and frightening. She could see they belonged to a very different world from hers.

The Millers' girls were drawn fourth. At least, thought Sandra, they would not have to go first. That would have been dreadful. But now they had a good hour to wait; adequate time to get thoroughly nervous. Sandra smiled at the girls encouragingly. They looked fresh and smart in their crisp white blouses. Sandra winked at them, and then they all turned to pay attention to the first team.

Sandra was delighted. The first team were bad, hopelessly bad. The Chairperson lost her place, apologized, shook her head, asked if she could start again. Sandra felt pity, wondered critically how well the girl had been trained. The main speaker read his speech, never looking up once; the cardinal sin. It was clear this team were out of the running.

The second team had chosen to speak on television situation comedies. It was an odd choice of subject. The main speaker spent most of his time recounting funny one-liners from well-known programmes. The audience and judges laughed, but Sandra was fairly certain that they would not do well. It was derivative and trivial; there was no point to the speech. Although the young speakers were engaging, they had clearly been left to their own devices in the writing of the speech, and it showed. Sandra knew things were looking better and better.

The third team was relentlessly dull. Sandra had never seen such wooden speakers. The three students stood rigidly by their chairs, bodies immobile, and delivered speeches in a measured monotone. Oh, it was worthy stuff – something to do with Japan, America, Europe and trade restrictions – Sandra wasn't really listening. The speakers had evidently learnt their speeches by heart; their teacher sat opposite them actually mouthing the words with them. It was appalling. The judges had their heads down, making notes. And then it was Millers' turn.

'My Lord Mayor, Lady Mayoress, Judges, Ladies and Gentlemen. Good evening. My name is Catherine McDonald . . .' Her voice was steady; she even stole a smile at Lucy. Sandra loved her.

'There are acceptable risks,' said Lucy in measured tones, 'and unacceptable risks. The risks that the nuclear power lobby ask us to take are unacceptable. I don't want to bring my children up in a world where we risk a terrible nuclear accident. We all discussed this and we all felt the same . . .'

No one in the audience could fail to see their quality, thought Sandra.

'And so I ask you to show your appreciation in the usual manner!'

The audience clapped. Sandra was certain that the clapping was louder than for any other team. And now it was time for tea. The audience and competitors would have refreshments while the judges decided. Relieved to get up and move about, Sandra approached the girls and warmly congratulated them.

'They did do well!' said Lucy's mother to Sandra. 'They came across so –'

'Authoritatively,' said Sandra. 'And you could hear every word they said. And they looked so –'

'Smart,' said Lucy's mother. 'Like proper young ladies. But at the same time they seemed –'

'So natural!' added Sandra. 'As if they meant what they said. Which they did.'

They must win. They must win, thought Sandra. Unless the judges like the humorous approach, and go for Redcliff High's 'Television Comedy'. No, they couldn't. It simply wasn't as good as ours.

Sandra didn't remember drinking her tea. Or whether she had a biscuit or not. She wondered how long it would take the judges to decide. Surely it was a foregone conclusion anyway. The grey-haired man – the Lions' President – approached Sandra and shook her hand.

'Well done! Lovely bunch of girls. Tell them I thought their speech was very interesting. Very interesting. Very lively.' Did he know the results? wondered Sandra. Had he been with the judges? She watched her girls drinking their tea. For their sakes, for their sakes alone, she yearned for victory.

And then he informed them that the judges had reached a decision, and that the audience's presence was required back in the chamber. Sandra thought, I can't bear this. I wish I was anywhere else. Relax. Relax.

She took her place in the chamber. The audience settled expectantly. The President bumbled on, about the high standard set that evening, the very difficult decision the judges had to reach, the confidence of young people. Get on with it, commanded Sandra. He commented on the performance of each team, blandly praising each. It must be us, thought Sandra. Us, or possibly the television ones. But it must be one of us.

'We have certificates for all the participants, and thoroughly deserved they are too. But the team in second place will receive book tokens, and tonight's winners will receive book tokens, a trophy, and a place in the regional final. And so, the moment you've all been waiting for. In second place, Redcliff High, for their talk on Television Comedy.'

It's us, Sandra knew then.

'And our winners - and a big round of applause, please, for the team from St David's and "Economic Trade Barriers".'

Sandra felt sick. It was a mistake. It had to be a mistake. But no. There were the St David's team - that collection of zombies - walking forward, shaking the hands of the judges, receiving their tokens and the cup, and then Redcliff, and there were her girls - she dared to look at them now - stunned, whispering to each other, trying to look brave. What had happened? They were so much better than anyone else. It wasn't fair.

Sandra spoke to the parents in shocked disbelief. Despite everyone's protestations that the girls had done wonderfully, that the judges' criteria were odd, that you never could tell, and other assorted clichés, everyone was badly disappointed. Sandra knew she could have cried. It just wasn't fair. But Stella had taught her to recognize that voice of her inner child, that emotional reaction. Sandra's internal Parent told her she hadn't tried hard enough, she hadn't been careful enough. Sandra's Adult told her that they had simply been unlucky, they had done their best and not succeeded. Listen to the voice of your Adult, Stella had told Sandra. Sandra did. We've done our best and not succeeded. She still felt like crying.

Outside, flurries of snow swirled round the departing guests. Sandra buttoned up the toggles on her duffle coat, swung her scarf around her. She felt heavy with disappointment, drained of energy. Which somehow seemed appropriate. She knew really the competition wasn't important, but just now, it seemed like everything. She entered the Town Hall car-park and there was her Fiesta with a frosting of snow.

On the top of the gas fire were two empty cans of Stones bitter. There were two more full ones in the fridge, and Sandra had every intention of getting them later. She had rung Zoë's number, and the babysitter had informed her that she had not returned yet. She would have rung her mother, but it was late, after ten, and she didn't want to worry her. Sandra was alone with it all.

It's not fair, she thought, on a wave of anger; the wave swelled, and subsided. What did those judges expect from teenagers? I hate judges, she thought to herself, her anger returning. And then, as the anger retreated again, she thought, what was the point of it all? And then she did begin to cry a little bit, for nobody was around. All that work, all that positive thinking – she rubbed the tears from her eyes and listened in astonishment to her own sobs – all that work, for nothing.

For nothing, she told an imaginary Stella. Those girls believed in themselves, and I believed in them, but we still lost. She said to Stella, you can think all the positive thoughts you want, and bad things still happen. So there.

And what would Stella say to that? Sandra asked herself. She imagined Stella sitting there, deflated. And she wanted to help Stella think of an answer, a defence for Sandra's destructive accusations.

All right, Sandra, she said to herself, would you have done it differently if you'd known? Would you have trained them to talk like zombies if you knew that would make them win?

No, Sandra told Stella-Sandra sheepishly.

And Sandra thought of the winning team with contempt. Thankfully the girls she taught were not like that. She was aware of a surge of affection for Millers', the girls particularly, and the staff too. OK, so the school was less than perfect, despite the fact that they all tried so hard to be perfect. She thought of Anne

Palmer's meticulous tiny handwriting on the duty lists. But school wasn't perfect. That's fortunate, thought Sandra, for I'm not either.

Nor's Stella, she realized, and nor are any of us. Nor's therapy. She was cheering up now. Then a thought struck her, and she laughed aloud. For those awful judges, those dark-suited tight-lipped judges, whose judgements were so devoid of humanity, were nearly all lawyers! And Sandra realized then that if she was to give up school and train for law, she would eventually be joining them – and perhaps not, for still she was not sure of herself – but she knew then, with a growing conviction, that she never wanted to be a lawyer; to have that kind of authority, it just wasn't for her; somehow Millers', as depressing and aggravating as it could be, was what she had chosen. And her mind cleared.

It's all right, she told Stella, as she was falling asleep that night, you don't have to be perfect. It's all right even if you lose. You get over it. That was what she would tell Stella, she decided sleepily. When she saw her. Whenever that would be.

CHAPTER NINETEEN

'So has she told you about this friend?'

'What friend?'

'She says she's got a new friend, and she's going to introduce us,' explained Marie, satisfied that at least she knew more than Harry. The traffic lights changing to amber caught Harry by surprise, and he jerked the car to a halt, flinging them both slightly forward. But Marie seemed accustomed to this.

'Do you want another sandwich, Harry?'

'I'll leave it till later.'

'We'll be there in half an hour. What do you mean, later? I'll eat it for you.'

Stella traced an imaginary line down Roland's chest with her forefinger.

'I feel you know them as well as anyone could. But you still might find them difficult, Roland. My mother has this insatiable need for dominance. She feeds on inadequacy. She has a very low opinion of men – because of my father, and because of her father. She tries to consume me too. But you know all this, darling.' She kissed his bare chest, and rose from the bed, and reached for her clothes. 'You were wonderful this afternoon,' she said. A few hours ago, they had nearly made love. Stella was certain this was because she had written to Richard. Roland found it difficult to handle deceit. 'Get dressed now,' she instructed him, cajolingly. 'My mother would die if she found you in my bed.'

'No, I'm telling you it's *left* at the roundabout! How many times have you come here? You should know the way to your daughter's house.'

'Keep your hair on.'

Marie exhaled sharply in irritation. Nobody knew what she had to put up with. He lives in his own world, she told an imaginary audience. Harry reversed into a side turning, and retraced his path to the round-about.

'Do you think she's missing him? Richard. She doesn't say much, if you know what I mean.'

'She must be missing him. It's a long time.'

Marie looked momentarily at her husband. She asked herself how she would feel if Harry was to go away for six months or so. Would she miss him? She wondered. She would cope. She learned to cope without Stella, and that was a blow, Stella leaving to live up here in the north. But she had come to accept Stella's odd little ways, her strange interests, her hypersensitivity. If only she would have some children.

Stella straightened the cushions, and then saw the picture of herself and Richard, and turned it to the wall. Roland watched her silently. She turned and approached him, and sat on his lap.

'I'll explain. You don't have to worry. She won't be angry with you. But she'll take it out on me. I know I'm a disappointment to her. She would have liked a daughter like my cousin Rosemary, with children, who stayed close. My mother's bitter, you see. Oh, I wish this was over.'

'Disempower your mother, Stella. You are an autonomous human being.'

'I'll try. Shall we meditate?' said Stella, brightly. 'And centre ourselves?'

Roland nodded.

'You missed the turning! Are you in a trance or what?' Marie demanded angrily.

'I'm sorry, I was thinking.'

'Thinking! You're supposed to be driving. So what were you thinking about?'

'This friend. Perhaps she's been keeping her company while Richard's been away.'

'I'm glad she has a girlfriend. It's nice for a girl to have a girlfriend. You remember Esther? My friend Esther with the glasses. They went to Bournemouth. I should have written.'

'I should have written. Then I wouldn't be confronting her like this, and putting myself at such a disadvantage. But don't worry, Roland, I'm sure they'll like you.'

'I'm sure to like her. Stella and I have the same tastes, you know that. Like mother, like daughter. Thank God we're here.' The car drew up suddenly, and juddered to a halt. Marie examined herself in the mirror while Harry got out and opened the boot, revealing a large maroon suitcase. He left it standing on the pavement by the car, while Marie got out. She walked up the drive and rang the doorbell. It was answered immediately.

Marie hugged Stella, feeling her thinner than ever. So she is missing Richard, Marie decided. Stella was hardly aware of her mother. Usually, as soon as her mother arrived, Stella sensed her encroachment, withdrew in a fastidious horror at her mother's bulk, suffered intensely. But now it was as if she was in a dream. Her father came up the drive with the suitcase. He put it in the hall.

'Give me your coat, Mum. And you, Dad. You both look well.'

Coats were taken off, coats in Stella's arms. She hardly knew what to do with them. Into the coat cupboard. Now what?

'Come into the lounge. There's someone I want you to meet.'

'Your friend! She's here already? Is she staying with you? That's nice. Keep you company.'

Stella opened the door. Roland rose from the armchair and walked over to Marie, his hand outstretched. She shook hands, looked around, puzzled.

'So where is she?'

'This is Roland, Mum. My friend.'

'Nice to meet you,' said Marie, automatically. She sat down. Her mind was racing. Unusual of Stella to have a male friend. But she does strange things. What would Richard say? It must be innocent – Stella would never have a lover. She's a funny girl – doesn't care what people think. A male friend. And so thin!

Harry joined her on the settee. He smiled; Roland smiled; Marie smiled. And then Stella moved over to the thin man and sat on his lap. On his lap!

'Mum,' Stella began, 'and Dad. I want to tell you

something. As you know, years ago I embarked on a programme of personal growth, which has meant that I've discovered all sorts of new things about myself and my relationships. I've had a lot of new understanding, and gradually I came to realize that my relationship with Richard was seriously dysfunctional. He denied my authenticity, stifled my growing spirituality and stunted my development. Not having children was both the symptom and result of this. When he left, I found I was free to grow again, and realized that our relationship acted as a sort of block. Then I met Roland. He was my therapist. We ... we ... have started this spontaneous ongoing supportive situation ...'

'Stella! I want to speak to you in the kitchen!'

At least, thought Stella, this would not be in front of Roland. Docilely, she followed her mother and entered her kitchen. She withdrew a stool from under the breakfast bar and sat there, passive. Marie did the same. Stella knew why her mother had chosen the kitchen. The kitchen - anyone's kitchen - was her territory. She was surrounded by food and the means of preparing food. If battle had to commence, Marie would make sure it was on her ground.

'Stella. Are you living with him?'

'Not living. He has his own house in the Quays, and he comes here –'

'Stella, I mean *living*!' Stella nodded.

'And does Richard know this?'

'I wrote him a letter.'

Marie felt winded. Her daughter - her own daughter – having an affair. Which was not something that happened in their family. The shame. The failure. And he was so thin. He needed feeding. What would she tell her sister Milly? Stella's marriage. What would happen to Stella's marriage? The shame. She would have to tell Milly. Mind you, Milly's Rosemary walked out on her husband. And these days, these days it was all different. Girls separated, divorced. In her day you stuck with your husband, for better, for worse. For worse. A stab of jealousy, and then she looked at Stella. Who was still her baby and didn't know what she was doing. What could you say to these kids? And besides, now, please God, she might have a granddaughter.

'What did Richard say?'

'I don't think he will have got the letter yet.'

'And you love this – what'shisname?'

'Roland. Yes.'

'Stella – it's not so easy to break up a marriage.'

'I know, but . . .'

'God knows what I'm going to tell Milly. But I'll think of something. I saw this coming, you know. I said to your father, they spend too much time apart. He'll lose her, I said. I knew it.'

Stella looked at her mother wonderingly. She seemed to have accepted it. There was no battle. Stella felt cheated. Perhaps, she thought, her mother had not seen the immensity of it, had failed, naturally, to understand quite what she felt for Roland, had trivialized it all in her own mind. It was all very odd. And Roland and her father were in the lounge together. Stella suggested they go back and join them.

The two women returned. Roland and Harry were still seated, Harry on the settee, Roland in the armchair.

The lounge was quite silent. Neither man had apparently said a word.

'I'll put the kettle on,' said Marie. 'Who wants a cup of tea?'

Roland had made the dinner. It was a lentil casserole with vegetables. Stella knew she would feel safe around Roland's casserole, because it was made with his love, and could not do her any harm. He had told her that when he was soaking the lentils. The bonus was, she discovered now, that she was not tempted to eat very much of it. She watched her mother with curiosity. Marie sprinkled her plate liberally with salt; tasted it; frowned; added more salt; raised her eyebrows at Stella. Now I know, Marie thought, why he is so thin.

Frankly, she couldn't see what Stella saw in him. Mind you, Richard was worse. Richard you never saw. Always away on business; even at home he would be working. So finally Stella was fed up. Maybe it wasn't so surprising. Marie still felt tremors of shock, like the after-effects of an earthquake. Stella with a lover! Stella's marriage over! It was a lot to get used to. But most of all, Marie was curious. How did it happen? Stella had not said a word. Secretive she always was. Marie continued to stow away spoonfuls of stew as quickly as she could in an attempt not to taste it.

'So where did you learn to cook, Roland?'

'I live alone,' he explained. 'I have to cook for myself.'

'He has to cook for himself,' Marie said, for Harry's edification. 'So you're not married?'

'No.' Roland shook his head and smiled.

'Tell me. How did you meet Stella?'

Roland pointed at his mouth to indicate that it was full. Stella interrupted.

'I told you, Mum. He was my therapist. After Gill left, I started with Roland.'

'So you're a therapist too? Don't tell me, you're not another one for this analysis and meditation and assert-iveness training? Ach, you'll suit each other. Listen, when she first told me about the TA I thought she'd joined the Territorial Army. So I'm supposed to know? So you like the therapy business?'

'Roland's writing a book too.'

'An author! Harry, he's an author! And what book is this you're writing?'

Roland cleared his throat. 'Ritual and Male Friend-ship Bonds.'

'And what's that when it's at home?'

'It's a study of the way in which men are most at ease communicating with each other when they are engaged in some sort of game or ritual   such as foot-ball, drinking, spectator sports. It's about male emo-tional illiteracy. It's the development of a paper I wrote for a psychoanalytical journal.'

'Do you come from Manchester?' inquired Marie, swiftly changing the subject. 'Were you born here?'

'Ormskirk. I was brought up in Ormskirk. But I went to university here.'

'And then you became a therapist. But you never got married. You had girlfriends?'

'Mum!'

'Don't be so sensitive. She's always been sensitive, Roland. Since a little girl. You got parents?'

272

'They still live in Ormskirk. They're retired.'

'We've retired, me and Harry. We had a shop – did Stella tell you? A ladies' wear shop. But we sold out, bought a ground-floor flat in Woodford. The shop's a Kebab House now, would you believe? We drove up there once, had a kebab. Not bad at all. Do you like kebabs, Roland?'

Stella admired Roland's poise under her mother's constant barrage of questions. She watched his face carefully for the least sign of discomfort. Had she thought that he felt at all uneasy, she would have done something, said something. But Roland, serene, mild-mannered, parried her mother's interrogation with a Christ-like calmness. Yes, he liked kebabs, he preferred Indian food, liked eating out, enjoyed walking, didn't watch much television, had a younger brother, his father had been a bank manager, his mother had never needed to work, no, she didn't get bored. Stella was learning more about her lover than she had ever known before. She listened to her mother with a dull resentment and with her fork made patterns in the lentil casserole.

'You don't mind me saying this, Roland, but you look like you could do with some weight putting on. You don't diet like Stella?'

Roland shook his head and smiled.

'Because, I'm wondering. She couldn't stop dieting, you know. That's why she started with all this therapy. I thought maybe you were a dieter. Men diet.'

'No. It was different for me.'

'So go on. How did you become a therapist?'

'My own experience in therapy led me –'

'So you were in therapy? For dieting?' Roland shook his head, flushing slightly. 'So what brought you into therapy? You had a problem?'

'Mum!' Stella was livid.

'No harm in asking.' But now Marie was quiet. She reached over and cut herself another slice of wholemeal bread, and glanced at Stella, who was looking at Roland with concern. And curiosity. For her mother had dared to ask the one question that she had lacked the courage to ask. Why had Roland gone into therapy with Gill? He had never volunteered the information, and she felt it was wrong to ask. One day, she was sure, he would tell her. She sensed his vulnerability, and was engulfed in a wave of tenderness. And he put up with her mother so well. She was interested to find out what he thought of her. She looked forward to hearing his analysis. But that would be after the weekend. There were still twenty-four hours to go.

Stella woke very early in the morning, alone in her queen-size bed. She was wide awake immediately; it was impossible to sleep. Roland had of course gone back to the Quays. This was the first night they had spent apart since the 'Mickey Mouse' weekend. Stella missed him. But she would not face her parents with their physical relationship. Besides, her mother put all thoughts of sex out of her mind. She always had done.

The stifled grunting she could hear was her father snoring. Marie complained constantly about this; she had bought Harry strange nasal devices to assist his night-time breathing, had got herself earplugs, but to no avail. Apart from the snoring, the house was quiet.

There was no traffic outside. Stella guessed it must be about seven o'clock. She lay there, alert, vibrating with tension.

I, Stella Martin, love and approve of myself. I, Stella Martin, have infinite patience, tolerance and goodwill. You, Stella Martin, have infinite patience, tolerance and goodwill. She, Stella Martin   The bedsprings creaked. Someone turned over. Her mother, by the sound of it. Stella could imagine her mother, her flabby, dimpled legs, those rolls of fat, covered by her floral nightdress, her face frowned and creased in sleep. Stella wondered how her mother must feel, being so fat, knowing now that she would always be fat, always. How did she live with it? Stella felt a remote kind of pity.

And she noticed that. I feel pity, she thought. She rolled over on to her side, opening her eyes to her bedside table and her book of daily affirmations. I feel pity for my mother. She ordered herself to stay with that. Gill had said, you will be better, entirely better, when you have reached forgiveness. Resentment must be dissolved. Your mother maimed you, but she did the best she could at the time, with the resources at her command. This you must accept. Stella had heard these words, but for her they were only words. Yet, this morning, she was aware of this new feeling, cutting through the swathes of resentment, repulsion, anger, alienation. Pity. And there was something else too.

For her mother had accepted Roland. There was no scene, no recriminations. It had all passed peacefully. It was simple. Admittedly, as soon as Roland had gone last night, she had pleaded tiredness, had gone straight

to bed. But Marie had not stopped her. She had simply
said she was tired herself. And then she had said, he's
a nice boy. Pity he's not Jewish, but he's a nice boy.
She liked him. Pity; yes, she felt pity. And gratitude
too. That was the second emotion. Pity and gratitude.
The bed in the next room creaked again, and Stella
heard footsteps. They grew louder, then softer. A door
shut; a few moments later a chain pulled. Stella lay
quiet. She ran her hands over her stomach to check it
was still flat – an automatic gesture. She would let her
mother go downstairs first, let her find some breakfast.
Stella reached over to her tape recorder and pressed
the play button. It was time for her morning meditation. She closed her eyes.

Marie found the light switch, pressed it, and Stella's
kitchen was bathed in a pale glow. Marie looked round
appreciatively. It was a spacious, modern kitchen, with
white marbled worktops, and every appliance Marie
could think of. Stella even had a dishwasher; a dishwasher for two! For a family, Marie could understand,
but when there were just the two of them? The two of
them. Marie reminded herself of the new reality. Stella
and this Roland. Marie padded over to Stella's slim
grey jug kettle, and switched it on. Her joints felt
slightly swollen today, but it was damp in Manchester.
She opened the cupboard to look for coffee. Inside
was a poster. It was of a tree. There were words, too.
Marie did not have to put on her glasses to read them,
because they were large. 'Once you learn truly what it
is to love, what it is to be, all is different – yet all is
unchanged.' It's too early in the morning, thought

Marie. Near the coffee were some cards, in Stella's writing. Recipes? Curious, she picked them up. 'I love myself deeply. I am completely lovable. I can give and receive love. The universe will support me always.' Strange girl. All this love. Look where it led to. She thought of Roland. The kettle gave a tiny click.

Marie turned to the fridge for milk. One thing she liked about her daughter's kitchen was the ease of it all. There was no bending or straining. The fridge was set into a unit. She opened the door, and found a half-full bottle of milk. But there was little else. What did she live on? Love? Marie could not understand how a daughter of hers could not have a fridge bulging with food. Food was affluence, and Stella was affluent. Food was security. Food was joy. And Stella only had some Edam cheese, a lettuce, a few tomatoes and half a bottle of milk. And love. Love she's got plenty of. Love, she won't go short.

Marie was restless. There was no one to talk to, nothing to look at. She was reading a detective story, but she had left it upstairs, and it wasn't worth the effort to get it. She couldn't sit there doing nothing. There in the sink was a casserole dish, full of water that was once soapy, but now had a layer of scum on its surface. It was obviously the casserole dish that Roland had used. It needed washing out. Marie was glad. She moved over to the sink, lifted the dish, ignoring the stabbing pain in her wrists, and tipped out the water, which gurgled into the sink. So where was Stella's scourer? She never had things where you'd expect them to be, that girl. Marie looked in the cupboard next to the sink, and there she found a box of Brillo pads. That would have to do.

When Stella entered the kitchen, her mother was elbow deep in soapy water. Stella stood in the doorway, observing her mother's back, her maroon dressing-gown, her mother's messy grey curls. Her mother at the kitchen sink. Pity. And gratitude.

'Hello, Mum.'

'Stella! You're up early.'

'I couldn't sleep.' Stella flicked the kettle on, and waited for it to boil. The dish was clean now, and Marie laid it on the drainer. She remembered the lentil casserole, its texture, taste.

'If I were you, Stella, I wouldn't leave him to do the cooking again.'

Marie settled opposite Stella at the breakfast bar. To Marie, breakfast bars felt extravagant, American. Time now, she thought, for some girl talk. Her daughter looked thin and pretty. To think she was already thirty-five.

'Have you thought what's going to happen to this house? It's a nice house.' Stella stared into her coffee. 'Because when Richard finds out, you might not be able to live here. Have you thought of that?'

'Roland has his own house,' said Stella. 'I'll be all right.'

'And how will you live? Money doesn't grow on trees.'

'Mum!' said Stella reproachfully. 'You forget I'm a qualified therapist. And so is Roland. We can earn money. I know I won't be so rich as ... as now. But Roland and I, together – well, there are all sorts of things we can do. We can run workshops together, and do joint therapy groups, and do relationship counselling.'

'There's money in that?'

'Plenty of money.'

'You mean people pay you for talking to them?'

'For listening.'

'A cushy job. They can ring me, I can listen. And I wonder what Richard is going to say to all this.'

Stella tried to breathe into her abdomen, in order to relax. 'I expect he'll be upset. I know he will be. But . . . but I can't help it.'

There was silence. Marie looked around this beautiful kitchen regretfully. This could be the last time she would ever be there. But that was life. When Stella was at school, her teachers had said that she could have applied to university. If she worked hard. But Stella had refused, said she didn't want to. And Marie had not put on the pressure. What could she do? If the girl didn't want to, you couldn't force her.

Stella sipped her coffee and stole a glance at her mother. Pity. Gratitude. And something else now, too. The time she had been dreading had come and gone. She had been alone with her mother, and Marie had said nothing, had accepted the situation. It was almost unbelievable. It was the result of those creative visualizations; it was the effect of all the positive vibrations from her meditation and affirmations; it was a miracle. What was that odd, warm feeling Stella had in her chest, that melting feeling? It was something she had not experienced with her mother before. It was a gentle, tender feeling. Could it be love? At last, would she be able . . . The end of therapy, said Gill . . .

'Mum,' Stella said, 'I want to tell you something.'

'So tell me.'

'Mum, I forgive you.'

Marie was mystified. 'What have I done?'

'I mean, for everything. All your mistakes when I was a child. I want to give you my love and forgiveness.'

'Forgiveness! You forgive *me*? You weren't so wonderful yourself! Do you remember the tantrums you had? The names you called me? You were such a perfect child? Listen, Stella, I had my work cut out. Forgive me?'

'Please don't spoil it. This is so important for me.'

'I forgive you, she says! So, tell me, what mistakes did I make? You turned out so badly? You're a funny girl, I know, but you were always a funny girl. You used to hide from the coalman, and from the dustman. I had to send you next door. And all this was my mistake?'

'You just don't understand!'

'You're right, I don't understand. What do you have for breakfast in this house? I'll have the Edam if you've got some bread.'

Stella watched her mother ease herself off the stool and lumber over to the cupboard. She loathed her. Absolutely loathed her. Why couldn't she see what that forgiveness had cost her? And to throw it back like that. Her mother completely failed to see how far she had come. Belittling therapy, and then blaming her. Always there had been this battle to impress her mother, and her mother was never satisfied, always wanted more. And now even her forgiveness was not good enough. Her mother did not recognize what Stella had succeeded in becoming. Stella thought of herself at her own therapy group, saw herself through Zoë's eyes and Norah's eyes and Carol's eyes. And through Roland's eyes. What was wrong with her mother's vision? I'm so hurt, Stella thought. She crossed her arms against her chest, like Gill had taught her to do, to ward off negativity.

Marie ambled back to the breakfast bar.

'This Edam is old. It would have kept better if you'd wrapped it in cling-film. It doesn't take a moment.'

She says all those hurtful things to me, thought Stella. And then it's as if it never happened. Nothing is serious or lasting with her. It's my mother, Stella thought resentfully, who needs the therapy.

'Has your father told you about the over-sixties club he's joined? So sociable, all of a sudden. I said to him –'

Cutting across Marie's chatter came the harsh ring of the telephone. The women jumped. They both thought, it's very early. It jangled insistently. A client in difficulty? wondered Stella. But she feared it wasn't. Roland? Answer me, demanded the phone. She lifted the receiver.

'Go on. What did Richard say? He was angry? Did he cry? I hate hearing a man cry.'

Stella sat on the settee, both her parents with her. She was stunned. She held the cup of tea her mother had made but did not think to drink it.

'It wasn't him,' she said. 'It was Gill. She said I wasn't to worry, because she was in love with Richard. He's been unfaithful to *me*!'

CHAPTER TWENTY

Zoë sat on the edge of her bed in her slip. She never seriously considered, even briefly, Stella's suggestion of meditating. She knew it would be impossible. She was as alert as the taut string of a bow. If she was to continue getting ready now, she would be a whole hour early. Laura was in front of the television, watching *Neighbours*. Normally this was banned in the Swann household, but tonight Zoë was grateful for Laura's uncritical absorption in affairs in Ramsay Street.

It was incomprehensible to her that she should be contemplating going out to meet a strange man. She tried to think forward to what might happen. Most likely, she thought, he would simply not be there. She and Sandra would arrive at the Players Theatre, and no man would be there wearing a yellow rose. They would have a drink, and she would fight off a sinking feeling, leaden limbs, and then they would go home. Or he would be there, and she would know, from the way he looked at her, that he was disappointed. He would invent some spurious reason for leaving early, and promise to ring her soon. And then she would go home alone.

She flicked the elastic band she was wearing around her wrist. Negative thinking! If she persisted in thinking like that, she knew she would never go. She was precisely aware of the location of his letter. It was in the bedside table, in the cupboard, tucked inside the last pages of P. D. James's *Devices and Desires*. Appropriate, she thought, grimly. She could see in sharp focus the blue ink, and printed letters of the single handwritten word 'John'. Tonight she would be meeting him.

She had already decided what to wear. She had abandoned weeks ago her new smart, assertive look. She opted instead tonight for a straight black skirt and a new cream blouse with a floppy collar. She thought she looked a bit like a waitress, but Sandra had said she looked unusually attractive, and slim, and besides, Zoë felt comfortable in a plain skirt and blouse. To wear anything too seductive might give the wrong impression.

All day she had been unable to concentrate on her teaching. In the middle of an explanation of a complex grammatical point, her mind would wander. What if I'm late, and I miss him? What will he look like? And she would apologize to the girls, and receive their bemused looks, and she realized they were similarly distracted. They hadn't been paying attention either. Her subject had never seemed more dry to her. She had looked at the girls and felt almost as if she was one of them again. She was fifteen, going out on a blind date, going to a party and hoping to meet someone and knowing – she always knew this – that there were many more attractive girls than her, that she should be grateful for any crumbs of attention. But always, there was that never quite suppressed hope. That bittersweet supposition, what if? As there was tonight.

Zoë tried to make herself think of school. The last

thing she wanted to do was to build her hopes up. She would not allow herself to imagine a positive outcome; she would be badly disappointed. School, school. The corridor outside the Latin Bookroom with the Junior sports results. The oniony smells from the Home Economics block. Girls emptying waste-paper baskets into huge dustbins in the caretaker's lobby. School. Anne Palmer had informed her that it would be hard to fill her timetable next year. It was a warning. Zoë would have to be prepared either to teach another subject, or discuss the possibility of part-time employment. Zoë's suggestion of Classical Studies had fallen on deaf ears. The Head felt enough Arts subjects were on offer. The school's participation in Science 2001 was conditional upon a certain number of girls taking science A Levels, Dr Young had told all the staff time and time again. Zoë was told she could consider teaching typing, perhaps, or Information Technology, under Debra. This was all bad news. Zoë had known it for a couple of weeks. But she had dealt with it by hoping it would go away. With Sandra's encouragement, she had looked in the pages of *The Times Educational Supplement* for a new post. But there was nothing in the area. The despair washed over her. And she reprimanded herself. She was supposed to be having a good time tonight. If there was one night it might be appropriate to forget about school, it was tonight. She shook her head to dispel her own thoughts, and stood, smoothing down her slip, wishing automatically for a larger bust, trying not to focus on her face.

She went to her wardrobe to find her skirt. Last night at the meeting she had rehearsed her words.

'Hello. You're wearing a yellow rose. I'm the lady you wrote to.' She had pointed out to Stella that you should never end a sentence with a preposition, but Stella had looked baffled. Then she had said Zoë oughtn't to sound too clever to begin with. Which was a fair point. 'Hello,' Zoë repeated. 'You're wearing a yellow rose. I'm the lady you wrote to. My name is Zoë.' Or was it, I'm Zoë? All of it sounded so artificial. In the group, Stella had pretended to be the man she would meet; David was asleep and Jim had not turned up. It was very easy with Stella. They had a textbook discussion about their hobbies and tastes in music. But it was a sham, and Zoë knew it.

She slipped into her black skirt. The doorbell rang loudly, and she heard Laura run to the door. She greeted Sandra loudly and enthusiastically. Zoë smiled involuntarily to herself. She put her old sweater back on and joined them.

'You're early, Sandra! I'm not ready and Suzanne's not here yet.'

'I know, but I prefer to be here than at my place. I thought you might like my company, anyway. And I didn't want you getting cold feet.' Laura looked up at Sandra, sensing the excitement. 'I'll put the kettle on and we'll have a drink. Laura, come in the kitchen with me and show me where the biscuits are and you can have one!'

As soon as she saw Sandra, Zoë felt better. She was grateful for the way Sandra breezed in, took charge, and made it all seem so much fun. She had missed her at school. Sandra had taken some sixth formers to a day of lectures on the A Level texts. No more brooding, she told herself. She followed her daughter and friend into the kitchen.

'Tell me about the meeting yesterday. Did I miss anything exciting? I don't suppose you're breaking the confidentiality rule if you tell me what went on, because I'm a group member, at least for now.'

Zoë laughed to herself, remembering. 'Stella said she was going to try a new analytical technique with us. It was strange, Sandra. She got us to pick a Walt Disney character we associated with, and she used it to pinpoint our problems. No, honestly, Sandra, at the time it all seemed quite convincing. I said I felt like Cinderella without a fairy godmother – but I had to say something. No one else would. I don't think Norah liked it when Stella suggested Pinocchio for her. Stella said that perhaps at some level Norah was being dishonest about an aspect of her life, and if she came clean, her consciousness of her nose would diminish. Norah got very frosty after that.'

'But it's not her who's the liar!' exclaimed Sandra. 'It's Jim! Everything he's said in every meeting is a complete fabrication.'

'That's what Norah said. Stella reminded her not to be critical of other group members, and really, Sandra, she looked astounded, as if it hadn't actually dawned on her that he'd been stringing her along.'

Sandra whistled. 'It doesn't sound like it was a good night for Stella.'

'Quite. She didn't really seem herself. I thought that. She was sharp with Norah. I put it down to the fact so few of us were there. Jim wasn't there, and nor was Angela. Carol came, but she didn't say much, just explained about this commune that she and Eric and Jim are joining. I must say it sounded lovely – in Turkey! I've never been to Turkey. Imagine going to Mount Ararat. One day, when I retire –'

'Did she say anything about me not being there?'

'She explained you were busy, but not otherwise. She had problems with David, too.'

'David? You mean he actually woke up?'

'Yes. Towards the end. Stella suggested he do some work with her, and asked him if he felt like the Dormouse from *Alice in Wonderland*. He yawned and said perhaps. She said then that it was his inadequacy, his sense of being smaller than everyone else, that led him to opt out, as it were. But this was the funny thing, Sandra. He said he didn't think so. He said that for the past few weeks he'd been doing two jobs – he'd been doing night work as a hospital porter. That was why he was falling asleep at meetings.'

'What did Stella say to that?'

'Nothing. She didn't react at all. It was odd. I felt sorry for her.'

'Yes, I feel sorry for her too. Has Kevin turned up yet?'

'The agoraphobic? No.'

'Poor Stella.' Sandra was thoughtful for a moment. 'Is it a good time, do you think, to tell her I want to leave the group?' Zoë looked at Sandra, alarmed. 'No, look, Zoë, you don't need me to go with you. You know everyone now. I just . . . I just feel I've had enough of it.'

'Why?'

A host of pictures crowded Sandra's mind. She saw

her sister's face, her parents, Angela and Carol locked in battle, Stella looking hungrily at the nuts, the unfairness of the public-speaking competition, and her knowledge that life was like that.

'I don't know where to begin. Yes, I do. How can I solve my eating problem by finding out why I've got one? Even if the analysis is right, how does knowing what caused it help me get over it? If a doctor tells you you've got pneumonia, and it developed from the bronchitis you had the week before, that doesn't make you better, does it? And all this positive thinking. How can I think myself slim? And if something bad does happen, how do you think yourself out of it? Pretend it's not bad? Which is silly. Or pretend you're not upset? Which you are. And all this concentration on self – it just makes you selfish – doesn't it? I mean, for me, I'm speaking for me, if I want to stop overeating I've got to *stop* thinking about me, haven't I? And my appetite. And Stella can't solve my life crisis for me – I've got to sort it out myself. I just . . .' Sandra trailed away. It was impossible to say precisely what she felt. One thing she knew for certain, however, was that she could not have any more therapy. Everything in her rebelled at the idea. Besides, she thought, and kept the thought to herself, it's not me who needs help, it's Stella.

'For me,' Zoë said quietly, 'it's been quite good. I know it's nothing like the real world' – Zoë smelt the onions in the Home Economics block again – 'but it's a nice world to retreat into, once in a while. And I do think I'm a bit more assertive. Aren't I?'

Sandra narrowed her eyes and looked at Zoë. Had

she changed? Perhaps. Once or twice since starting the group she had stood up for herself. And to put the ad in the *Guardian* had taken a certain sort of courage. Yet Zoë's job was still in danger. Can people ever change? Sandra wondered. She was right to be indecisive, she realized. The world was full of unanswerable questions.

'Yes, of course you're more assertive,' Sandra said. 'You carry on going. What's worrying me, though, is telling Stella. I feel as if I can't explain my real reasons. Because it would be like pulling everything away from under her feet. I don't feel resentful. Actually, Zoë, I like her. But I will explain. I'll explain to her as best as I can. Next week.'

The doorbell rang again. 'Suzanne! And I'm not even properly dressed yet. You do Laura, Sandra, and I'll finish myself off.'

'Look, Sandra, I don't want to be early. Are you sure we're not going to be too early?' Sandra's car bowled along the empty road, heading for Manchester. They flashed past a brightly lit garage, past a large public house.

'No chance,' said Sandra. 'We've got to park, haven't we? And if we are early, we'll go for a drink ourselves, anyway.'

'Because I don't want to be waiting for him to come in.'

'Well, shall we aim for quarter to nine?'

'No, no! Let's be exactly on time.' Zoë clutched her handbag tightly; in her high-heeled shoes her toes were clenched tight. She felt as if she was going into hospital for an operation. This was all far worse than she had anticipated. Manchester at night looked alien to her. It was another city to the one whose bookshops she browsed in, whose cafés she drank coffee in. To her, just now, it seemed full of young people, in laughing groups, assured, self-possessed. She felt she had no right to be there.

On either side of the car rose tall buildings, their upper storeys dark now, the window displays of the stores lit like a picture show. Bars, restaurants, dark chapels, the anonymous blankness of office buildings. High up in one, Zoë noticed, there were a few lights. She saw a man working late, perhaps on a night shift. She wondered what he could be doing. She thought how nice it would be, to be at work now, manning a phone, checking some figures, alone on the twelfth floor. It seemed an infinitely preferable situation to her own.

'I wonder what he does for a living?' asked Sandra.

'Well, it's an insurance office,' explained Zoë, 'so it could just be overtime.'

'How do you know he works in an insurance office?' said Sandra, surprised.

Zoë paused, reorientated herself. 'Oh, you mean John! No, sorry, I don't know what he does. That doesn't worry me. I mean, as long as he doesn't do anything illegal! Or immoral!'

Sandra was pleased to hear Zoë attempting to be humorous. She was feeling fiercely protective now, secretly doubtful about the wisdom of the whole thing. Men weren't the most trustworthy creatures. And she couldn't bear Zoë to be let down. But at least this man read the *Guardian*; he would be politically correct, no doubt. Was that a free parking meter? Sandra noticed a space between a row of cars parked at an angle along the road. That would do. She slid in, parked, turned off the engine. The two women sat there.

'It's quarter past eight,' Sandra commented.

'Too early,' said Zoë.

'Shall we go and wait in the theatre foyer?'

'No!'

Sandra could not see why not. She knew the Players Theatre well. It had its own small theatre company, whose plays tended towards the avant-garde. But in common with the other theatres in Manchester, it occasionally staged something mainstream, something that was likely to be on school syllabuses, in order to fill a few houses. So Sandra had taken parties there to see *The Rivals*, *She Stoops to Conquer*, and *Death of a Salesman*. They were reasonable productions. She had been there by herself to see some Brecht while she was a student. It was a cosy theatre, with a small, tiered auditorium. It lacked grandeur; it also lacked the alternative, studenty feel of some of the other city theatres. It was a neutral sort of place to meet.

That night there was a performance of Beckett's *Endgames*. Sandra would have quite liked to see that. A rather depressing setting, she thought, for Zoë's romantic encounter. But then, it clearly wasn't his intention to make her see the play. The bar would obviously be quiet during the performance; it was a cultured, neutral, intelligent sort of place to meet. Sandra could see it now, in her mind's eye, its walls adorned with posters of past performances, the high stools around the perimeter.

Or would he be sitting at a table? thought Zoë. At one of the tables on the upper floor, looking out over the square. Waiting for her, wearing his yellow rose. Perhaps he would be at the bar. Or standing at the entrance to the bar, conspicuous with his yellow rose. That would perhaps be more likely. The car's digital clock flashed 8.21.

'Let's go over this,' murmured Sandra. 'We walk in together, right? I stay in the background, I'll turn and examine a poster. You look for him. If you see him before he sees you, point him out to me. Then –'

'No. Let's pretend we don't know each other. You come in after me. You'll be able to work out what's happening.'

'I feel like a private detective, Zoë!' 8.22.

A couple walked past the car. Zoë felt suddenly itchy, scratched the back of her neck, squirmed on the seat. Sandra was overcome with impatience. 'Let's go!' she commanded, and removed the key from the ignition, and the car's clock faded into darkness.

The foyer of the theatre was empty. The performance had begun. Two usherettes were talking by the ticket office, and looked up with mild curiosity at Sandra and Zoë. Sandra moved over to the board that displayed the reviews of the production of *Endgame*. She read it with real interest. Zoë tried to occupy as little space as possible beside her. It was conceivable, she thought, that this man, this John, would come in while they were in the foyer. And he might wonder whether she was the woman . . . Was he lonely too? she mused. Would he be as shy as her? Perhaps, she thought, with rising spirits, he would feel as inadequate, as lost, as terrified as she felt now. He did say he was interested in personal growth. Hopes, and fears, jostled for dominance in Zoë's mind. She pulsed with nerves.

'It's time,' Sandra whispered.

The bar was on the left of the foyer. Sandra and Zoë had to walk down a short corridor, and there was the main drinking area, with its flight of stairs leading to a mezzanine floor. The bar was not empty. At several tables sat figures drinking, and Sandra and Zoë stood at the entrance to the bar, undecided.

'I know!' Sandra's voice was low. 'I'll go to the bar and get myself a drink, and then you come in and look around, to see if anyone's wearing a yellow rose. OK?'

'OK.' Zoë was hoarse.

Sandra moved decisively to the bar. A barman, in a decorated waistcoat, his hair smoothed back with Bryl-creem, came up to her. She ordered a half of bitter. She dared not look round. Dared not see what was happening to Zoë. Her drink arrived. She paid, not thinking to check the change. Should she look now? If she turned, what would she see? It was impossible to wait any longer.

When Sandra turned, she saw that the man at the table facing her, reading a copy of the *Guardian*, wearing a yellow rose prominently in his lapel, was Dr Young. And Zoë was approaching him.

'It's you,' she said. 'It was me.' Dr Young looked confused, annoyed. 'I mean, hello. I'm the lady who wrote the ad ... The yellow rose ... You're ... the personal growth ... It's me, Zoë ... I –'

The Head stood up. Sandra saw that his face was

completely devoid of colour. It was all unbelievable. And Zoë persisted.

'But what about your wife – and children? Does she know? Oh! I see. You wanted to meet another woman. And you answered my advertisement. Sandra!' Her voice rose. 'Sandra, it's the Head. Of course, you're a John too. Sandra, come here. Look who it is.'

Well, thought Sandra, this changes everything.

CHAPTER TWENTY-ONE

The Head had the door of his study shut all week. He's very busy, the office had explained, when Sandra had attempted to make an appointment to see him about another public-speaking competition she was considering entering. Sandra had goaded Zoë into trying to make an appointment to see him. Tell him you're concerned about your timetable next year, she had said. Zoë got as far as the Head's secretary, who informed her that he was busy on a statement for Science 2001, and had given orders that only those people whom he wished to see could interrupt him. In fact, the staff had commented on this, and made ironic remarks about his putting Science 2001 before the welfare of the school. Sandra and Zoë knew better. They had discussed all weekend whether to make their adventure public or not – had, in fact, been speaking of little else. But they had decided to do nothing; not for a time, at any rate. Sandra rather enjoyed the feeling of power the knowledge gave her. It was remarkably easy to sit in the staff room, her hand over her mouth, listening to her colleagues pulling faces and talking about Dr Young. Occasionally she would amuse herself by winking at Zoë and watching Zoë blush.

She smiled to herself, thinking these thoughts, as she walked along the shopping precinct. There were some things she needed at home: bread, washing powder, and a pair of shoelaces. Errands that necessitated visiting several shops. Occasionally she was passed by pupils, who had also decided to come to the precinct after school. They eyed Sandra uneasily. They knew they were not to loiter after four o'clock, but to go straight home. But perhaps Miss Coverdale would not tell.

That was when Sandra had the idea about the chocolates. It was a wicked idea, and she knew it. But she immediately covered herself. It's not going to be easy, she reasoned, explaining to Stella tonight why I'm leaving. I really don't want to hurt her feelings. And it's not only that, I want to show my appreciation for what she's done for me. I want to buy her some sort of present. She lifted her chin in determination. On the way to the supermarket she knew there was a small chocolate boutique, as it called itself, that sold hand-made Belgian chocolates. Those would be perfect. She need only buy a small box. She would pick them her-self, just a dozen or so. It would be a token for Stella, a token of her appreciation.

It was done. Sandra carried in her hands a small gilt box, tied with a purple ribbon. Inside were twelve rather expensive chocolates. Sandra hoped Stella would open them there and then, and offer her one. But Sandra reprimanded herself. These were for Stella. They had cost Sandra a tidy sum, but, she thought acidly, less than a therapy session.

Zoë was not going with her tonight. It had proved impossible to get a babysitter. Suzanne was poorly with a chest infection, and it was somebody's eight-eenth, and all the girls were going to that. But Zoë said she was quite happy to stay at home and catch up with her marking. She seemed happy to Sandra. She had seemed a lot happier since the night in the Players Theatre. Secretly, Sandra was glad that she was giving the group a miss. She rather relished the idea of telling Stella herself what had happened to Zoë – would that be professional? she wondered. Well, the Head certainly wasn't very professional! Also, it would be better explaining herself privately to Stella, saying her goodbye alone. Sandra looked down at the chocolates.

The chocolates sat beside her on the front seat of the car. Sandra had found a card to go with them too. Its design was a star. Appropriate, Sandra thought. For she knew that *stella* was Latin for 'star'. That afternoon she had been teaching *Antony and Cleopatra* to her upper sixth. She loved that play. She had studied it at university too, and she knew it very well. Now, teaching it, lines would stick in her mind. And thinking of Stella's card, she said to herself, 'The star is fallen . . . And time is at his period.'

When she reached 8 Lincoln Grove, the house appeared to be in darkness. Sandra was surprised. Admittedly she was early, as she wanted to catch Stella alone, but in the past when she had been early, there had been a number of lights, from Carol's flat, from the front room. But now, just darkness. Yes, it was Thursday, of course it was. She wondered what could be wrong.

She rapped at the door, holding the chocolates and card in one hand. She waited, rapped again, disturbed. Then she heard footsteps. Stella opened the door. She looked completely different. She wore no make-up, her eyes were puffy, as if she had been crying, she looked scared. She hardly seemed to see Sandra. She ushered her in, said she was not quite ready yet, and Sandra was to wait in the front room.

Sandra switched on the light herself. The room looked dishevelled, as if it had not been cleaned or tidied since it was last used. There were crumpled tissues on the floor; cushions and bean bags were scattered untidily. There was a faintly musty, dank smell – no incense, or any hint of Stella's usual fragrance. And the house was quiet. She seemed to be the only person there. Where was Carol? Where were the others? She felt uneasy, and disobeying Stella, she returned to the hall. Now she could see that there were suitcases out there – one rather elderly box suitcase, and a smarter, large leather one. There was a rucksack too, with a sleeping bag attached. These preparations for departure unsettled Sandra. She listened carefully in case she could hear Stella. But there was not a sound. She returned to the front room.

She looked at her watch. It was well after eight, and no one else had arrived. Something was certainly wrong. Stella had made no attempt to come down. So Sandra returned to the hall again, and called to her. In a few moments, she reappeared, and came slowly down the stairs, holding on to the banisters as if she was frightened of falling.

'Are you all right?' Sandra asked, worried now.

'Yes, yes.'

'Where's everybody else?'

Stella's reply sounded rehearsed, distant. 'Carol is leaving tonight. She's not coming. And Norah and

David are not coming back. Kevin hasn't come. There isn't a group any more.'

'It doesn't matter, Stella!' Sandra said, as brightly as she could. It was clear now, what was wrong. For a variety of reasons, the group had folded. Naturally Stella felt bad about it; she probably felt unwanted, unloved, and Sandra guessed that all her positive thinking wasn't enough to dig her out of this one. She felt worse now, knowing what she was going to have to say to Stella. Perhaps tonight wasn't the right time after all. Sandra stood there hesitantly.

'So there isn't a meeting tonight?'

She saw a tear roll down Stella's cheek.

'No, Stella, don't cry! They're silly, all of them. There'll be other people coming along. You'll have another group.'

'It's not that,' she said. 'It's not the group. It's . . . something else.' And then she broke down completely.

Right, Sandra thought, it's time for action. She pushed Stella into the front room and got her to sit down on a bean bag. She sat with her, her arm around her, and let Stella cry. This is the real thing, she thought, remembering all the historic tears that had been shed in group meetings. This distress was real. And Sandra's concern was equally real. She waited until Stella was ready to talk.

'I've had a letter,' Stella said, and then was quiet again.

'I think,' said Sandra, 'it would help if you talked about it.'

'I can't,' Stella said.

'Look, Stella, I won't tell anyone. We'll have a

confidentiality rule, OK? But whatever it is, you must confront it.'

'I am confronting it. But I just can't face it!'

'Can I get you a drink of anything? Is there anywhere I can make a cup of tea?' Stella mumbled something about a kitchen at the back, and Sandra went to explore, and sure enough, in a back room was a kettle, some mugs and some coffee. Before long she had returned, with two mugs of black coffee. She handed one carefully to Stella, who accepted it gratefully. Sandra's was too hot to drink. She spoke again.

'Is there anything I can do? Please tell me, because I'd like to help.' Stella shook her head. Then she spoke sadly.

'I can't ask you for help! You're my client. You're the one with problems.'

'Yes!' Sandra said with enthusiasm. 'That makes me the best person, don't you see? Because how can you understand someone with a problem unless you've got a problem too, and anyway, it gives me a chance to do something for you!'

Stella did not seem to understand. She sniffed loudly. From her jeans pocket she extracted a letter. It was a long letter, written on air mail paper. Stella left it folded, held it as a talisman. She began.

'This is a letter from Gill. Gill was my therapist. My first therapist. She left England. She lives in California now. She started up the TransFormation Foundation and she introduced me to him. That's the awful thing, she meant it to happen! I feel so manipulated!'

'I'm sorry, start again.'

'When Gill left, she arranged for me to continue my

300

therapy with Roland. And I did. He had been in therapy with her too, you see. I fell in love with him. And Richard – Richard is – was – my husband. He went to California – on business. And he went into therapy with Gill. And they're in love. And –'

'But that sounds OK to me. You've just swapped partners.'

'No, no. Look!' Stella thrust the letter at Sandra.

DEAR STELLA,

I wanted to write as soon as I could to explain my phone call to you. Richie and I sat up late, reading your letters to us, and we felt so glad things had turned out this way. Richard is wonderful, Stella. I've never told you, have I, what he's done for me and TransFormation. He not only got the accounts in order, but arranged a loan *and* invested a sum of his own money in it – which I think we both see as a huge spiritual commitment. Of course, when I first met him, Richie was a sick man. I've asked him about this, and he doesn't mind me telling you. Your marriage was a sham. I'm glad you've recognized this too. I worked with him intensively for weeks. These were some of the most meaningful and fulfilling sessions I can remember taking. I got through to the hurt, damaged little boy, who was so scared of rejection that he held himself back, built this wall of money around himself. Now you can see why your distance, your own blocks on intimacy, made this so much worse. With your need for perfection, you placed very high demands on Richard. He could never meet them. He felt a failure. So he simply went on making more money. It was his defense.

Sandra flinched at the American spelling.

He felt you did not want him to follow you into the

experience of therapy; he said you pulled up a drawbridge behind you. That was when I first met him. We made a connection. He's made so much progress, Stella. We've been lovers for two months now, and he is so warm and virile. He has been able to let go now, let go of his inadequacy, and he has let go of his neurotic fixation with his money. He has learnt how to spend and give. We have built a new rebirthing block at TransFormation, which I am calling the Richard Martin Campus. He thought it best if I tell you this. He knows how well you and I understand each other, and how this is easier coming at you from a woman.

Sandra looked at Stella, who was staring dully ahead of her. What a bitch this woman is, Sandra thought. She was certain, by the sound of things, that this Richard was not worth the trouble. But even then! She read on.

Now you can see why I was so glad you found Roland. I knew that your natural generosity would enable you to make progress with him. I think at this momentous change in all of our lives we can afford to speak openly. I want everything to be known by all of us, so that we can move forward in complete honesty and fearlessness. Roland Temple was one of my very first clients. When I first started as a person-centered therapist in your country, I worked chiefly in the field of psychosexual counseling. Roland came to me because of problems with impotency – erectile failure. It didn't take me long to discover what lay at the root of this – I'm sure I don't need to tell you all this – I know you and he will have discussed it. His first sexual experience was with a girl in Blackpool when he was only fifteen. It was a girl he met at a funfair, he told me. He took her on a ride – the Alice in Wonderland ride – and then, aroused, he went into a back alley, and they made love. But they were discovered by his father. This left Roly with two problems – firstly, a belief that sex was wrong and dirty, which has led to his erectile failure, and secondly and conversely, as you will understand, he can only become aroused in some sort of fantasy setting. When he was my lover, I used to read him fairy stories. This had the effect of convincing him that sex was pure and innocent, as well as being reminiscent of his earlier experience. I am telling you this as I am sure you will find it useful!

While he was with me, Roly was never able to fully resolve his problems. I embarked upon a physical relationship with him because I believed this would unblock him, but I could see after a time that this one was not working for me, and a relationship must be a two-way thing. I need a much more assertive lover. I did, however, publish a very successful paper on the connections between sex and childhood fantasy, although I knew at the time Roland felt uneasy about sharing at that level, as the paper was based chiefly on his experiences. If you're interested, the paper is being reprinted shortly by Schumansky and Thomas, as part of their ground-breaking book *Modern Myth and Mickey Mouse*. They told me they found my paper inspirational.

I was glad Roly took an academic interest in psychotherapy, as that helped him to get over the loss of me, for I felt the need to move on, and that was when I conceived the idea of TransFormation. I want to say to you, Stella, that I am so happy to share Roly with you. I am so certain you are right for each other. I'm sure he is reassured by your reluctance to engage in intimacy; I'm sure you don't mind knowing now that I pointed out to him, when you commenced therapy with him, that you would make a very suitable partner. I think a therapist has the right to use her influence in a positive way.

Richard and I are thrilled for you both, and we want to reassure you that we will support you both in everything you do together. Of course you understand from what I have said that your allowance from Richard is being put into TransFormation. We did not ask your permission because we both knew how pleased you would be to be part of the Foundation. We both want to remain close to you, and when I come over to England with Richard, I hope we can meet and celebrate.

I love you, Stella,
GILL

At first Sandra thought this was an elaborate joke, and looked swiftly at Stella, expecting her to start laughing, and say 'April Fool', or something like that. But she sat staring blankly in front of her. Sandra thought she had better check her facts.

'Was Roland the man you were with at Angela's party?' Stella nodded. 'Did you know all this, I mean –' Sandra blushed, 'about his problems?'

'No!' Stella burst out. 'That was the awful thing. He never told me. I never knew he slept with Gill. Or anything. Except now I can see, I can see why he never . . . All this is true. I feel so dreadful, Sandra. So used. Listen. She's had each one of us in therapy, she knows us all!' And knowledge is power, thought Sandra. 'I've been her puppet. I thought these things were all my choice, Roland and leaving Richard and everything, but she meant all this to happen. And maybe Roland doesn't really love me,' Stella wailed. She commenced sobbing again. Sandra's mind was still reeling. She repeated the facts aloud.

'So your ex-therapist has had both your husband

and your lover, and she packed you up and sent you as a present to her ex-lover.'

Stella nodded.

'And your husband is stopping your money. What is this TransFormation thing anyway?'

'A New Age therapy centre in California. It's Gill's.'

'That must have cost some.' So she's using your husband's money, Sandra thought, as well as the money you paid her, and Roland paid her, when you were in therapy with her. No wonder you're all part of it! I suppose TransFormation's her personal growth. Sandra breathed in audibly.

'Oh Sandra, what shall I do?' Again Stella was convulsed in sobs. Sandra hugged her, filled with anger against this appalling American woman, against the therapy business, and also with a fierce protectiveness. She knew she would do anything for Stella.

'I feel so alone,' Stella went on. 'I mean, I love Roland, but it's all different now, and I don't have Gill any more and no therapist and no group and —'

'I'm your friend,' said Sandra.

'What will I do? What will I do about Roland? I thought he was so perfect, so perfect for me. And how can I carry on as a therapist now?'

'Look,' said Sandra, 'I don't think it matters about Roland's impotence.' Then a thought struck her. 'Have you had sex with him?'

'Oh yes. Twice.'

'Well, then. There's hope, isn't there? Better than living with a man who never leaves you alone. And it doesn't matter if he's not perfect, Stella. I thought he looked a nice bloke. Have you seen him since getting this letter, which, incidentally, I think ought to be ceremonially burnt?'

'No. It came this morning, and I came here to be alone. He doesn't know where I am, I think.'

'Well, I think you ought to see him and get all this out into the open. He's as much a victim as you, and neither of you have anything to be ashamed of. Even if she did suggest you as a partner, he wouldn't have taken you on if he didn't care.'

'Cruella de Vil!' murmured Stella. 'He said she was Cruella de Vil.'

Sandra ignored that remark. 'And you don't have to give up therapy. It helps some people. Look at Zoë – you know, Zoë, my friend, in your group. You've done a lot for her.' Now Stella looked at Sandra with attention. 'Yes!' continued Sandra. 'You gave her the courage to go out and meet a man. And guess what?'

Sandra judged the time was right to distract Stella. So she told the story of their brief encounter with the Head, and was delighted to see that Stella listened, and smiled, too, at the climax of the story.

'So you see,' Sandra concluded, 'you're better off with Roland!' Stella smiled again. 'Go and see him. And write back to this Gill and tell her what a bitch she is. That'll be therapeutic.'

Stella said, 'Thanks, Sandra. You're so decisive.'

I've cheered her up, Sandra realized. And she felt good. That was when the chocolates caught her eye. They reminded her what it was she was going to say to Stella tonight. Perhaps now was the right time after all.

'Stella. You're not alone, you know. There's me as well. I want to be your friend too.'

'But you're my client, and . . .'

'I think it might be better if I wasn't your client, but we still saw each other, just as friends. I think we have a lot in common.'

Stella looked down at herself, as if to say, but how could you like me, seeing me like this? It was an eloquent look, and moved Sandra.

'I like you!' said Sandra. And she meant it. 'Look!' she continued, 'I've bought you a present. To cement our friendship!' And she handed the small gilt box to Stella, who accepted it curiously. 'Go on, open it!'

Stella carefully removed the purple ribbon. She did not know what to expect at all. It was kind of Sandra to get her a present. What could it be? The top of the box felt empty; whatever it was had settled at the bottom. She felt the way the weight was distributed. She unfolded the gilt cardboard. There, nestling in crushed Cellophane, were twelve exquisite chocolates. Stella blanched in horror.

'They're for you.'

Stella panicked. It was rude to refuse a present, but really, Sandra ought to have known that she would never, never eat anything with so many calories as . . . She could not afford to get fat. She looked at Sandra with momentary disgust. But Sandra had been so kind to her. She was so nice about Roland.

'Go on, Stella. Have one. It won't kill you.'

'But I can't eat these.'

'Why?'

Stella thought. It was a very, very long time since

she had had a chocolate. She wondered what one tasted like. She was not sure she remembered. She picked a diamond-shaped chocolate, a plain one. She put it in her mouth and bit, her teeth sinking into the centre of the chocolate, which crumbled, and gave way, and immersed her tongue in a cloud of dissolving sweetness. She could not even recognize the flavour, but the taste and sensation were electrifying.

'That's not so bad, is it?' said Sandra. 'Look, I'm doing it too.' Sandra took a chocolate and popped it in her mouth. It was white chocolate, like the Milky Bars she ate as a child. At the bottom was an almond. She sucked it, feeling the ridges with her tongue. She ate the rest of the chocolate slowly. She realized, as she savoured the sensation, that she usually ate chocolate very quickly, guiltily, stowing it away as if to pretend to herself she hadn't had it. This deliberate enjoyment was alien to her.

'Shall we have another?' Stella said. They both reached into the box.

When Sandra had finished her second selection, from which a chocolate-covered stalk of a cherry had extended enticingly, she asked Stella whether she was feeling any better. Stella nodded, was about to reach for a third, and stopped.

'But I shouldn't be doing this, Sandra! Eating for comfort!'

'I don't see why not. Not if it works . . .'

'But . . .' Stella's voice trailed away. Sandra knew what she was thinking. But if you eat for comfort you'll get fat. And of course Stella was right. If you did it a lot you would. But if you did it a little – this was Sandra's new discovery – if you did it just a little – you would only get a little bit fat. And who wanted the perfect figure, if there was such a thing? Sandra didn't honestly know if it would be possible for her to only overeat occasionally, but she decided she might give it a try. Perhaps now wasn't the time to discuss this with Stella, but she looked forward to a time when she would. Meanwhile, she took another chocolate. So did Stella.

Stella wasn't talking either. It was partly the narcotic effect of the chocolate, partly her thoughts. She would tell Roland about this, about the agony and the passionate delight of eating chocolate. He would help her. And perhaps then he would talk about his problem. And she could help him. Perhaps they weren't absolutely perfect, but even then . . . She looked at Sandra, glowing now. Sandra was clever. She had shown her a way forward. They both took another chocolate. There were only two left, but that didn't matter. Stella realized that Gill had never really understood her difficulties with food. How could she, when she had never experienced them herself? She watched the intent, abstract way that Sandra ate. Sandra understood.

They each had their final chocolate.

'Sandra,' Stella began, 'I can remember eating chocolate like this on the way home from school. On the bus. And it felt so good especially if we'd been made to work very hard.'

'Yes!' said Sandra, her voice alight with recognition. 'And sometimes I'd eat biscuits while I was doing my homework, and I could get through a whole packet. I didn't even know I was doing it. And my mother would joke.'

309

'But it wasn't a joke!' Stella said. 'And if I'd been out to a party and no one asked me to dance –'

'Yes! I'd make a peanut-butter sandwich or something to have before bed.'

'And did you ever pretend to help your mother with the cooking, so that . . .'

CHAPTER TWENTY-TWO

Sandra was looking forward enormously to her dinner with Stella and Roland. She had not seen them for two weeks, as she had been busy marking the summer exams. Now it was not long to the end of the school year, and Sandra's thoughts strayed with increasing frequency to the summer holidays, her summer holidays. Some old school friends had rented a house in Cornwall, and she was joining them. But now, as she strode through the Quays, on her way to Stella and Roland's, clutching a bottle of Shiraz-Cabernet, she was full of a much more immediate source of gratification. She had so much to tell them.

Life could be awful sometimes, she thought. And unfair. But sometimes it was just the opposite, splendid things happened too, all of their own accord. She thought back over the last few weeks.

Was it about a month after their meeting with the Head? Something like that. A typewritten notice went up on the staff bulletin board, announcing that he had been offered a consultancy with Science 2001, and that he was accepting, and so would be leaving Millers'. By and large, the staff were delighted. Sandra almost felt cheated at the time, she had to admit, but she and Zoë had kept their secret.

Then of course the governors had to advertise for a new Head. Everyone had thought that Anne Palmer would apply, but she declined the opportunity. She had confessed to Sandra that she hadn't been sleeping properly, that it was all getting too much for her, trying to keep control of the school. She was now looking forward to an early retirement. But Debra Wentworth had applied, of course. It was then that Sandra realized how much she was generally disliked. It was hard not to join in the barbed conversations that the staff had about her, and Sandra reflected how difficult it was to be in a position of authority and to retain popularity.

When the governors announced their decision, from the two hundred applicants, there was an outcry. They had appointed another man. The governors assured the staff both publicly and informally that Adrian Hawkshead really was the best applicant. But at least Debra had not been selected. She had said, subsequent to Mr Hawkshead's appointment, that she had decided to start a family. Having a baby was bound to be so much more fulfilling than being a wage-slave. Then Sandra was offered Head of General Studies for next year! She wondered whether it was some sort of bribe. But it was a good promotion, and it delighted her parents.

But that wasn't it. Stella and Roland knew all that already. It was what had happened this week that she was dying to relate. First of all, on Monday, Debra had announced that she was pregnant. And she had told Zoë that it would therefore be impossible for her to take the Athens trip – just in case there were complications. Would Zoë mind? Zoë did not mind. All week she had been more cheerful than Sandra had seen her for ages. Even though she had made good progress in her self-esteem sessions with Stella, this one piece of news seemed to have an even more electric effect. But today the new Head had visited the school.

He came and met the staff informally in the morning break. They learned he was a classicist – had an Oxford degree in Latin and Greek. He had previously been a Deputy Headmaster at a well-known boarding school. He was single. This surprised Sandra – although the rumour had spread that this was the result of a recent divorce – for he was a good-looking man, middle-aged, but good-looking.

Then in the afternoon he had asked to see Zoë. He explained to her how strongly he felt that a good classical background should be the springboard for learning. Even more so today, he argued, now that once again we were poised to share in the cultural affairs of Europe. He was appalled to see how little provision was made for the classics at Millers', and what did Zoë think? He promised to advertise immediately for a new Latin teacher to assist her. She was in his study for an hour. When she came out to tell Sandra what had happened, she was in a daze. They had spoken of Catullus, of Ovid, of Pompeii. He was so easy to talk to. And he had asked her if there was room for him on the Athens trip. It was some years since he'd been there, and it would be an opportunity to find out more about the sixth formers, and the school. How could you refuse the Head-designate? Zoë had said to Sandra. She didn't have the courage to say 'No' to him, Zoë had explained, and had said she would arrange another staff place with the travel company.

That was what Sandra wanted to tell Stella and

Roland. She felt hungry. She hoped Roland would not be cooking tonight. But Stella, she knew, would be preparing the dessert. She increased her pace as their house came into view.